Tao Lin

Leave Society

Tao Lin is the author of the memoir *Trip*; the novels *Taipei*, *Richard Yates*, and *Eeeee Eee Eeee*; the novella *Shoplifting from American Apparel*; the story collection *Bed*; and the poetry collections *cognitive-behavioral therapy* and *you are a little bit happier than i am*. He was born in Virginia, has a B.A. in journalism from New York University, and is the founder and editor of Muumuu House.

Also by Tao Lin

Leave Society

Leave Society

Tao Lin

VINTAGE CONTEMPORARIES

VINTAGE BOOKS

A DIVISION OF PENGUIN RANDOM HOUSE LLC

NEW YORK

A VINTAGE CONTEMPORARIES ORIGINAL, AUGUST 2021

Portions of this work first appeared, in different form, in the
following publications: "Upset" in *NOON* (2020) and "Catatonia"
in *Pets: An Anthology*, edited by Jordan Castro, published by Tyrant
Books, New York, in 2020.

The Cataloging-in-Publication Data is on file at the Library of Congress.

Vintage Contemporaries Trade Paperback
   ISBN: 978-1-101-97447-6
eBook ISBN: 978-1-101-97448-3

Book design by Nicholas Alguire

www.vintagebooks.com

Printed in the United States of America
10 9 8 7 6 5 4 3 2 1

Nothing is as it appears to be. This is not glib.
—Kathleen Harrison

Contents

Year of Mercury

Surgery

The day Li arrived in Taipei for a ten-week visit, he and his parents went to a surgeon to discuss his chest deformity. The surgeon asked Li what he did. Li said he wrote novels.

"Knows about everything, then?"

"I write novels so I know *nothing*," said Li, who normally might've replied, "Ng," a grunted word meaning "yes," "right," "okay," or "I see," but was on a quarter-tab of LSD.

Li's mom laughed a little.

The surgeon opened a computer presentation on pectus excavatum, which affected around 1 in 125 people and had no known cause. First described in print in the sixteenth century, it gave one a sunken, undersized chest, crowding and flattening the heart and lungs. Surgical correction began in

1911. This surgeon had done the Nuss procedure, in which curved metal bars were embedded behind the ribs and sternum for up to four years, around six hundred times.

Li had felt deformed since grade school. In Florida, among scant Asians, he'd usually been the smallest boy in each class. His six-years-older brother, Mike, had called him fish lips, buckteeth, mutant, and other names that had made him feel self-conscious and ugly. In high school and college, he'd been a frail, gloomy, awkward, anxious, troublingly shy loner. When he learned at age twenty-three that his chest was deformed, he'd rejected surgery, deciding instead to use the insight as motivation to be healthier, but now, at thirty-one, he was reconsidering. Maybe he'd be happier and stabler, with less back pain, if his chest wasn't concave. He lacked money and insurance, so had talked to his parents, who'd suggested he, who lived in New York City, fly to Taiwan, where healthcare was inexpensive.

It was November 4, 2014. Li got a CT scan. The surgeon looked at images of his chest and said he'd have a sixty-year-old's heart when he was forty unless he got surgery. The prognosis seemed uncompelling and somewhat vague to Li, who'd recently estimated he'd live to only around fifty.

That night, at his parents' fifth-floor apartment, Li read "We Are Giving Ourselves Cancer," a *New York Times* article that said CT scans gave up to one thousand times the radiation of an X-ray and that 5 percent of future U.S. cancers could result from "exposure to medical imaging."

He ordered four ebooks on radiation. Nuclear power plants continually produced waste that stayed radioactive for hundreds of millennia, he read. People didn't know what to do with the toxic material. Some was put into plastic bags. The best containers lasted for only around a century, and leaks were common.

Li read by holding his phone above his face while supine in bed with bent knees. Back pain had restricted him to a small set of robotic postures, except for when he was on cannabis or LSD, strong anti-inflammatants. He preferred cannabis but had feared getting caught sneaking it into Taiwan, so had brought scentless, tiny LSD instead. It was his only reliable reprieve from pained disillusionment. He used it daily.

After reading for a while, Li realized CT scans emitted electromagnetic radiation and that he'd bought four ebooks on nuclear radiation. He didn't seem to know the difference, or what the word "radiation" meant, but he felt confident he could learn.

In the past year, inspired by philosopher Terence McKenna to try to understand his own reality, Li had begun to pay less attention to fiction, newspapers, and magazines, and more attention to scientific journals, independent researchers, non-profit organizations, and nonfiction books. The world seemed more complex, terrible, hopeful, meaningful, and magical than he'd previously thought or heard.

From *The Chalice and the Blade*, in which Riane Eisler coined the terms "partnership" and "dominator" to describe the two underlying models of society; *The Archaic Revival*, McKenna's argument for restoring aboriginal (a word derived from the Latin "ab origine," meaning "from the source") values; *When God Was a Woman*; and other books, he'd read about the global culture's forgotten backstory: people across Eurasia seemed to have lived in peaceful, egalitarian societies, worshipping nature in the form of female deities, for at least thirty millennia as hunter-gatherers and five millennia as farmers, before the dominator model, introducing war and sexism, emerged in conquering form around 6,500 years ago, nadiring three millennia later with Yahweh, whose tantrums (punishing women by making them be ruled by men, threatening people with eternal hell) the species was still trying to recover from.

Misogyny, materialism, corporations, and pesticides had supplanted cooperation, animism, nature, and psychedelics, but the grim chaos seemed to be leading somewhere. Humans seemed to be deep into a brief, failable transition called history—a fifteen-millennia release from matter into the imagination, a place that was to the universe as life was to a book: larger, realer, more complicated.

One reason Li liked this worldview was that it asked him not to worry or panic but to stay calm, like a midwife, and try to facilitate the birthlike, surreal, and probably cosmic process. Hundreds of species, possibly, were flashing out of the galaxy every few millennia in an inconspicuous metatwinkling, a shower of lifedrops joining the ocean of immateriality.

Five days after seeing the surgeon, Li and his parents went to a cardiologist, who said, "Some Japanese live in small houses, some in big houses. One's not better than the other. It's the same with chests." Li had below-average cardiopulmonary functioning, according to tests by the surgeon, but below average wasn't abnormal, said the cardiologist, who recommended push-ups.

Outside, Li and his parents praised the cardiologist. Li's mom, who was sixty-one and had always stressed avoiding surgery due to the risk of coma or death, seemed happier than Li had seen her in years. She asked Li if he was happy that surgery wasn't required and that the deformity wouldn't, according to the cardiologist, shorten his life.

Li said no, not especially, because he'd already suspected those things and had already mostly decided against surgery. He wanted to work on his general health. The CT scan seemed to have given him diarrhea, mouth sores, nausea, and heavier night sweats than normal. He'd been waking filmed in cold sweat multiple times a night.

On the train home, Li continued reading about radiation. He'd finished two of his four ebooks. He'd learned that increasing amounts of radioactive atoms from nuclear, coal, oil, and gas power plants; wars; weapons tests; cars; smoke alarms; TVs, and other societal ephemera were in everyone, ejecting destabilizing particles to attain stabler states.

Drawing in his room that night, Li heard his mom in his dad's office, which was also the TV-and-dining room, saying she was allotting him some money for stocks. "Write down what you want to buy and bring me the paper," she said, sounding somewhat annoyed, and returned to her office.

She'd gained control of their finances over the past decade, during which Li's dad had been imprisoned for money laundering and then gotten repeatedly scammed—delivering gold bars to the family of a man he'd met in prison, flying to Belize and Nigeria to give cash to strangers who'd emailed him.

A minute later, Li heard his dad in his mom's office, half of which was filled with his dad's cardboard box hoard, saying which stocks he wanted to buy and how. Despite having no money to invest, Li's dad followed the stock market obsessively, emitting a near constant stream of bickering-fomenting advice.

In bed at 2:30 a.m., Li reminded himself to merge with nature's experimental creation of portentously ambitious art, scalarly tunneling through matter on the surfaces of planets, toward the unknown other side, because what else was he going to do?

He didn't want to specialize in embodying and languaging confused alienation anymore, as he had for a decade, writing existential autofiction. He didn't want to forget that angle either. It seemed auspicious to have distrusted preconceptions, groups, and ideologies for so long. He had less to unlearn.

"Nature isn't mute," he thought in distracted review. Something mute wouldn't unfurl a universe in which to evolve singularityward. Something mute wouldn't speak people from atoms. Li wondered when he'd be asleep. His pillow-propped feet felt unpleasantly warm and heavy, as if blood had gathered at the wrong end of him.

Teeth

On his ninth day in Taiwan, Li closely examined his mouth's interior for the first time in maybe five years. His gums seemed scarily receded. A canine was turning black. Teeth zapped with pain when touched. He hadn't been to a dentist since the nineties and still didn't want to go, didn't want X-rays, etc.

He searched "natural cure tooth decay" on Amazon and bought *Cure Tooth Decay: Heal and Prevent Cavities with Nutrition.* He read that cavities were caused by malnutrition, not bacteria; that modern humans got less than a fourth of the minerals and a tenth of the fat-soluble vitamins that their aboriginal ancestors had gotten; and that the main service of conventional dentistry, "a profound failure," was to drill holes in teeth to fill with a half-mercury amalgam of toxic metals.

Li didn't have any fillings. He'd somehow never gotten a cavity, maybe because they'd been in his eight pulled teeth, or, with 25 percent fewer teeth, each had gotten more nutrients. He suspected his parents had fillings, but he felt unready to ask.

He focused on reading more books and on persuading his parents to use natural toothpaste, soap, and cosmetics; drink green smoothies; and add fish liver oil, ghee, seaweed, chlorella, sprouted seeds and nuts, and fermented vegetables to their diets.

On day fourteen, he ran out of LSD and began to feel grumpy most of the time. Sometimes his frowny face felt like the main problem, brainwardly fuming sullen petulance.

At dinner on day seventeen, Li's dad couldn't seem to stop criticizing Li's mom's panfried fish. The skin wasn't crispy—a complaint he'd been making for decades.

"From now on you cook," said Li's mom, staring at the TV, which they ate facing. On the news, police cars chased a minivan containing ketamine and amphetamines.

"Need to figure out why the skin sticks," said Li's dad.

"Tonight you're washing dishes," said Li in the tone he felt his parents were using on each other.

Li's parents seemed startled, looking at Li.

"You can't speak like that to Dad," said Li's mom.

"You don't help," Li told his dad. "You just complain."

"He can only complain," agreed Li's mom.

"So tonight you'll clear the table and wash dishes," said Li, and, to his moderate surprise, his dad began clearing the table.

"Once a week, not every night, can't do it every night," said Li's dad.

Li asked his mom when his dad had last washed dishes.

"Never," she said, and told Li to apologize to his dad.

As Li apologized, his dad averted his eyes and said Li should apologize to Dudu, their seven-year-old, four-pound white poodle, who was seated on the sofa with her right foot turned out, seeming a bit sassy.

Dudu had hair loss on most of her body. Her skin was a grayish pink. Her tassel-like tail resembled a rat's tail. She had the most hair on her head.

"Sorry for being loud," said Li. He and his parents liked to imagine that Dudu viewed all human speech as being directed to, or about, her.

Dudu stared at Li with her cloudy, cataracted eyes. She liked only three people—Li's parents and Auntie, as Li called his mom's sister.

On a pre-dinner walk three days later, Li talked about statins—a type of cholesterol-lowering drug his dad, who was sixty-six, was on. Statins, he'd read, caused cancer, depression, amnesia, dementia, and other problems, like twitching.

"My eye has twitched for twenty years," said Li's dad.

"You've used statins for twenty years," said Li.

"It doesn't matter what happens to us," said Li's dad. "When we're old, we won't remember anything. We'll have no worries."

"That's not what happens," said Li. "You'll feel very not good." In Chinese, people said "not good" instead of "bad."

"You wish for us to be healthy," said Li's mom.

"You won't be able to do anything," said Li. "Other people will need to care for you."

"We'll hire someone to bathe and feed us," said Li's dad.

"How you two are in ten years matters to me because I'm going to take care of you two," said Li, somewhat blurting something he didn't feel committed to doing, but which, after saying it, seemed, calmingly and hearteningly, more possible.

That night, Li's mom emailed Li, "I was very moved by you saying you will take care of us. What more could I ask for from a son? However, we don't want to become your burden when we get really old. Therefore, I understand it is important to follow the healthy way of living which you have been working to teach us."

Li woke sweating at 3:30 a.m. He maundered dysphorically through the small apartment, in which most sounds could be heard from anywhere else, finding toxic things to discard. Dudu growled quietly, in her high-pitched voice, from Li's parents' bed. She was most awake at night, when she guarded Li's parents as they slept.

Li carried the microwave into the elevator, down six floors, into the trash room. Back in the apartment, he emailed his mom two articles on the negatives of microwave ovens, including that they leaked radiation. He peed and returned to bed.

The next night, Li's dad entered Li's room, opened Li's third novel, and correctly pronounced "Xanax." He'd read around a hundred pages of Li's writing in the form of random selections. He was the CEO of two medical laser companies and the inventor of the flying-spot scanning laser technique for LASIK vision correction. He stood reading silently for a minute, then left.

Li was drafting an email to his mom, suggesting she switch from Levoxyl—the synthetic thyroid supplement she'd been on since her thyroidectomy in 2006, the same year she was diagnosed as prediabetic—to natural thyroid, like Hillary Clinton. Convincing her would be a long-term process, he anticipated with some dread.

Li disliked trying to change others. Since college, he'd derived inspiration from a passage in *The Book of Disquiet* on how people who are concerned about evil and injustice in the world should begin the campaign against those things at their nearest source—themselves—in a task that would take a lifetime.

But he felt differently with his parents, health-wise, because they seemed near dementia and other miserable problems. Li's dad's eye twitch, brain functioning, and weight seemed to be worsening. He often said he was carrying ten Dudus of extra weight. Li's mom was chronically dizzy, tired, and unable to sleep. Her doctor wanted her to take diabetes drugs.

Yoga

Thirty tabs of LSD arrived on day thirty-five. "On first LSD in three weeks while healthier and emotionally stabler than maybe ever," typed Li on his phone that afternoon, walking to his tenth day of yoga class, which he'd started in part as back-pain therapy. "Sensing new things that superimpose, giving the illusion of distorted perception," he typed.

He'd been taking notes for his fourth novel, which he wanted to be autobiographical, like his other novels, for more than a year already. For a few months, he'd considered abandoning autobiography, but he liked its self-catalyzing properties too much—how it made life both life and literature, imbuing both with extra meaning.

At the beginning of the yoga class, Li blacked out during a backbend, returning in a kneel. None of the other students seemed to have noticed. Soon, yoga began to seem entirely mental. They weren't bodies in a room on the eighth floor of a building; they were minds controlling bodies from outside space-time.

Li felt vaguely astonished as he seemed to leave even his mind, as if waking from a thirty-one-year dream. He sensed he was "reading" the life of an organism embedded deep in a history, then reentered the dream with what felt like a complex yet infailable shift of attention.

For mesmerizing minutes, sweating profusely, he seemed aware of only his pleasurable exertion, tirelessly trying harder than in any previous class, gliding in and out of poses in time to the class-patrolling teacher's voice.

The teacher tightened Li's yoga band to a degree that normally would've felt excruciating but currently just felt different. "Didn't I just say, '[words Li didn't understand]'?" she said.

Li focused on seeming normal. He noticed a student's disgusted face and immediately felt it was about him. Was he unconsciously acting offensive or unseemly?

In child's pose at the end of class, he synesthesiated perspiration as a crunchy, oceanic blare. Leaving the studio, he felt tranquil and a little absent.

Descending in the bright, mirrored elevator, he looked in his mouth to check on his blackening canine. He felt shocked by what he saw. All his teeth seemed porous with cavernous holes. How had he overlooked this?

Focusing on a dark spot atop the canine, he realized with

vertiginous relief that it was a dragonfruit-seed fragment and that the other dark areas must also be seed pieces. He tried to fingernail the particle away, but it wouldn't move.

He felt disappointed and frightened, realizing his teeth *were* hole-ridden. He recalled that *Cure Tooth Decay* said general health was determinable via teeth and gums. He began to accept that his teeth and maybe organs were rotting.

Walking home, he typed, "Feel renewed motivation to be healthier after seeing teeth on LSD." Concrete reality faded in and out of partial transparency. Parts of his mind seemed to be drifting away in undirected exploration, taking the senses with them.

Keycarding open the gate to the ten-story building where his parents lived, Li began to feel like he was in a realistic, many-scened, calmly mystical novel in which he and his parents were sympathetic, amusing characters.

Deshoeing, Li sensed he was perceiving his mom anew due to LSD, which was much stronger after three weeks' abstinence. She seemed disconcertingly "schizophrenic," he thought as she asked him about yoga. She seemed less cohesive than he remembered, but also livelier, he acknowledged as she said, "It's very good you're doing yoga every day," twice, the second time to Dudu in a nonsensically pedantic tone.

Li focused on walking to his room.

"Why'd you use that bag today?" said Li's mom.

"Huh?" said Li, sounding comically oafish to himself.

"Don't you usually use a green bag?"

"No," said Li, entering his room. Putting his gray bag in his closet, he saw the green bag. Confident he'd never used it, he thought "schizophrenic" again, then thought "tetched," a word he often thought about himself but had never said aloud or written.

In the bathroom, he touched the dark spot on his rotting canine with a dental pick. With a slightly sobering recognition that he was very high, he realized he'd already realized it was a seed fragment. His teeth *weren't* full of holes.

Showering, he wondered if his mom was on drugs. Five months earlier, at his brother Mike's apartment in Brooklyn, he'd seen Xanax by her bag and then later had emailed her asking if she remembered warning him against the drug years earlier, saying it caused brain and kidney damage. She'd replied, "I took it for a short time, a long time ago. I remember I emailed you once saying that Thin Uncle"—her brother—"said people should never take drugs for sleep. You were on a drug spree at the time and were angry because you thought I was trying to tell you not to take drugs. I was very scared every minute when you were on drugs. I was afraid your health would be damaged."

Li had been addicted to amphetamines, benzodiazepines, and other pharmaceutical drugs for three years. He'd ended the increasingly life-threatening phase by isolating himself in his apartment in Manhattan, replacing pills and friends and most of culture with cannabis and books, and finding his new interests: history, nature, psychedelics, the imagination, his parents, and his body—six things he'd previously mostly ignored. When he got to Taiwan for his current ten-week visit, he'd been ensconced in stoned hermitude for fourteen months, during which he'd begun to view himself as recovering not just from pharmaceutical drugs but from nearly everything. Recovery—healing himself from the mental and physical effects of dominator society, which included himself—had become his main focus in life.

After showering, Li stood in the bathtub looking down. He could see his squished, lopsided heart beating against his chest's dentlike depression. His body lurched a little with each beat. He studied the translucent, question-mark-shaped, inter-eye things drifting inconspicuously across his vision. From their motion, he briefly sensed the curve of his eyeball.

In the kitchen, he blended jalapeño, celery, ginger, and coconut water. He poured the drink into two cups. He handed his mom her cup, then quickly drank his portion, not realizing how bitter it was until his mom, coughing, said he might've made it too strong.

"I didn't mean to make it this strong," said Li, esophagus burning with a quickly fading spiciness. He laughed, then felt almost unbearably endeared by his mom's laughter, which sounded uncharacteristically carefree and whole.

For a few startling moments he felt like they were adolescent or teenage friends, talking in a kitchen on a Friday night. They decided to go buy Li's dad, who was in China for business, and whose old, run-down laptop had seemed near irrecoverable breakdown for years, a new computer for Christmas, which was in two weeks.

In Taipei Main Station, they walked past cosmetic-surgery

ads. One showed giant, shiny, female faces. One showed a row of smiling doctors in white coats.

At the store, as his mom paid for a MacBook, Li stared at his palms, which kept undefinably and entrancingly shifting while seeming continually about to resolve into the normal, wallpaper-like appearance of human skin.

Dentists

On the first day of 2015, Li's dad revealed he had a toothache. Li provided peppermint oil. It was his eighth week in Taiwan, and he still didn't know if his parents had mercury fillings. He'd delayed asking due to having a backlog of health concerns to address—for himself, his parents, and Dudu— and because he dreaded the belligerent process of convincing his parents mercury was toxic if they did have fillings.

His procrastination ended as he realized he could find a dentist for both the ache and the mercury. He emailed his mom, asking if she and his dad had fillings. As he'd worriedly assumed since reading *Cure Tooth Decay* six weeks earlier, large amounts of mercury had been implanted in his parents' teeth in Florida in the eighties and nineties.

Over four days, Li showed them a *60 Minutes* exposé called "The Hazards of Mercury Fillings," a video titled "SMOK-ING TEETH = POISON GAS," and selected online articles, interspersed with his own emotion-muddled rhetoric, which became fear-based frustratingly often. He stressed he was telling them good, empowering, actionable news.

On a list titled "5 Holistic Dentists in Taipei," he found the only dentist in Taiwan trained by Hal Huggins, who'd pioneered mercury replacement in Colorado in the seventies.

At the dentist's office, Li's dad browsed certificates on the walls. "The dentist is only forty-six," he said, carrying Dudu. "Acupuncture," he read.

Li saw the dentist in a hallway. They smiled at each other. She moved out of view, into a side room, seeming kind and gnomish.

Li sat by his mom, who was filling out forms. The dentist's assistant, who seemed around Li's age, asked Li's mom if Li spoke Mandarin.

Li remembered high school, when many of his peers had treated him as if he were mute, telling one another that he didn't speak.

"Why don't you ask him?" said Li's mom.

"I can, but not that good," said Li, who spoke a crude, ungrammatical Mandarin-English mix with his parents, using the simplest words from each language, though they were fluent in English.

After getting X-rayed in a phone booth–like room, Li's dad reclined in a dental chair. He asked the dentist if she used lasers.

She made a vague, inward noise.

"My son told me to read a book," said Li's dad, who'd read thirty pages of *Cure Tooth Decay*, which Li's mom had read in its entirety. "It said modern dentists use lasers."

"Your son should read more books," said the dentist, organizing her tools.

"The book only mentions lasers a little," said Li. "The book and I think like you do. My dad doesn't believe you. I had to convince him and my mom. I believe you. They don't. They do now but not before."

The dentist laughed.

Li's dad had nine fillings, two crowns, and three fake teeth. Eight months earlier, his dentist had replaced his three front teeth after two of them cracked when he bit into a chicken bone.

"Looks like you've been to your dentist too much," said the dentist. "Hal Huggins said, 'Never make friends with your dentist.'"

As the dentist cleaned Li's dad's teeth, Dudu sat on Li's mom's lap, though the assistant had said she should stay in her enclosed container, which had wheels and was mandatory on trains and buses.

"Why are poodles called guìbīn?" Li asked his mom.

"That's just what they're called here."

"What does it mean?" said Li.

"'VIP,'" said Li's mom in English. "'VIP' or 'honored guest.'"

"Hm," said Li, smiling at Dudu, who'd switched that week from drinking Ensure, a toxic-seeming shake for elder humans that a vet had recommended years earlier, to drinking raw eggs.

Li's dad's foreign oral materials were photographed in a special room, and then Li's mom told Li to distract his dad while she discussed payment with the dentist.

"Let's go over here," said Li, leading his dad to the reception area, grinning a little.

Minutes later, Li and his parents entered a small room, where the assistant opened a PowerPoint presentation, which said Li's dad would need to get blood-tested before the procedure. Depending on the results, he might need to detox first, using supplements sold by the dentist. Li felt his parents' suspicion toward the safety measure. The assistant skipped two pages.

Four pages later, Li asked about the skipped pages. The assistant scrolled back. The pages said patients should consume organic produce, naturally raised animals, and bone broth (which Li's mom served nightly), and that lifetime abstinence from seafood was mandatory due to cumulative mercury contamination since the industrial revolution.

Dudu coughed and shifted on Li's dad's lap.

The assistant discussed crowns and bridges.

"Generally, most people—the masses—agree that you don't need to get those replaced, right?" said Li's dad.

"What?" said the assistant after a moment.

"Can you explain why those should be replaced?" said Li.

She said mouth metals made electrical currents that interfered with brain functioning.

"Does the dentist practice acupuncture?" said Li's dad.

"That's not relevant," said the assistant.

"Is the dentist certified to practice acupuncture?"

"Why do you ask?"

"I'm a physics professor. I've taught at National Taiwan University. I can listen to you on teeth, but when you talk about electricity—no, I need to say something. Do I not make sense?"

"I didn't make the presentation," said the assistant, seeming bemused. "Do you want to talk to the dentist?"

The dentist appeared at the entrance to the room, which couldn't nonawkwardly fit more people, and began arguing with Li's dad, who asked how it was possible that poison had been implanted into millions of mouths. The dentist said toothpaste, mouthwash, fluoridated water, and root canals were just as unbelievable. They began talking over each other.

"I argue with him every day," said Li, somewhat exaggerating.

"Many of my patients are like this before mercury removal, very negative," said the dentist to Li, with "very negative" in English.

"Okay then," said Li's mom. "Let's bicker at home. It's embarrassing in public."

As she paid for the visit with the assistant, Li's dad called the dentist a liar, the dentist said other dentists had lied to Li's dad, and Li said his dad needed to stop believing lies.

Outside, it was dusk. Forested mountains surrounded the city, which from its side streets could seem benign and serene. Looking closer at the mountains, one saw steel lattice towers, power lines, temples, homes.

"Now what are we going to do?" said Li as they walked toward the main street. He couldn't stop thinking they'd "stormed out" of the ideal dentist for their needs. He and his dad berated each other. They got in a cab.

"We left halfway through the PowerPoint," said Li from the front seat after not speaking for a while.

"No," said Li's mom. "We finished it."

"No," said Li.

"No?"

"No. I was looking at the scroll bar. Dad started fighting with the dentist halfway through. It's funny."

Ten days later, at the office of the only other dentist on "5 Holistic Dentists in Taipei" whose phone number worked, Li's mom filled out forms for the new dentist as Li's dad criticized the first dentist's teeth-cleaning price to the new dentist's assistant.

"That's really too expensive," said the assistant. "Who is she?"

Li's dad said she'd been trained in the States.

"So has our dentist. What's this dentist's name?"

"Don't need to talk about her," said Li, standing behind his parents. He'd run out of LSD again the previous day. He'd wanted to be on it all the time—life felt painful and bleak without it—and had quickly developed a tolerance, using around a tab a day in quarter-tab doses.

"It's in the past," said Li's mom.

"So, how did you learn about mercury removal?" said the assistant.

Li's mom said it was all Li.

"Oh," said the assistant. "Are you . . . a dentist?"

"No," said Li. "It's because I read some books."

As his dad got X-rayed again, Li looked at neon tooth-paste and fluorescent mouthwash in a glass display, longing for the first dentist. They were lucky, he told himself, to have found another mercury-removing dentist.

He sat, opened *Bugs, Bowels, and Behavior* on his phone, and read about dysbiosis, a damaged microbiome, which most people had and which led to leaky gut and brain barriers, causing or worsening most-to-all modern diseases. He highlighted "If you suffer from the stomach flu, food poisoning, or other pathogenic illness related to the gut, how well can you function at work?"

Maybe more people needed to go to the edges of society, and observe and think from there, looking out and in, for humans to survive long enough to reach the end of history, he thought while reading about a 2011 study on how 43 percent of U.S. children had one of twenty chronic conditions, including autism, asthma, and diabetes.

Li's dad rinsed with antibiotic mouthwash. The dentist briefly looked in his mouth. The X-ray appeared on a screen. The dentist said everything foreign should be replaced with ceramic. He had a master's degree in biomaterials from New York University.

Li's mom asked if he could explain why it wasn't good to have mercury fillings—a question Li had asked her to ask.

"You already know, or you wouldn't be here," said the dentist, seeming suddenly shy and vulnerable. "Right?"

It was "improper and unethical," according to the American Dental Association, for dentists to extract fillings "for the alleged purpose of removing toxic substances." Slowly, though, the dentist, who chaired the dental departments at

two universities and was sixty-eight, began to answer. He'd
seen a video showing that fillings fumed at normal mouth
temperatures and that fuming increased with hot liquids,
like soup or tea. He had friends with health problems—
dizziness, headaches, amnesia, tremors—that had resolved
after demercurization.

Li's dad and the dentist left the exam room laughing and
patting each other's backs. "Go make back our money!" said
the dentist, who knew someone who'd help Li's dad sell dental lasers in China.

"They're like old friends," said Li's mom, and Li smiled.

As Li's mom paid, Li's dad criticized the first dentist and
praised the new one to Li in a giddy, seemingly gloating
manner.

"The first dentist was better," interrupted Li. "You
ruined it."

"Huh?" said Li's dad, seeming confused.

"I'll talk about it outside," said Li, moving toward the
elevators, regretting ruining his dad's mood and marring the
positive dental visit.

Outside, remorse dissolved, revealing self-pity and irritation.
"Instead of thanking me you make me feel like I did something wrong by bringing you to the first dentist," said Li.

"The first dentist was a scammer," said Li's dad.

"Without me you might have no teeth in five years," said
Li. "Your teeth were breaking apart!"

"I bit a chicken bone too hard," said Li's dad.

"No," said Li. "You didn't have enough minerals and
vitamins."

"We're grateful for your attention and research," said Li's mom.

"I just want to help prevent future suffering," said Li, and talked about Thin Uncle, whose hand had tremored conspicuously at a buffet earlier that week. Neither of Li's mom's brothers was thin or fat, but as a child Li had named the shorter one Thin Uncle and the other one Fat Uncle, and the names had endured.

They rushed aboard a packed train. "I'm going home alone," said Li, glancing at his mom's face, which looked anguished. He stepped off the train through closing doors.

Alone on the platform, he closed his eyes and told himself it was wise to self-isolate when upset. He was returning to New York in four days.

Barcelona

Back in his small Manhattan studio apartment—number 4K—after twenty hours of travel, Li smoked cannabis, thought about his parents, and cried. With his just-ended ten-week visit, he'd unknowingly entered an annual cycle of, roughly, winter in Taiwan and the other seasons in the United States. It was mid-January.

In early February, he began teaching a weekly craft class on the contemporary short story to MFA students at Sarah Lawrence College. He got too stoned before the first two classes and couldn't stop laughing, but also taught well, he felt, invoking a vibrant, relatively unawkward environment. His students read about characters with generalized fear, relationship instability, and severe yet calm disillusionment.

Li had taught the class once before, years earlier, when he often wished to die instantly, by comet or asteroid impact, while also fearing death—what if it just made things worse?

In 2015, he no longer wanted to die, but also wasn't averse to dying, which he now feared mostly out of timidity and unreadiness instead of neurotic pessimism, because it had gotten increasingly plausible to him that death was a microcosmic history—a personal untethering from time-paired matter—meaning it might feel like reading a novel's last sentence, as you involuntarily returned to the more daunting and consequential world of your life.

In late February, Li got an email from his mom that said, "The second dentist was not a good dentist at all. He did not cover Dad's face or use an oxygen mask when removing Dad's mercury. On the second visit, we asked him about safety. He got angry and shouted he would not continue to remove Dad's mercury. He then recommended a third dentist, who did a great job. Dad's mercury was sucked out today. Mercury-free at last." She was next. Auntie and Thin Uncle had made appointments.

One night in March, walking to the train after class, Li saw a raccoon using a sidewalk. In 4K, he turned an eight-by-eight-inch paper ninety degrees thrice, seeing four iterations of an in-progress mandala. "Which one makes me feel the least lonely?" he thought with loneliness-reducing amusement and stimulation. He'd been drawing mandalas for fourteen months, transculturally occupying himself for up to ten hours a day, which had been good for recovery.

He remembered in middle school when, before an assembly in a gym, he showed a friend a rare Magic card he'd gotten called "Fork." His friend had mock-strangled him. His mom had descended the bleachers and scolded the friend. Li had censured her for years, citing the event as overprotection. The way surprising memories arose while drawing made Li suspect he was always subconsciously reviewing his past, seeking details and scenes to insert into the thousands of stories directionalizing his life.

Around midnight, pain in his back and hip became suddenly excruciating. Supine with one leg bent, he played *Civilization* on his phone for two hours. The game began in 4000 BC, which was when textbooks said civilization began but seemed to be when dominator culture—in which the sexes were ranked with a bias that then, Riane Eisler argued, infected every relationship—emerged.

In the morning, unable to stand without holding on to furniture, Li felt familiarly defeated. His hip-and-back pain, which had gradually worsened since appearing in his early twenties, had always shifted and toggled in severity and location for mysterious reasons.

In April, Thin Uncle emailed, saying he'd been diagnosed with Parkinson's. "As you may know, there is no cure, all medication is only to try to reduce further degeneration. I have read various websites, as, however, I trust that you may provide more accurate information, I am seeking your help." He and Li's mom had studied English in college. Li gave dietary advice, and Thin Uncle said, "I have been much depressed, as if I would live in darkness with panic in the near future, but now I feel warm comfort." Li forwarded his mom the emails and said they needed to regularly review what they'd learned or else, saturated in the opposite information, they'd forget, then forget they'd forgotten. "Uncle said you are his savior," she replied.

In May, on the last day of class, Li gave his students wine. They discussed a Lydia Davis story in which an urban woman seemed to go quietly insane over months, feeling surprised one day when her omelet didn't speak. They discussed a Lorrie Moore story about disenchantment and read an interview with Moore from which Li learned that the last nine words of her story, which he'd read around ten times since college, were literal, not metaphorical—"she was gone, gone out the window, gone, gone."

In June and July, Li expanded his notes on his recent Taiwan visit into a hundred pages of a novel, which he sent to his editor along with a pitch for a nonfiction book on psychedelics. They decided to try to combine the two books into one. Li updated his pitch and sample pages, and his editor said it wasn't working because it seemed like a collected works.

Li agreed, then made a third pitch that included even more of his works—mandalas, lists, an essay on riding a universe-riding body. His editor said it still wasn't working. Li reseparated the book into two books, as in the first pitch—two flimsy, inchoate books. He lacked the motivation to write the nonfiction and the material to finish the novel.

A week later, he left space and maybe time for five minutes by inhaling vaporized DMT in 4K. It was the furthest he'd gotten from culture—the deepest into the mystery. When he returned, he was terrified for hours, believing his friend who'd brought the DMT worked for the CIA. He posted an account of the experience on his website.

"How is DMT beneficial to humans?" his mom emailed him, seeming worried, and Li replied he'd think about it.

Four years later, when he still hadn't answered her question, he'd decide to put the answer in his novel's last chapter.

In September, three weeks after smoking DMT, Li flew to Barcelona for a four-day vacation with his parents, who were there for an eye conference. He swallowed two cannabis capsules, fell asleep in a hotel room, and woke to his parents entering with luggage of unsold lasers.

Hugging his mom, Li felt abstract and surreal. Something seemed different about her face.

"This is very not good," said Li in the bathroom about Crest toothpaste.

"I know," said Li's mom. "It's Dad's."

"It's much worse to use Crest than water," said Li.

"Water is better?" murmured Li's dad.

Seated at a restaurant, Li thought, "Fuck it," about trying to improve his parents' health. He would stop pestering them with unfortunate information and just be their friend, like before he read *Cure Tooth Decay*. He felt conflictedly relieved. Cannabis was lifting him out of the bomb-shelter-like place where he normally existed, carrying him eerily away, into mental wilderness. He stopped wanting to give up.

His mom's eyebrows seemed higher on her forehead than he'd ever seen them. He told himself to consider what to say and say it later, like maybe the next day.

"Between your eye and eyebrow looks different," he said a minute later. "Did you do something to it?" Drafting this scene years later, he'd realize he hadn't noted and didn't remember his mom's verbal response. She held her balled fists in front of her cheeks, as if trying to hide.

"What do you think?" Li asked his dad.

Li's dad said he opposed the surgery. He'd learned of it when he returned from China and saw Li's mom in bed with a bandaged face.

"She's gotten surgery before," said Li's dad.

"No," said Li's mom, seemingly automatically.

"When?" said Li.

"When you were in college," said Li's dad.

"He knows about that time," said Li's mom, who'd read a story Li had published online in 2006 in which a character suspected his mom had gotten face surgery.

"Now I can't tell as much what you feel by looking at your face," said Li, worried about what was happening. His flustered mom seemed helpless and under attack, and he didn't seem to be helping.

"I've felt pressure from you," said Li's mom to Li's dad, who said, "I've said you could gain some weight. I haven't said to do anything to your face."

"Have other people said anything?" said Li.

"People have told me I look tired," said Li's mom.

"I feel you look very energetic and alert," said Li, and smiled.

"Really?" said Li's mom, smiling a little.

"Yes. Your eyes look very wide, like you're surprised."

"Is that good or not good?" said Li's mom.

"I don't know," said Li, looking away to hide a large grin, relieved and happy to have begun to feel playful and compassionate and friendly, instead of just gloomy and distressed. "I feel it's good. You seem like you're paying a lot of attention."

"Really?" said Li's mom.

"Really," said Li.

After their food arrived, Li's mom said she'd told Auntie she was getting surgery, but hadn't said what for, and that Thin Uncle had learned afterward; the three siblings met for coffee most days.

"What did they say?" said Li.

"Nothing," said Li's mom.

"They didn't say anything?"

"They said, 'Ng.'"

"Ng," said Li, and looked down at salmon on his plate. Eating it with a fork, he felt emotional, imagining his mom secretly getting surgery. He privately thanked cannabis, without which he might not have mentioned anything until after the vacation, by email.

After dinner, walking on La Rambla, a wide pedestrian street, Li felt calm and positive and energetic. His back pain, which he'd told his parents was gone—cured by nutrition, yoga, posture control, and rarely sitting—felt more stimulating than bothersome.

"How old do you two think you'll live until?" he said.

"Eighty-five," said Li's dad.

"Don't know," said Li's mom. "What about you?"

"Don't know," said Li, who'd reestimated when he'd die from fifty to sixty or seventy due mainly to diet. He'd been confused about what to eat for optimal health, changing in his twenties from vegetarian to vegan to raw vegan, until reading about aboriginal diets in *Cure Tooth Decay, Nutrition and Physical Degeneration*, and other books.

Li's dad approached an international chain ice-cream store. Li said their ice cream, which he'd eaten from 2010 to 2013, was a little healthier than most ice cream.

"Then let him," said Li's mom. Until that year, she and Li had merrily encouraged Li's dad to eat anything, thinking he was protected by statins.

"Wait outside," said Li to his dad.

In the store, Li and his mom stood in line.

"Get Dad something with nuts," said Li's mom.

"He said chocolate and the red one," said Li.

"Dad likes nuts. Get him nuts."

"I should get what he said," said Li.

"Okay." Li's mom went outside.

Li tried to invisibly spy on his parents by mentally examining the patch of his peripheral vision in which they moved in and out of view outside the glass storefront. His playful attempt at new behavior made the wispy edges of his consciousness creep into other worlds. He felt nearer "the mystery," a term referring to the empirical evidence that things existed outside culture—electrons, stars, trees, birds, minds—that couldn't be explained, in terms of who made them, why, and how.

When Li first heard of the mystery from McKenna two years earlier, it had seemed poetic. Gradually, he'd realized it was literal but hard to understand from inside dominator society, which over six millennia had barricaded itself from the mystery's two known forms (nature and the imagination) with a radially growing wall of truth-costumed lies. Dissolving the interposition daily with solitude, books, and cannabis, he'd regularly, if tenuously, sensed the mystery as a humbling, friendly, joinable presence.

In bed in the hotel, he thought about his mom's first face surgery, twelve years earlier. She'd been alone in a large house in Florida with two elderly toy poodles, Binky and Tabby. Li had been at college; Mike at grad school; their dad in prison. She'd endured, holding together the loose, estranged family—in which the others seemed to naturally drift apart from one another—with calls, letters, emails, prison visits.

Was she in a crisis again? Li didn't seem to know. He told himself to compliment her eyes more, so she wouldn't think the surgeon had botched it, which could lead to more surgery and spiraling despair.

Minutes after waking in the morning, Li began talking to his mom about her face. He reminded her she'd always said to avoid surgery. She said she wouldn't do it again. She called Li "guāi," which meant "obedient and well-behaved," for noticing and mentioning the change.

At Aquarium Barcelona that afternoon, Li's torso began to feel heavy and sandbaggish. As his dad walked around photographing fish, Li and his mom sat and talked, affirming, as they often did, that they should learn from his dad in terms of being able to do anything with childlike enjoyment, make friends with seemingly anyone, fall asleep whenever, and (except when doing business) not worry.

Later, in a cathedral, Li asked his mom when she'd brought him to church. She said when he was nine or ten. Parents of kids at Chinese school, which he'd attended weekly for two years, had recommended it. They'd gone twice. Li remembered believing in God while there. Seated "Indian style" with around twenty kids, taking orders from a man on a stage, he'd closed his eyes, told himself he believed in God, and asked God and/or Jesus to forgive him for his sins.

Growing up in Florida, reciting "one nation under God" daily at school, seeing God promoted on money, stickers, billboards, and signs, hearing everyone constantly thanking and/or cursing God, he hadn't realized that God was just one deity out of millions. He'd stayed somewhat confused through his twenties about God, Jesus, Christianity, and the origins of the world. Did things somehow begin at AD 0?

He'd finally gotten less confused by reading Merlin Stone's *When God Was a Woman*. God was Yahweh, a god who'd emerged at a time (1500 BC) and in a place (the Near East) where a preexisting supreme deity had already, for five-plus millennia, been "revered as Goddess—much as people think of God," wrote Stone, who argued that the pagans whom Yahweh targeted when he said, "Destroy their altars, break their images, and cut down their groves" had been Goddess worshippers.

The next day was the National Day of Catalonia. Stores were closed. At a beachside casino, Li won four hundred dollars on blackjack. His dad lost one hundred dollars. Li walked on the beach, thinking about his novel. Maybe it could end in Florida, where he was going in two months, or in Taiwan, where he was returning in three months.

Maybe after Taiwan he'd move to California and his novel could end there, with him starting a garden. He'd planned to move the previous year but had gotten occupied with the possible chest surgery, then had stayed to teach.

He floated in the sea, thinking about his mom's recovering upper face. It made her seem vulnerable and childlike, reminding him she had struggles outside family.

In the hotel, he fell facedown onto a bed.

"Du is tired," said Li's dad. "Li is tired." Li's parents somewhat often called Li "Du" by accident. They seemed to have a category, represented by Dudu, for "beloved other."

"Are you tired, Li?" said Li's mom.

"No," said Li, bouncing into a sit.

At dinner in a busy restaurant, Li's mom praised an elder who was eating alone, with wine and a book. She said she liked doing things alone, unless with family or close friends. She was a "loner," she said in English. Li said he was even more of a loner.

On La Rambla, he asked his mom if she could crack her knuckles. He demonstrated with his hands. She couldn't.

"I couldn't until weed," said Li. His inflamed hands had felt achy and doughy. "Weed is good for inflammation."

"I know," said Li's mom. Li had praised weed, as they called cannabis, many times to her by email, saying it had helped him stop the other, destructive drugs.

"Dad might like weed very much," said Li.

"Will it make me sleepy or energetic?" said Li's dad.

"It can do both. It might make you want to exercise."

"I want to smoke it, then do work," said Li's dad.

"You can do that," said Li, becoming increasingly stoned. He walked away a little and said, "Barcelona," to himself in an Italian accent. He said it louder, laughing.

Swinging his arms, he sensed the controllability of certain of his pelvic muscles for what felt like the first time. The muscles seemed unconsciously tensed. He realized he

was subconsciously reluctant to move in ways that had once
hurt because he'd internalized the worst of his pain.

He felt lost in stimulating contentment, inner space twinkling with capturable insights. He made himself half a foot
taller by walking on the fronts of his feet, amusing himself
and his parents.

"Why do you have so much energy?" said Li's mom.

"Did you eat weed?" said Li's dad, torquing suddenly
toward Li to see his face.

"No," said Li, turning away, grinning widely.

"He's laughing," said Li's dad, smiling. "You can't bring
it on planes. Police will get you."

"I didn't," Li lied. "Don't worry."

"Police will snatch you up," said Li's dad.

"No need to worry," said Li.

"Snatch you up," said Li's dad.

In the hotel room, Li smiled with unfocused eyes, glad
he'd been helpful and calm regarding his mom's surgery—
asking questions, having a sense of humor, listening.

"What happened?" said Li's mom.

"Nothing," said Li, moving away.

At the airport the next day, Li was chosen to have his luggage
searched. He didn't have anything illegal because he'd swallowed his last cannabis capsule that morning.

Back in apartment 4K, upside down on his inversion
table, he felt happy and moved that he missed his parents.
He fantasized about ending his novel in Barcelona, smiling
in the hotel room.

Florida

Two months later, in November, Li flew to Orlando for a five-day vacation with his parents, Mike, and Mike's three-year-old son, Alan. On day two, in a rental SUV in Cocoa Beach's parking lot, Li gave Alan, the ostensible main reason for the vacation, a carrot.

"What did you give him?" said Mike.

"Carrot," said Li.

"Don't let him eat it. It hasn't been washed."

"Some people think soil bacteria can be good," said Li, retrieving the carrot. He'd been eating unwashed organic produce for years, so had overlooked that Mike might disapprove.

"When you have a child you can raise it however you want," said Mike.

"Okay," said their mom. "There's no need to say that."

As the others ate lunch in a restaurant on a pier, a moderately stoned Li absorbed electrons through his feet on the beach.

In London fourteen months earlier, on their previous whole-family vacation, he'd ordered just a salad at dinner in a restaurant, and Mike had said, "You always have to be different," in a disgusted-sounding voice. Li had leaned across the table and lightly slapped Mike's cheek—a technique he'd gotten from Mike, who, as a teenager, in jolly moods, had slapped Li while saying "Don't be a baby" or "Turn that frown upside down," snapping Li sometimes out of dour grumpiness. It hadn't worked in London in part because Li, peaking on back pain, hadn't felt jolly. Mike had left dinner, cabbing back to the hotel. Their parents had seemed unbothered and even energized, agreeing with each other that fraternal conflict was normal.

Li joined the others in the pier restaurant. His dad was eating fried shrimp from a red plastic cup. His mom was pouring thick dressing onto a crouton-heavy salad. Mike and Alan had tacos and milk.

Li looked at pelicans on the pier and remembered how weird they were, with their handbag-like beaks. As a child, he and his parents had fished on the pier almost every weekend. Mike had been busy skateboarding with friends.

After Mike and Alan left for the pier, Li reminded his

mom about their family-vacation agreement. In July, he'd emailed her, "I want to go to Orlando, but I would like to choose where we and Dad eat. Mike can choose everything else." She'd emailed Mike, "Li agrees to go, but was worried you and him might disagree again on his diet. Thin Uncle changed his diet, no more trembling. My blood sugar is near normal. It really works." Mike had said, "I will make sure not to mention anything about food."

On the pier, Li's dad caught three small fish. Alan reeled in the third one and held it for a photo. A plan formed to buy fish at Cape Canaveral to cook in the hotel for dinner.

In the SUV, Mike, the only family member with a driver's license, seemed to ignore the plan. Maybe he didn't know about it. He was driving in the other direction.

"We're going to Whole Foods at some point," said Li from the third, backmost row of seats, next to Alan, who was strapped into a rear-facing child seat.

"We aren't going to Whole Foods," said Mike, sounding and appearing, Li saw in the rearview mirror, offended.

Li moved to the middle row, crowding his parents. "Do you know what someone with diabetes should eat?" he said. "Mom is prediabetic. Have you researched diabetes? I have." He gabbled disjunctively on blood sugar and diet. He saw disbelief on the side of Mike's face and felt self-conscious of how upset he'd suddenly gotten.

Mike parked on the side of the highway.

"What are you doing?" said their mom.

Mike got out of the car. "Get out," he said.

"Why?" said Li.

"Don't yell in front of Alan. Get out."

"I shouldn't have done that. Sorry."

"Get out of the car now," said Mike.

Li retreated to the third row, where Alan seemed asleep, but might have been pretending, and apologized again.

Mike continued driving. No one knew where he was going. Born in Taiwan in 1977, he was six months old when his mom left for the United States, where his dad had been for a year, working on a physics doctorate. Auntie's family had cared for him until he was two, when his mom brought him to Rochester, New York, where he met his dad.

Li stared out his window at the ocean, thinking about his microbiome. It was hard to change his microbiome because the first microbes to colonize his body had formed biofilms—microbial communities protected by self-produced polymer matrices. The past was like a biofilm, he thought experimentally. It couldn't be destroyed or suppressed. It had to be replaced gradually, with emotion-charged information, story-embedded ideas, memorable stories.

Mike parked in front of a Bonefish Grill. He and Alan went inside and ate as the others waited in the SUV.

Back at the hotel after a stop at Whole Foods, Li and his mom made a dinner of beef, bok choy, and fish soup.

At Disney World the next day, they parked in "Villains: Hook," got checked for weapons, and entered the Magic Kingdom. "Here, find Winnie the Pooh," said Mike, holding a map toward Li without eye contact. Li unfolded the map, located the ride, and silently began walking there, feeling disgruntled.

As his mom, brother, and nephew queued for the Winnie ride, and his dad stood in place using his phone, Li walked around eating celery, carrots, and almonds. If imaginary entities could read lives like books, who, he wondered, was reading his life? His post-death self probably wasn't, he sensed with some surprise. He clamped his nostrils and pushed air into his head.

Visible reality dissolved with a boingy, abstractly tickling, noiselike sensation. He kneeled, touched paved hot ground, didn't know where or what he was, stood, and felt energized and refreshed. He'd begun fainting in this way— in which, instead of losing consciousness, he seemed to ride the untethered vessel of it elsewhere, like in a smoked-DMT trip—around a year earlier.

The first time it happened, he'd been in 4K on his hands and knees after doing ten crude handstand push-ups on his sofa with his heels against a wall. He'd learned to trigger it by forcing air into his head, breathing deep and corseting his torso, and other simple methods. In Taiwan, it had happened regularly during yoga, so he'd termed it "YG." Compared to his painful, unpredictable malfunctions, YGs seemed safe and friendly, allowing him to inconspicuously leave culture and matter whenever.

On the It's a Small World ride, seated by his mom in a boat, Li noticed they were in a giant room whose ceiling panels reminded him of middle school, which made him think of asbestos—the toxic building material that was in a third of U.S. schools and that caused asbestosis, a long-term inflammation and scarring of the lungs.

After two more rides, Li and his mom sat in muggy heat, eating brought food. Li's mom wondered if always-happy people existed; she thought not. Li said modern people should feel unhappy, due in part to toxification. A 2005 study by the Environmental Working Group, a nonprofit with the motto "Everything Is Connected," had found an average of two hundred types of industrial compounds, including car emissions and banned pesticides, in the umbilical cord blood of American babies, he told his mom.

Li had suspected since middle school that he was constantly being poisoned and/or that he was cursed. Tracing his feelings back to things and culture, to molecules and ideas, the past two years, he'd sometimes felt a surreal wonder, realizing that both and more seemed to be true—he was radioactive, malnourished, dysbiotic, degenerate, brainwashed, brain damaged.

The others emerged from the food court. Mike pushed Alan in a covered stroller. Alan began crying. Mike asked if he wanted to return to Under the Sea, where it was cooler. Alan didn't seem to know, but after being asked more times seemed to convey he did. On the way there, he started crying again. "Where do you want to go?" said Mike. Alan stopped crying, seeming dazed. Mike asked if he wanted to return to the food court. Alan seemed to nod. Mike pushed. Alan cried.

Watching this, Li realized it was impossible for small children to know they existed in an uncomfortable phase-shift called history—a period of time, beginning with permanent settlements and ending with immateriality, that humans hadn't adapted to function well in—and so they absorbed the misattribution of their discomfort by adults around them to location, temperature, the lack of certain things or food, and, later in life, themselves, others, or life itself.

An hour later, on Tom Sawyer Island, Li's dad and Alan seemed entranced in the same aloof, mollified way while eating chocolate-coated frozen bananas.

"Is this real?" said Li's dad. "Did Tom Sawyer live here?"

"None of this is real," said Li.

Alan repeatedly crossed a shaky drawbridge, laughing.

"Children naturally seek complexity and novelty," thought Li. Pointing at a yellow leaf, Alan said it'd become a banana.

"Alan," said Li, holding a leaf. "Look how tiny this is."

"Tiny," said Alan, giggling. "What is it?"

"A leaf," said Li, startled by his nephew's gleaming eye contact. "It's just a tiny leaf. It's smaller than the others."

At Animal Kingdom the next morning, Mike politely, with a friendly smirk, asked Li if he'd navigate again that day. Li said yes. He liked good-mood Mike.

Walking to the "Africa" area of the theme park, Li and his mom recalled Mike's shoplifting arrest at age sixteen. Li, who'd stolen thousands of batteries in his twenties to sell on eBay, learned that Mike had stolen batteries, not, as he'd somehow believed, pants. After a night in jail, Mike had been grounded for a week, during which, one day, he and Li had gone fishing at a pond near their house. When they got home, their mom had asked Li if they'd spoken to each other. They hadn't.

In line for a safari simulation, Li felt unsettled, seeing his mom zoom in and out of her face in photos on her phone, as she'd been doing compulsively that trip, seemingly due to the surgery she'd gotten months earlier. He remembered staring at his own face and head with self-conscious despair as a teenager and older while alone in bathrooms, using multiple mirrors when available.

Later, petting a chained cow across a fence, Li thought, "Nature minimizes cruelty." For four eons, life had been riveting and blissful. Earthlings had enjoyed nested cycles of flowing variety, linked in ancient webs of mutual benefit, before dying, usually in awe-saturated, euphoric shock, as perfect food for grateful others.

History was the cruelest phase—life increasingly endured pain from known, unknown, and misattributed sources before dying confused, with many people burying their corpses in expensive containers, away from the natural cycles—and so the briefest. If Earth were seventy instead of 4.54 billion years old, history at fifteen millennia would be the last twelve minutes.

At Altamonte Mall the next day, Li's parents asked Li if Barnes & Noble had his books. Usually, with Mike present, Li would demur, not wanting the potentially envy-inducing attention, but, freshly caffeinated, he blithely ignored Mike's feelings while also suspecting his normal meekness was misguided.

The store didn't have his books.

"Where's Dad?" said Li's mom. "Go find Dad."

Li's dad was browsing a book on ancient Egypt.

Li asked if he knew what "mainstream" meant.

"The masses," said Li's dad. "Most people."

"The mainstream is wrong about the pyramids," said Li. "They weren't tombs. There were no bodies in them."

"Then what were they for?" said Li's dad.

"I don't remember," said Li after a moment.

Li's dad was looking at a photo of the Sphinx, which Li had read was at least 12,000 years old, not 4,500 years old.

"Many mainstream beliefs are wrong," said Li, vaguely recalling his dad expressing similar rhetoric in the past.

Li's dad opened *The Mind of God* at random with a focused expression. Li recognized the book. As a teenager, he'd spent many days and nights in bookstores' philosophy and supernatural sections, seeking a way out of his life. Many books had included "God" in the title, which had alienated him. Nature, continuously transcending itself, was supernatural, he'd since learned. No one knew how far it had already gone.

Li found his mom browsing a picture book of dogs with funny haircuts. He told her the bottom half of his head was undersized due to malnutrition, giving him a long face, unlike his parents, Thin Uncle, and Auntie, who had square faces.

"Americans have sharp faces," said Li's mom.

"I know," said Li. "It's due to malnutrition."

"I thought it was from sleeping on one's side."

"No. How could it be that? Pillows are so soft."

"It's what I thought," said Li's mom, walking away.

Li said modern people had to get their wisdom teeth removed due to facial degeneration, which had once been attributed to interracial breeding, as he and his mom had read in *Nutrition and Physical Degeneration* a year earlier.

"Seems like you're not listening to me," said Li, amused

to feel like an annoyingly didactic character. He wanted to talk about how the deeper humans got into history, the more deformed their bodies, the stranger their malfunctions, the weirder-seeming and actually weirder their realities.

An hour later, Mike seemed rushed and bored, driving the family through Willow Run and Stonehurst, the subdivisions where they'd lived from 1988 to 2007.

They passed a pizza restaurant where Li in eleventh grade had seen a commercial promoting a drug for social anxiety disorder. He'd been there with the marching band (he played snare drum) after a football game. An extroverted trumpet player, looking around a large table, had said, "That's what happens to people with social anxiety disorder—the room literally spins. It's SAD. Really. That's what it's called." Terrified that someone would notice he had social anxiety and confront him about it—the worst thing, it had seemed for years, that could happen—Li had experienced a kind of negative DMT trip, receding into catatonic mortification. The room had almost vanished in darkness. The people too.

At a red light, Mike told Li to call Wekiwa Springs—being commanding again, Li felt. The state park was closed. Mike said he'd told Alan, who was asleep in his child seat, they'd go canoeing.

"Let's go buy fish at Cocoa Beach," said Mike and Li's dad.

"Why would we go to the beach to buy fish?" said Mike in an exasperated, agitated tone, as if his dad had suggested attending a Ku Klux Klan rally.

Li recognized the tone from when Mike had said, "We

aren't going to Whole Foods," and realized he'd inaccurately thought Mike had used it specifically on him.

Calmed by the realization, Li remembered he'd used the same tone on their parents for most of his life, that he still struggled to avoid it, and that it was the tone their parents usually used on each other.

At the DMV, Li sat by his mom, who wanted to renew her driver's license, and said, "I'm not going on vacation with Brother anymore. Not until he changes."

"People don't change," said Li's mom.

"I did," said Li. "I am."

"You're completely different, more at ease, like when you were small. You even smile and laugh now."

"It's because I'm healthier and stopped drugs and am more positive now," said Li, not mentioning the main reason, he felt, for the personality change—being on cannabis or LSD half the time while with his parents the past two years.

"I know," said Li's mom. "It's very good."

"I've also been talking more because I've been writing about you and Dad more."

"You're much more open now," said Li's mom.

"I'm still changing. It takes years to change. I still get upset."

"Everyone gets upset."

"I don't want to," said Li.

"There's a Chinese saying—it's easier to change a dynasty than a personality."

Year of Pain

Hands

Li returned to Taiwan on December 5, 2015, a month after the Florida trip, with six tabs of LSD and forty-four capsules of baked cannabis. He was back for an eleven-week visit because he liked being out of New York City, which he associated with bleakness and his pharmaceutical drug phase, and because living with his parents felt slightly surreal in a way that was satisfying for both his life and his novel.

"So now you'll visit every year," said Li's mom. "You'll add a week every year."

"I don't know," said Li, feeling defensive. "We'll see."

On day three, he saw the movie *Irrational Man*, then deep-breathed in a crowded plaza while waiting for his parents, who were in a Frankenstein movie. He'd been habitually doing improvised breathwork to strengthen his chest and lungs—breathing to internal counting, breath-holding during various activities—which had led to regular YGs.

"Du," said Li's mom. "Li. Have you been waiting long?"

"I just was right here," said Li in a distracted slur, returning to a tenuous-seeming reality after briefly losing visual input.

"Your movie just ended?" said Li's mom.

"Yes," said Li after a long-feeling pause.

"Did you like it?" said Li's mom.

"Yes," said Li, and began to walk. Vehicles, people, colors, and lights wobbled and vibrated along a stable axis, as if they could be turned off to reveal something else.

Li's dad couldn't remember *Irrational Man*, which he'd seen the previous week, even after Li said it was about an unhappy professor who murders a judge with poisoned orange juice.

Li wondered if his mom, who seemed quiet, had noticed his strokelike drawl or general confusion. "Now we're going to the piano store?" he said.

"Right," said Li's mom. "We're taking the train. We'll browse today, research at home, and go back another day."

"We should just buy today," said Li.

Li's mom said they should rent.

"Rent," said Li, troublingly upset.

"You're here only three months," said his mom.

"You two are so greedy," said Li, whose parents often accused each other and themselves, and sometimes Li, of greed.

They descended stairs into the station.

"Then we'll just not get a piano," said Li.

"Don't be like that," said his mom.

"I'll go myself, then," said Li.

"We'll go together," said his mom.

"Let's go tomorrow," said Li, realizing he was being like Alan when Alan had cried in a stroller at the Magic Kingdom. Instead of tears, he was crying dejected sentences.

"We should go today," said his mom.

"Okay," said Li with a softening expression. "Renting is better. I wasn't thinking before. I thought we were buying, so when the plan changed I felt not good."

On the train, he apologized for calling his parents greedy. He emailed himself, "Parents seem taken aback by my outburst, and I also feel taken aback. If I saw Mike doing what I did, I would view him as very grumpy and bad."

They bought an electric piano, then Li's dad left to buy batteries. His frequent battery trips and Li's mom's frequent trips to the bank reminded Li of the protagonist of *American Psycho* recurrently lying, "I have to return some videotapes." He'd imagined his parents secretly eating, gambling, having affairs, seeing doctors.

Back in the station, Li flung his palm-up arm around like a tentacle. "Dad used to do this more," he said. "He does it less now."

"You've noticed that?" said Li's mom.

"In the past, his whole arm would seem numb after movies."

"So you're really good at observing," said Li's mom.

"So the fish oil and other things really help," said Li.

"Of course," said Li's mom.

An electronic, jazz-inflected, dreamy variation of the first four bars of Chopin's second nocturne, written in 1830, played in the station, signaling the train's arrival.

On the train, Li held his breath and pulled in his stomach, unintentionally cultivating a YG.

Disembarking in an underground station, he felt himself leaving his body. He could still function in physical reality, he noticed with interest as he calmly joined an escalator queue. He seemed fully gone for a moment.

Returning, his first sensation was a strong urge to hold his mom's hand, which he hadn't done since he was maybe ten. As his hand glided toward hers to gently clasp it, memory and identity returned. Startled, he pulled his hand back to his side.

Bunun

Li was relatively calm from days four to seventeen, getting significantly upset only twice—when his mom said his favorite grocery store's frozen organic chicken looked "scary," and when he said her Neutrogena hand cream smelled toxic and she called him oversensitive.

Dehoarding some of his dad's cardboard boxes one day, he found sheet music from his childhood and inaccurately played Chopin's second nocturne. Stoned in yoga class for the first time, he felt like a complex rubber band, gently stretching itself. Alone in a park on LSD one night, he emailed himself, "Tell parents not to worry if they start tremoring or have dementia, it can be helped with diet."

For a day and a half, he fantasized about writing a thousand-page novel based on his growing notes, which had gone from irregular to daily to almost hourly, but otherwise he didn't think about his novel. He'd decided to write the nonfiction book on psychedelics first, and had been working on it inconsistently. Without a contract, he was somewhat losing interest in both books.

On day eighteen, Li and his parents rode a train and a cab to a B & B on a mountain in southeast Taiwan. The B & B was owned by an elder man with a large garden and three rental apartments. In his office, a TV and three computers showed stock prices. Li's dad said, "Farm in day, stock at night," and Li's mom laughed.

Walking in the garden at dusk, Li tried to hide a nosebleed. His mom noticed and said he should see a doctor if he kept bleeding. Li reminded her that Dr. Chan, their family doctor in Florida, had scalded the inside of his right nostril when he was twelve with hot metal in a dubious procedure that had led to even more nosebleeds.

As a child, his nose had bled near-daily for years. He'd stood aside, clamping his nostrils with tissue paper or a paper towel, as others played. After each nosebleed, reassuringly coagulated globs of blood had oozed into his mouth and throat, private evidence of survival. Nosebleeds had seemed potentially deadly: Dr. Chan had mentioned fatal blood loss. Bleeding had gradually decreased since ninth grade, except during his drug phase, when he'd snorted cocaine and heroin.

Li and his parents ate at a buffet with twenty-two types

of greens. They drank a grass-jelly beverage on a moonlit patio. Dudu quarterheartedly chased lizards, staying closely aware of Li's dad, her favorite person. If he vanished, she'd run to increasingly distant spots with anxious energy, standing briefly in each with darting eyes, emitting squeaky whimpers.

At the B & B that night, only Li's dad slept well. Li slept for two or three hours, waking repeatedly to his dad's snores and Dudu's growls. Li's mom didn't sleep, which wasn't especially unusual.

In the morning, they rode a cab to a place where they biked to a tree that had been in a famous commercial for a Taiwanese airline. Standing under the tree, Li felt emotional, seeing his mom zoom in and out of her face on photos on her phone.

They cabbed up a mountain to an aboriginal village, where they watched a show with dancing and polyphonic singing. The show's MC joked that they, Taiwan's fourth-largest indigenous group, were called Bunun, which meant "person" but sounded in Mandarin like "cannot," because they were incompetent.

Li felt amused but showed no reaction because his midsection had begun to feel bulky and viscous, as if turning into marble. After the show, browsing the village's store, he walked at half speed to hide the change from his parents.

In a cab, Li's mom said Li could live with the Bunun for two months—teaching English, learning Bunun, practicing Mandarin. Li said he'd like that.

————

Back at the B & B, he lay in pain on a hard bench, feeling worried, then returned to his and his parents' room and saw his mom using SK-II, a brand of noxious cosmetic he thought he'd convinced her to discontinue the previous year. In the bathroom, he found statins, more SK-II products, and a package of teal capsules.

On the MacBook he and his mom had gotten for his dad the previous year but that his mom used because his dad disliked Apple products, Li learned the capsules were Nexium, a proton-pump inhibitor that his mom said Thin Uncle had recommended. It was the fourth-best-selling drug in the United States. The second-best seller was Li's dad's brand of statin, which he said his doctor had made him keep taking. First was a brand of the synthetic thyroid compound Li's mom was still on. Researching statins for the fifth or sixth time in a year, Li slammed the computer on the wood floor.

On the undamaged computer, seated together on a bed, he led his parents on a ninety-minute multimedia research session, guiding them through dystopian data on drugs and corporations. He stressed he was showing them helpful, potentially brain-damage-reducing information. They gave sustained attention—hard to get from his dad on health. The night began to feel productive and intimate.

In the morning, Li helped the B & B owner plant mango seedlings, moving through pain to not seem lazy or disinterested. The B & B owner invited Li to live with him for a month to learn organic farming.

On the train back to Taipei, seated in his own row, Li rested facedown on a tray table. Facedown on arms was probably his commonest sitting position so far in life. He liked its socially acceptable, portable, free privacy. His face, leaking tears and mucus, felt like the low sky of a muggy, cramped world. Inflammation made him emotional.

It was Christmas Eve. Li wondered if his pain had worsened again that day due to sitting in damaging positions the previous night while upset. Pain had returned hard despite his varied efforts, which now included sleeping on the floor, daily inverting and stretching, and the Gokhale Method—aborigine-based techniques for posture and movement he'd begun doing from a book.

At around one a.m., on an inversion table he'd ordered and had sent to Taiwan, he felt sudden, paralyzing pain in his sacrum, as if something had cracked. Holding himself very still, he felt self-conscious disbelief. He dimly remembered feeling similarly confused in high school when his chest would suddenly hurt, indicating his lung had collapsed.

He gingerly dismounted the table and shuffled slowly through the dark apartment, quiet enough to not elicit barks or growls from Dudu, who was in his sleeping parents' bed.

Wincing and sweating, he lowered himself to his bed—blankets on the wood floor. When his heart stopped pounding, he began to test the pain with tiny, coaxing movements, trying to learn about it.

Hospital

In 2001, when Li was a senior in high school in Florida, his right lung collapsed three times. The first time, he was in his room above a three-car garage. He went downstairs and told his mom his chest hurt. She said to lie down. He returned to his room.

At the hospital, a nurse said he had a "lung scrape," which happened after colds. Li hadn't had a cold. Flu? No. A nurse listened to his breath with a stethoscope and walked away. A third nurse approached and said Li had pneumothorax—a spontaneously collapsed lung—and would need a chest tube.

Li was wheeled behind curtains. He asked if anyone had done the chest-tube procedure before. A nurse had seen it done once, but no one had done it before. Li's mom was told not to watch. The tube's position needed to be gauged by pain, so only local anesthesia, for slitting Li's side, would be used.

A nurse asked Li if "a few" interns could watch. He said yes, thinking the nurses would be more careful if watched. A nurse arrived with a plastic-wrapped package that seemed bought from Walmart. Inside was a sharp-tipped tube that looked stiff and thick as a garden hose and was attached to a suction machine.

Li was surprised this was the solution. He lifted his head. Past seven or eight interns and a half-closed curtain, his seated mom was weeping. He focused away from the scalpel, toward a nurse holding his left hand, and felt a searing, raking pain. The tube had to be shoved in gradually.

After, Li's mom entered with a wet face, as if her pores had opened like tiny faucets. Li had never seen her like that. She held his hand. Li's own wet face felt peaceful and warm and alert. Normally he looked and felt troubled, aggrieved, or tensely self-conscious.

That night, the tube seemed to expand in his chest as he lay in a hospital bed on intravenous painkillers. He propped his body with pillows in slight variations, hoping to reduce the severe pain. Over hours, he found a bearable position, but then the pain returned. He tried to show no reaction because his mom was seated by him.

After a while, he said he needed more painkillers. His mom left the room. A nurse entered with two needles and injected both into Li's IV. The pain didn't decrease, so the nurse brought pills. The suction machine gurgled, filling with frothy, bloody fluid.

For a week, Li lay in bed, eating, sleeping, watching TV,

and listening to his CDs, most of which were by punk bands who criticized corporations, governments, inequality, and war while promoting creativity and nature.

The day the tube was supposed to be removed, Li and his mom learned their doctor, whom they'd met once, was in Hawaii.

The doctor appeared three days later, said he'd pull out the tube on the count of three, yanked it out on "one," and tossed a large jumble of tubing, stitches, tape, and suction machine into an uncovered trash can.

Li walked out of the room, aware that he didn't feel any happier.

At home in their large, sunny house, Li stood at the doorway to his parents' bedroom, or a few feet inside, two to four times a week, blaming his mom for his unhappiness as she lay in bed trying to sleep. She'd spoiled him too much, he said, parroting his brother, who was at grad school, and his dad, who was rarely home that year.

Sometimes Li stressed it wasn't her fault, that he knew she loved him and only did things for his benefit. Sometimes she seemed afraid of what they'd become. Sometimes she apologized—usually with sarcasm but also, a few times, while crying and seeming devastated—for being a bad mother.

Sometimes as Li tried to involve her in his tortured reasoning (she could fix him, he felt, by disciplining and punishing him) she became unresponsive with closed eyes, supine with the blanket up to her neck, and Li, usually already crying, would get louder.

Finally, she'd say in a blunt voice that she was exhausted

and wanted to sleep. Li would stand there weeping with a swollen face and numb throat, nose dripping snot, then wander back to his room, bleary and confused.

Sometimes he'd return to her, blubbering, and say he was wrong and sorry and didn't know what to do, and she'd tell him to lie down in his room, and he would.

At school, Li wanted to be in the hospital, where the problem had seemed simple and clear. He was in cooking class when his lung collapsed again.

In the hospital, a nurse opened a package containing a tube that seemed half the circumference of the first tube, making Li think the first tube had been the wrong size.

To avoid slicing scar tissue, the slit was made between different ribs that time. The tube somehow wouldn't go in, even after the slit was enlarged.

Li was held down, and the tube was shouldered in with shockingly hard thrusts, jolting his body. He anticipated the tube piercing his heart. The pain felt disturbing.

When it was done, he still felt the same level of pain. A refrigerator-sized X-ray machine was wheeled in, used on him, and wheeled away.

An hour later, a nurse said the tube was in too far. After two more adjustments and X-rays, Li got IV morphine and was wheeled to the second floor, where a nurse asked if he wanted to watch *Survivor* or *Friends*.

His mom was in his hospital room so much, seated in a chair against the wall, that Li felt claustrophobic and annoyed. He asked her to go home. She said no. Someone needed to be there for emergencies.

He said breathing and talking hurt, as she knew, and that being loud was making things worse. He shouted to please give him privacy. She became unresponsive, looking straight ahead.

He began crying. He yelled that if he kept yelling his lung would recollapse (stress, nurses had said, was a big factor) and that it would be her fault. He yelled louder, almost shrieking.

Two days later, they met their new doctor, who said Li's lung had "relapsed," which shouldn't have happened. He looked at Li with a face that seemed to say, "You are a terrible person. There is something deeply wrong with you."

Antibiotics were injected into his chest one day to obliterate his pleural space so that his lung would adhere to his chest wall. He couldn't breathe that night. His torso and neck, then parts of his limbs and face, felt both numb and smoldering. He didn't sleep. Air trickled in somehow.

He was alone one day after the pleurodesis. His mom was feeding the dogs or buying food. He carried the suction machine like a briefcase into the bathroom, looked at his reflection, and thought he looked handsome.

Three years later, when he wrote about his lung collapses in an unpublished short story, he couldn't remember the one or more times when his dad visited. He remembered liking his dad's absence. It was one less thing to worry about.

In his room above the three-car garage, he threw his electric pencil sharpener and other things at his walls. He did it in the dark, somewhat experimentally, with irregular pauses. He tossed a splash cymbal at a wall. It bounced off, onto the carpet.

Li's dad knocked on Li's locked door. "Li," he said meekly. "What's wrong?"

Li stopped moving. He imagined entering one of the holes he'd made in his walls. His things—his drum set, computer, books, CDs—seemed to be watching him. His dad knocked again, then went downstairs.

Li lay on the floor until he felt cold, then moved to his bed. He wrapped his blanket around his head and squeezed it with both hands until he was tired. He felt like a heavy, dirty towel was trying to get somewhere and he was in the way.

He had no friends. He couldn't stop being debilitatingly shy. His awkwardness and gloominess, his inability to speak and be normal, annoyed people and made people uncomfortable—he could see it on their faces—which made him want to be alone.

Sometimes he thought he could be okay, even happy, as a mute hermit, eating and sleeping and doing small, private things related to art and fantasy, but this didn't seem like an option because he felt that his mom wouldn't believe he was fulfilled.

The third time his lung collapsed, he was showering before school. His mom was in bed. Her head, nested in dark hair, looked like a strange, egg-shaped organism. She seemed asleep. She got up.

They tried to talk the nurses out of a chest tube. After the tube was inserted, Li was wheeled to the second floor. Instead of staying in his room this time, his mom wandered the halls. She saw a lung doctor she'd gone to once for a cough. The doctor said Li should get surgery.

Happy the new solution didn't involve pain (he'd be unconscious), Li became talkative. He and his mom discussed how no one else had mentioned surgery. They criticized the other doctors and praised the new one. They became quiet. News was reporting on a school shooting in California.

Li's mom asked Li what he wanted to eat. Li said he'd think about it. After a while, he said a McDonald's fish sandwich and strawberry milkshake. When his mom returned with the food, they continued reveling in how good it was that she'd encountered the lung doctor in the hallway.

Li felt happy that he was happy and that it was making his mom happy. He'd stopped being talkative with her when he was eleven or twelve, except when lecturing and blaming her, but now he was smiling and there was an eagerness to his voice.

Home after the surgery, Li and his mom began to communicate via handwritten notes, which at first seemed better than their verbal arguments, with clearer language, less recursion, and no yelling, but quickly became just as despair drenched.

In writing, Li's blame-based logic often reached its dubious endpoint: To fix him, she had to force him into difficult situations, and she had to do it convincingly of her own volition. She had to factor in everything he'd said about what to do, then do something transcending all that, something surprising.

Li felt more doomed than ever. He wrote with angry,

vexed, and worried expressions, usually through tears. He dramatically slammed down the paper next to his mom, then walked away to wait for a reply. It continued all day and night sometimes. They used notepad paper, writing replies below replies, filling many pages, which Li stapled and referenced and began to tape on doors and in drawers. The notes embarrassed him. He feared other people seeing them.

He increasingly wrote notes to himself. He wrote that he should never blame anyone again. He quickly realized that change was a nonlinear process, destined to fail repeatedly, but he didn't give up. He wrote more notes, telling himself what he should do, and began to feel empowered to not be a helpless, unhappy, unknown recluse.

A month after the surgery, they visited the lung doctor, who showed them a jar of cloudy liquid and said it contained "blebs," which he'd excised from Li, creating holes that he'd stapled shut. Li wondered what blebs were—weak areas on the delicate membrane covering the lungs, he'd learn years later—and if he needed them.

At college, the lung collapsed around seven more times. Li felt very worried the first two times, imagining dying alone in bed, not wanting to go to a hospital for a chest tube, which had been the worst pain he'd ever felt, but each time his body healed itself over weeks to months, during which he couldn't sate his breath.

He began to trust doctors less, and to want to strengthen himself. While searching online for ways to independently reduce depression and anxiety, he learned of "natural health," which focused on preventing and curing disease through ancient, DIY methods, like food and exercise, instead of on relieving symptoms with expensive surgery and drugs, as in Western medicine. He started to realize his body wasn't defective; rather, his society was damaging.

For three or four years after college, he had bolts of pain in and around his heart that made him stop moving and stay still for minutes, afraid to rupture, tear, or puncture something. Whatever the problem was (the pain was in his left chest, away from the collapses, pleurodesis, surgery, scars, and staples) also healed on its own.

By late 2015, the heart pain became motion-stoppingly severe only around once a year, when it would remind him in a humbling way that his chest problems used to be much worse. Usually, it manifested as a mild, not-unpleasant ache, lasting seconds to hours. He sometimes couldn't tell if he felt pain, despair, restlessness, or loneliness.

Massage

But now he had a different chronic pain—in and around his back—which had grown through his twenties, as if the chest pain hadn't left, just migrated and evolved.

He hid the pain for a few days, then told his parents his back had begun to feel "cramped." After saying for months that he'd healed his back, the truth seemed too disappointing to share.

He decided to get massaged once a week. At his first massage, acute pain felt stimulating and vaguely pleasurable due to cannabis and the belief that the process was therapeutic.

"You should drink milk," said the masseuse, a young man whose name at work was "21."

"Milk gives me indigestion," said Li.

21 admitted milk gave him diarrhea.

At home, Li told his mom, who'd recommended 21, that he would've liked to talk less during massage, but otherwise it had been good.

Three days later, on January 2, 2016, Li's mom said, "Du goes to the elevator to say bye," and carried Dudu out of the apartment.

"Because she's elevator dog," said Li's dad, who was going to China for four days.

"Bye-bye," said Li's mom while making Dudu's leg wave.

Li felt moved by his parents' sly, Dudu-mediated tenderness.

On a walk later that day, Dudu seemed strangely relaxed. Normally, she refused to walk without Li's dad. She sniffed a tree, glanced at Li's mom, strolled to a concrete bench.

"Her eyes really gleam now," said Li's mom.

"They do," said Li.

"The fish oil is so good," said Li's mom, who'd been rubbing it on Dudu's gums thrice weekly.

"It is," said Li. "And the raw eggs."

Dudu stood still with her tail down, seeming to have begun to miss Li's dad, though when he was there she still often stopped moving during walks.

"Let's find Happy!" said Li's mom about another dog. "Happy's mom will give you chicken!"

Dudu, who'd never worn a leash, resumed walking.

"The good thing about having a dog is that they understand everything you say," said Li's mom.

"They can't understand," said Li, smirking a little.

"Can," said Li's mom.

"Maybe. Right, they can," said Li, deciding he preferred his mom's perspective, which made him feel closer to Dudu and also the mystery, which he'd been sensing less due to pain, but also more due to using more LSD and cannabis for pain relief.

At a lunch buffet the next day with Auntie and Thin Uncle, Li's mom said only she and Thin and Fat Uncle had gone to college. Their other five siblings had only finished grade school. Auntie, the second-youngest sibling, said she'd skipped school by climbing and hiding in trees. Li's mom, the youngest, said Auntie had skipped school once by hiding in a giant pickling jar.

Li laughed. It was his first time stoned around his mom's siblings. He asked Auntie what she'd done all day.

"It wasn't just me. It was a whole group of us. We played in the mountains."

"That's good," said Li. "What's the biggest animal you saw?"

"Lamb," said Auntie after a few moments.

"Lamb," said Li.

"When we did go to school, we often got zeros on tests," said Auntie, laughing.

Li's mom said parents of her generation, especially dads, had paid little attention to their children.

Li asked Thin Uncle about his hand. After implementing Li's dietary advice, beginning to exercise more, and getting his mercury fillings replaced, his hand had stopped tremoring except when he tried to write more than his signature.

"Did you call the language center that I mentioned in my email?" said Thin Uncle about a place where one could practice Mandarin with non-native speakers.

"I haven't," said Li.

"You can make friends there," said Thin Uncle, whose wife had died of breast cancer in 1988, when their kids were in grade school. "You can meet a girlfriend there."

Li, who was married but separated, said he'd think about it. He refrained from saying he didn't want to meet any more people, as he'd told his parents.

He wanted to heal his pain, so he could do adventurous, nature-based things, like live with the B & B farmer or the Bunun tribe.

On LSD at his second massage, Li felt amused and increasingly incredulous: 21 seemed to be massaging him with one hand, weakly and floppily, like a moribund fish, while silently using a phone with his other hand.

Had 21 been offended by Li's mom telling him days earlier not to share "the teachings"—his personalized massage wisdom—with Li but to just massage him?

21 began a set of heavy, unambiguously two-handed massages. "You're in Taiwan for a few months, right?" he said.

"Ng," said Li. "Almost three months." It was his thirty-first day in Taiwan. He was out of LSD and had already used half his cannabis. Due to pain, he'd stopped yoga and returned to sleeping on a mattress. He was prostrate in his room most of the time.

"Whenever you have problems, come to me," said 21.

"Okay," said Li, and turned over.

21 manipulated his lower body into various positions, producing intense pain.

Dazedly stoned on a pre-dinner walk the next day, Li told his parents he felt suān (cramped) but not tòng (pained).

Distracted and enervated by pain, then, he began to zone out in the opposite way of a YG (unmysterious, demoralizing, concrete), mumbling curt answers to his mom's questions about massage. He heard his dad, who'd returned from China that morning, say his mom was jealous of Dudu.

"I wouldn't be jealous even if you got another wife," said Li's mom.

Li's dad said something Li didn't hear.

Li's mom poked him with an umbrella handle.

"Don't hit me," said Li's dad.

"Hmph! That's called hitting?"

"You're not allowed to eat pig's feet tonight," said Li to his dad, resonating Yahweh with a little conniption of punishment.

Li's parents laughed, somewhat to Li's surprise.

Dudu walked onto grass and pooped.

Li's dad wiped her butt with a paper towel.

"Dad has the most patience for Du and you," said Li's mom.

Li said his parents were "bù xíng le"—a term, literally "not able anymore," his parents used to describe dead or dying businesses, life-forms, and situations in a similar way that Li used "fucked" or "doomed"—in terms of being patient with each other.

"You're right," said Li's mom, smiling at Li, who felt con-

flicted and nauseated. Usually, he argued against his parents'
pessimism about being more loving to each other.

At dinner, Li saw his mom touch her jaw. He asked if it
hurt. She said it had hurt ever since she bit into a spare-rib
bone in Florida, two months earlier.

The next morning, Li's dad left for China again, this time for
five days. He seemed to leave more when home life got tense.

At dinner, eating broiled fish, brown rice, homemade sau-
erkraut, and lotus-root soup, Li revealed he had sores at the
creases on both sides of his mouth.

Li's mom implicated the massage table. She said she
always asked 21 to use clean towels, which she supplemented
with paper towels from the bathroom.

"I'm not getting massaged anymore if you tell 21 to
change his behavior again," said Li.

"You don't need to threaten," said Li's mom. It didn't
make sense, she said, for Li to quit massage to punish her for
telling 21 not to share his teachings, which she'd done for
his benefit.

"You're right," said Li. "Sorry. I'm in a not-good mood."

After dinner, he ate spoonfuls of sweetened, alcoholic rice
that he'd found in the refrigerator.

He woke in the morning in what felt like a warm burrito of
pain, surprised. "Ahh," he said, trying to move.

Crutching himself with walls and furniture, he left his
room, traversed the hall, entered the bathroom, and heard his
mom say, "Let's go walk Du."

"Don't rush me," he said, carefully peeing. He heard his mom say, "Don't be *too* worried," to Dudu in a playful, theatrical voice. "We're leaving for a walk in a moment."

"I'm not walking today," said Li after shuffling stiffly into his room. He slept for three hours, then read a note from his mom saying he should stop getting massaged if he felt pain and not just cramped.

At dinner, Li said describing his pain would increase his mom's worry and that pain was hard to discuss in Mandarin. She said he could use English. He said English wouldn't be accurate either.

"In America, they rate pain from one to ten," said Li's mom.

Li said his pain was always changing.

Li's mom suggested, for the third or fourth time in three weeks, getting X-rayed.

"I want to see a chiropractor first," said Li. "When my back is truly bù xíng le, I'll get an X-ray."

"It doesn't hurt there anymore," said Li at his third massage as 21 worked on his right thigh.

"That means you've been listening to me."

"But my left side hurts now," said Li.

21 didn't say anything.

"It hurts the most in the morning," said Li.

"Are you having trouble breathing?" said 21.

Li lifted his head, said his nose was stuffed up.

21 said that was normal, due to facing down.

"Now is very painful," said Li as 21 massaged his left thigh. 21 said it was good he felt "very cramped"—it meant the massage was working. Li was surprised 21 had edited "painful" to "cramped." "Ow, ow," he said, fearing he might scream. Then it was over.

21 massaged Li's forehead.

Li hobbled around the massage table.

"Do you still feel pain?" said 21.

"I do, but it's better." It was what he'd decided to say after every session.

That night, after dinner, Li crept in and out of the kitchen, eating almonds, ghee, and sweetened rice. Li's dad, who'd gotten home from China while Li and his mom were eating dinner, then had immediately left to buy batteries, was using his laptop computer, parts of which were held together with tape. Li's mom was telling him to eat dinner so that they could go for a walk.

"You don't need to bother him," said Li, siding with his dad, which seemed to instantly sadden his mom. Sometimes he felt his capriciousness, shifting alliances near-daily, was a beneficial, balancing influence, allowing each parent to empathize with the other through him, but mostly he viewed it as frustrating and everyone-destabilizing.

On a rare post-dinner walk, Li felt deep inside the caves of himself. The world sounded distant and abstract. He realized he was ignoring his parents' communications, not even grunting or mumbling, "Don't know"—his stock parent-response for most of his life.

He started flapping—an exercise he'd discovered where he swung his arms—in a slow, minimal way. He'd been compulsively flapping to help his current and future moods. A glob of optimism dropped into him, and he felt open and calm.

"I should move through pain if I want to recover," he said.

"Isn't that the opposite of what 21 advises?" said Li's mom.

"No," said Li automatically, with an unpleasant sensation of mental dysfunction, and felt irritated again. "Stop pressuring me to do things differently."

"Then I won't say anything," said Li's mom. "We'll all keep our mouths shut."

"No," said Li, and started flapping again.

"Who is 21?" said Li's dad.

"The person who massages me," said Li, wrapping his arms around his shoulders with each careful, huglike flap. People in the distance were also flapping. Many Taiwanese adults and elders flapped. Li hadn't seen it in New York.

"Getting massaged too hard is dangerous," said Li's dad.

"No it isn't," said Li, annoyed.

Li's dad blamed Li's mom for upsetting Li, then walked away, talking to Dudu.

"I'm going home to write things," said Li.

"You two go home," said his mom. "I'm going to walk."

"Fucked," thought Li in English and Mandarin, lowering himself to bed over fifteen minutes, retreating five or six times to safer positions after encountering impasses of spasm-causing pain.

He lay breathing heavily and sweating. Pain had gradually

worsened since the Bunun visit three weeks earlier. Massage wasn't helping. Nothing seemed to help.

When his mom got home, she gave him an electric heat pad, which he accepted through his slightly ajar door with a noncommittal grunt.

Machines

On a pre-dinner walk three days later, Li's dad photographed a plane. A cloud. Some birds. He liked to photograph things when outside and not carrying Dudu or engaged in business. He stopped walking, typed on his phone for a minute, and resumed walking.

Li said his dad was the oldest member of "facedown troupe"—a Taiwanese term for people who looked at their phones in public. Li's dad said he'd seen older members. Li said no one else stood in place midwalk, emailing as their companions waited.

"I'm bathing tonight," said Li's dad, who bathed around twice a month. Self-consciously patting Li's mom's shoulder, he told her to "run the water" later, after dinner.

Li's mom seemed very upset.

"He didn't sound like he was being mean," said Li. "We all help each other. You told Dad to clear out the ice in the refrigerator."

"I'll do it," said Li's mom—she'd fill the tub by turning a knob. "I just don't like how 'run the water' sounds." She said it was what servants were told and that Auntie had told her not to do it.

"So it's Auntie," said Li's dad. "Ayo."

"You two are older than me. You should be responsible and not bicker."

"You're right," said Li's mom.

"You two bicker more than me. No wonder I'm like this."

"We didn't bicker that much when you were small," said Li's mom. "Did we?"

"You did," said Li.

"How did you hear us?" said Li's mom, almost to herself.

"I heard bickering all the time," said Li. He'd heard his sobbing mom tell his dad in a warbling voice, "She doesn't love you—only I love you," about a woman he seemed to have met in China. She'd driven away at night, not telling anyone where she was going. Li's dad had slept on a sofa for weeks or months. Poodle shit and piss had accumulated in the house.

"He can hear us talk, of course he can hear us bicker," said Li's dad, who one night, sending a fax, had turned to an adolescent Li, who was eating ice cream and watching TV, and said, "Mom wants me to die. Should I kill myself? Do you want that?" Li had made an annoyed noise and turned back to the TV. It was the closest he'd seen his dad to crying.

"It takes two to bicker," said Li's mom.

"Dad didn't say you were to blame," said Li. "He said 'us.'"

At their building's gate, the security guard had a package from FedEx with a form problem.

"I'll take care of it," said Li's mom, taking the form.

Dudu jogged toward the building in a slight gallop.

In the elevator, Li's dad talked rapidly about the form.

"Stop talking," said Li's mom. "I can't think."

In his room drawing, Li heard his dad in his mom's office, asking if she'd copied the form, telling her to do it, pontificating on FedEx and the need for copied forms, muttering, "Never listens."

Li's mom hissed some words conveying it was disgraceful and absurd for Li's dad to feign knowledge on FedEx. She did all the shipping, payments, and bookkeeping for his companies.

"Heh," said Li's dad, and entered Li's room. "Li. Where are my scissors?"

"You're washing dishes tonight," said Li, speaking Yahwehistly to kin again, though he'd been trying to resonate more with nature and other partnership teachers, like his Paleolithic and Neolithic ancestors, Daoism, ethnobotanist Kathleen Harrison, and Jesus, who seemed to have promoted the opposite of Yahweh's values.

"Why?" said Li's dad.

"You don't need to be upset," said Li's mom from her office.

"Because you're not being nice to Mom," said Li.

Li's dad said Li's mom had thrown pillows before.

"When?" said Li.

"She threw a pillow into the TV room and made me sleep there."

"If you were nicer, she wouldn't throw pillows," said Li.

"Did you copy the form?" said Li's dad.

Li's mom didn't respond.

"Mom always keeps copies of forms," said Li.

"She's forgotten three times," said Li's dad.

"Remember when you've told me to be nicer to Mom?" said Li. "Now I'm telling you to do that."

Li's dad said scolding worked.

Li said encouragement worked.

"Have you had employees?" said Li's dad.

"Yes," Li lied. "Encouragement works."

Li's dad said employees never changed unless yelled at. Li said his mom wasn't an employee, and that he was going to fire his dad, then, for being a "not-good" dad.

"There's nothing wrong with you," said Li's dad. "So how am I a not-good dad?"

Thinking with barely perceptible humor that there was not "nothing wrong" with him, Li said everyone was to blame. He said his mom worked morning to night, maintaining the home, caring for Dudu, cooking, cleaning, helping his dad with his businesses, while his dad slept thrice a day.

"I work at night," said Li's dad. "When no one is bothering me." He worked after his post-dinner nap, sometimes until five a.m., usually with the TV on.

"Maybe the hours worked are similar," said Li, still thinking his mom worked more. "But you bother us with noise from the TV."

"She'll keep doing it wrong if I don't scold her," said Li's dad.

"Mom isn't perfect," said Li. "No one is."

"That's why people need to be scolded."

"Does Mom criticize your machines?" said Li.

"She calls them ugly all the time," said Li's dad.

"And you haven't made them look better," said Li, who'd once defended the machines, saying ugliness underscored functionality, which his mom had been happy to hear, saying, "Your own son understands you."

"I have," said Li's dad. "Look at them." On the table where they ate dinner were three machines resembling airplane armrests. He'd finished building the infrared diode lasers, used to treat glaucoma in pets and humans, days earlier.

"You need to be nicer to Mom," said Li.

"She doesn't understand. It's not the look that matters for these."

Li's mom came out of her office holding a form and her phone in one hand. Li told her she was also to blame, which he instantly regretted, seeing her incensed, beleaguered face.

"Everyone is to blame," said Li.

His parents began yelling at each other.

Li swept his arm hard across the table, pushing off the machines. Seeking more business ephemera to destroy, he entered his mom's office, took a form from a scanner, crumpled it, and carried it into his room.

He stood still behind his door, heart thwacking.

"Give that back," said Li's mom.

"You don't need it," said Li.

"I need it to resolve the situation."

"You don't need to resolve it," said Li.

"I need the form," said Li's mom.

"It's not important," said Li, walking aimlessly into his dad's office. His dad was kneeling on the floor, between the table and the TV, gathering his machines.

"These are twenty thousand dollars each and they've been paid for," said Li's dad. "If they're broken, I'm going to make you pay for them. Child thinks money is easy to make. We need these machines, because otherwise we'd have no money."

"I don't believe you," said Li. Since 2003, when his dad was imprisoned, his mom seemed to have earned all their money through stocks and real estate. The three of them sometimes joked that Li's dad should write a book titled *How to Lose Money*; the joke was possible because he'd been the original source of the money.

Li wandered into his room, then back to his dad.

"Fortunately, they're durable," said Li's dad, arranging his machines. "I built them good. I can tell the doctor: I know these are strong because my son threw them against a wall and they didn't break."

Grinning convolutedly, Li returned to his room, where he spacily worked on a mandalic portrait of Dudu, marveling at his dad's ability to view things positively.

He empathized with his mom, hearing her on the phone with FedEx in her office across the hall. She went downstairs to give a FedEx employee a form.

Li sat by his dad on the sofa. "You and Mom are getting older and might start forgetting more. You can't treat Mom like this if she starts forgetting."

"Mom's brain is still good," said Li's dad, seated on the edge of the sofa, facing his small, dirty laptop, which was on a stack of ophthalmology textbooks.

"You can't be like this if Mom forgets things due to age."

"No, I can't," said Li's dad.

"How will you know if she's forgetting due to age?"

"When we're old, we won't bicker. We won't remember anything."

"She isn't forgetting on purpose, to hurt you, right?"

"I won't say anything then," said Li's dad in an annoyed voice.

"You should encourage, not criticize," said Li.

Li's mom returned. "I haven't thrown a pillow once in the seven years we've lived in this apartment, and he's still talking about it," she said, and entered the kitchen to prepare dinner.

"Be nicer to Mom," said Li. "Okay?"

"Okay," said Li's dad.

"When Dad is being mean, you can try to ignore him," said Li to his mom.

"A lot of the time, it's me," she said. "My temper is not good."

"Okay," said Li. "You've both agreed to be nicer."

At dinner, Li's mom commented on TV and food in a strainedly happy voice to a monosyllabic Li. When he disputed one parent, the other seemed to become both disconcerted and enlivened, with his mom getting more disconcerted than his dad.

Li's dad typed on his phone with a fierce expression. Li's

mom seemed to be refraining from pressuring him to eat. News was reporting on an elder woman who'd gotten heavily fined for stealing cabbage from a farm.

Li calculated he'd used cannabis three hours earlier; he became unstabler, he'd noticed, thirty to ninety minutes post-LSD and two to three hours post-cannabis. He asked his mom if her jaw still hurt. She said it had gotten better.

Li's dad began to viciously berate someone—Li's mom? The tirade sounded strangely vociferous and despairing. Li realized his dad was talking to his phone, on which he was text-messaging with one of his three employees.

Li's dad called the employee, who was in China, and berated him slightly less irately than before. Li and his mom heard Li's dad berate employees near-daily. They often told him to focus on writing papers instead of doing highly stressful business.

After dinner, Li lay supine in his room in pain. He used another cannabis capsule and felt despair at his dwindling supply. He'd been meaning to order more LSD. He was almost out of money.

He slept for an hour, then apologized to his dad, who interrupted him, saying there was no need to apologize: Li had helped him find weaknesses in his machines. One had come apart.

"What is it?" said Li's mom warily.

Li's dad explained.

Li's mom smiled at Li.

In his room, Li typed an account of the night. He entered the kitchen and saw his dad torqued toward him from the

sofa, saying, "You can't throw things. You can't and Mom
can't. Mom has thrown dishes before. You two can't do that."

"You're right," said Li.

"Didn't you throw my computer once?"

"I hit it on the floor," said Li about the MacBook he and
his mom had gotten for his dad, but which his mom used.
"When I found out you were using statins again and that
Mom was using Nexium."

"Can't do that," said Li's dad.

"I know," said Li, admiring his dad's characteristic method
of initially showing humor and forgiveness, then later seri-
ously discussing his disapproval. "I don't want to."

"No one says throwing things is good," said Li's mom
from her office.

"Throwing pillows is okay, not expensive things," said
Li's dad.

In bed, where he increasingly spent his time, Li remembered
he had steel staples in his lung. He'd read that biofilms survived on iron, that steel was mostly iron, and that pathogenic
biofilms caused "cognitive impairment, processing abnor-
malities, and memory problems." It seemed strange that a
lung could be stapled. Wouldn't the staples just slide out?

He focused around ten feet past his closed lids, expecting
to see something. After a few minutes, the slipperily wisp-
ing contours of a small dog appeared in unsteady motion, as
if trotting on a treadmill seen from above in shifting angles.
He sustained the vision with a mental-physical effort that
felt like he was merging his two eyes into one. The dog disappeared after six seconds. Li stared more but saw nothing.

He'd dabbled in this visionary practice for three years. It relaxed his eyes and helped him sleep. He'd seen landscapes and city skylines before—startlingly realistic grayscale panoramas, scrolling across his imagination screen, the nearer parts passing faster than the farther parts, as if he were in a train or helicopter, looking outside through absurdly dark sunglasses. He usually went from seeing to sleeping or dreaming, making it harder to remember the visions.

He couldn't sleep. He felt uncomfortable from lying on his left side for too long. He began the arduous process of rolling over without triggering excruciating pain. Supine had stopped being a good position. He made it onto his right side after what felt like fifteen minutes. Only his face, arms, and below his knees seemed uninflamed.

Until that year, reluctant to think about it, he'd reductively viewed his nearly full-body pain as "hip and back pain" or "back pain." Was it a muscle, bone, tendon, nerve, brain, and/or mind problem? Why did it change sides sometimes?

Four days later, at Li's fourth massage, 21 held and talked into his phone while massaging Li with one hand. When he got off the phone, he said he was starting work at a different parlor soon, so was calling his clients to inform them of the change.

That night, when Li's mom was on her nightly walk, Li entered the TV room. Taiwan's new president, the first female leader of a Chinese-speaking country except for Wu Zetian 1,350 years earlier, was giving her acceptance speech.

"Mom hates this one," said Li's dad. "Female. Why does she hate another female?"

"Don't say that," said Li. "Mom already said she doesn't hate her."

"She does. She's always criticizing her."

"Then say she criticizes, not hates," said Li, who didn't understand Taiwanese politics or history. Years later, he'd learn that Taiwan had been part of the mainland until rising waters islanded it around twelve thousand years ago. His ancestors had arrived there from China sometime after China claimed the island in 1683. In 1949, the losing side in the Chinese Civil War, called KMT, retreated to Taiwan and ruled authoritarianly, under martial law, until the eighties, when the DPP emerged. The new president was DPP.

"I hate someone else," said Li's dad. "Mom hates this one."

"Don't say that. You know it makes her unhappy. Don't say that when she's here."

"I can say it when she's not here?" said Li's dad, grinning.

"You say it every time the president is on TV," said Li. "Stop saying it."

He went into the kitchen to make fermented beet water. Weeks earlier, he'd introduced beet kvass and apple cider vinegar to his mom to replace Nexium for relieving acid reflux.

"Tell Mom to let me hug her," said Li's dad, miming hugging.

Li put beet pieces, sea salt, and mineral water into a glass jar.

"Whenever I go to hug Du—hug Mom, she doesn't let me," said Li's dad. "That's not good."

It was the first time Li had heard his dad confuse his mom and Dudu.

Later that night, Li stood in the kitchen stirring brown rice, which he was fermenting to decrease its phytic acid, an enzyme-inhibiting chelator, and increase its GABA, an antidepressant neurotransmitter.

The kinetic oven, which Li's mom had gotten to replace the microwave, dinged. Li removed almonds and walnuts, which he'd baked with ghee for his dad to bring to China. His dad was going to China the next morning for the third time that year.

"Your own son made you nuts," said Li's mom. "Are you moved?"

"Yes," said Li's dad in large dark glasses, testing beeping, flashing lasers.

"And fish oil and chlorella," said Li, putting capsules and tablets in a plastic bag.

Eating lunch with his mom the next day, Li said he was stopping massage because the parlor contained toxic fumes and because 21 had used his phone while massaging him.

"Aiyah," said Li's mom, shaking her head and glaring. "He should not do that."

"He's very busy," said Li.

Li's mom said Thin Uncle's back had once hurt so much that he could only crawl; after six months at a physical rehabilitation center, he was pain-free.

Li didn't respond. He'd heard the story three times that year. It seemed designed to passive-aggressively get him to go to the rehab center.

"Have you tried the heat pad?"

"No," said Li, frowning.

"Why don't you try wearing it to sleep?"

"Because I feel it's dangerous to do that and because I switch sides a lot at night and I don't think it will help."

"Then don't use it," said Li's mom.

"I found a chiropractor online. Can you make an appointment for me?"

Ankylosing

The next day, Li woke at around noon to his mom outside his room saying she'd made a 3:30 p.m. chiropractor appointment and was going to the bank to wire money to Li's dad's employee.

"I'm sleeping more," said Li quietly.

"I'm leaving," said Li's mom from the apartment's front door.

"I'm sleeping," mumbled Li inaudibly.

"I'm leaving," said Li's mom a minute later.

"Mom," said Li. "I'm sleeping. Let me sleep."

Two hours later, he moved bathroomward slower than ever, feeling vaguely humored by his decrepitude. He had to move delicately, with vigilant restraint, to avoid stabbing pain that seemed capable of making him spasm and fall.

He left the apartment in a stiff limp, cringing from body-control focus. He couldn't turn his neck or bend forward. He rode two trains and four escalators and saw his mom, smiling and waving.

The chiropractor was a large American man who'd lived in Taiwan for thirty-seven years. Li told him about his parents' mercury fillings. The chiropractor had also gotten his fillings replaced in Taiwan.

Li got X-rayed. The chiropractor said he and Li both had six lumbar vertebrae instead of five, making their spines sensitive. He said Li's coccygeal vertebrae were crooked, his right leg was shorter than his left leg, his bottom vertebrae were thinner in back than in front and were fusing to his sacrum, and that he should get a custom sole.

Li agreed to visit the chiropractor thrice a week, then lay prone on a machine that mechanically stretched his back, giving pain a wavy, cyclic quality.

The chiropractor pushed Li's skeleton, producing cracking noises. He made molds of Li's feet, told him to drink three liters of mineral water a day, said Taiwanese masseuses used too much force, and recommended tai chi.

Outside, Li told his mom that in 2007 he'd seen a doctor about his pain who'd also said his legs were different lengths. Instead of buying an expensive custom sole, he'd padded his right shoe with paper towels and toilet paper for eight years, until switching to shoes with minimal soles the previous year.

That night, Li's dad called from China. Li's mom handed her phone to Li, who told his dad about the chiropractor and returned the phone to his mom, who said, "Okay, talk to Du a little more, say bye."

Li's dad asked Dudu about her day, then he and Li's mom talked leisurely for a while. Their small talk moved Li, who'd recently felt more compassion toward his dad by considering how he seemed to have no friends. He only talked to Li's mom, Li, Dudu, his employees, people he saw on walks, and, rarely and formally, his two sisters.

In bed, Li thought about chronic illness, which was worst in the States and rising globally. Maybe health problems would end U.S. domination, weakening the country into a new kind of partnership society—a meek, in-turned place of diseased people caring for one another—and also, eventually, history.

Humans everywhere were being nudged and shoved and pulled and lured away from matter, toward the increasingly friendlier dimension of the imagination—away from inflamed, deformed, poisoned bodies and the ad-covered, polluted outdoors, into beds, books, computers, fantasies, dreams, memories, and art.

On a walk the next day, as Li and his mom approached a turn, she said it seemed like Li's pain went away—he seemed to walk a little faster—whenever they got there.

"It doesn't get better here," said Li, surprised by the flighty logic, which he sensed could, layering with his own uncertain attributions, lead to hopeless levels of confusion.

"No?" said Li's mom.

"No. Why would it?"

"I don't know," said Li's mom.

"You shouldn't track my pain."

"I'm not. I'm just talking."

"It's not good to track my pain."

"I'm not," said Li's mom, and told the story of Li running into a table when he was two. She'd asked him if it hurt a lot. He'd said it hurt "just right"—not too much, not too little.

"It's very hard to talk," said Li.

"You're very good at talking," said Li's mom.

"No," said Li.

"Articulate and eloquent," said Li's mom in English.

"No," said Li. "You're thinking about my writing."

Entering the kitchen very stoned that night, Li snickered, realizing his mom couldn't hear his approach.

"What's funny?" she said.

Li said he felt like a ninja. He put fermented kohlrabi on top of fermented rice and returned to his room.

At the chiropractor's office the next day, Li lay prone on the traction machine. The chiropractor used something resembling a handheld vacuum on his back, seeming to electrically stimulate it, then hastily passed a rumbling, blow-dryer-like machine over his body and limbs, then pushed his skeleton in various places, then taught him a leg stretch and asked if his pain had decreased.

"No," said Li.

"Did you drink three liters of mineral water a day?"

"No." It hadn't seemed sensible. He would've had to pee probably six to ten times per night. It took twenty minutes sometimes to get out of bed and up to an hour to nestle back into positions where pain settled into a sleepable ache.

"Did the chiropractor do the same things as last time?" said Li's mom at dinner.

"Yes," said Li.

"Nothing new?"

"No," said Li.

"Then he makes easy money," said Li's mom.

"If he hasn't helped me by the time the sole comes, I can stop going."

Li's mom suggested seeing a Chinese medicine doctor.

"They'll want to give me drugs," said Li.

"They don't use drugs. They use Chinese medicine—goji berries, ginseng root, things like that."

"That's good," said Li, dimly surprised he'd forgotten what Chinese medicine was. "I want to see a Chinese medicine doctor. Wasn't your dad a Chinese medicine doctor?"

"Yes," said Li's mom, whose dad had died when Li was five. She and Li had flown to Taiwan for the funeral. A big black butterfly had landed on the coffin above her dad's head and died there.

"Why are you smiling?" said Li's mom.

"I like seeing doctors," said Li. "It's good for my novel." He'd gotten increasingly interested in what seemed to be his new, simpler life. He'd imagined staying in Taiwan indefinitely, supported by and supporting his parents, tripping in bed, seeing healthcare professionals, abandoning his novel and nonfiction book for stories and poems—forms more suited to chronic pain, with which he could write for only an hour or two a day. The prospect had calmed and sometimes excited him.

"You look very handsome when you smile," said Li's mom.

News was reporting that a ceiling at the airport had caved in. There'd been no injuries.

"Don't let the chiropractor touch your neck," said Li's mom. "I had a classmate who was paralyzed by a chiropractor. You should never let any type of doctor touch your neck."

Li said he didn't think that was a good rule, but that he'd follow it so that she wouldn't worry.

"Who cured Thin Uncle's back?" Li asked his mom the next morning, mnemonically muddled by pain. "A Chinese medicine doctor?"

"No," she said. "The physical rehabilitation center."

An hour later, he held her arm for support as they rode the elevator and went outside to wait for a cab to take them to the rehab center.

It was raining. They stood under an umbrella.

"Even though I can barely move, I don't feel depressed," said Li, with "depressed" in English.

"Why?" said Li's mom.

Li said due to his GABA-enhanced rice and to eating a lot of fermented vegetables, which contained microbes that made serotonin, melatonin, B vitamins, and other calming compounds.

Li's mom shared a Chinese saying—the chronically ill become their own doctors.

At the rehab center, a doctor examined the chiropractor's X-rays of Li's spine. He asked if Li felt stiffest in the morning. He did. The doctor said he might have "ankylosing spondylitis," which Li and his mom hadn't heard of before.

"I'll inject him with steroids, then," said the doctor.

"He doesn't want shots," said Li's mom.

"Then what does he want?"

"The other therapies," said Li's mom.

"The electricity and heat lamp," said the doctor.

"Right," said Li's mom.

As the doctor began to leave, Li asked if his legs were different lengths. He and his mom had agreed it was wise to wait until the ends of visits before asking questions.

The doctor looked at the X-rays again, then at Li's feet. He said Li's left foot was flat and that the length difference was due to standing askew during X-rays due to pain.

Li sat backward in a chair with a lamp at his hip and electrodes on his back, researching ankylosing spondylitis on his phone.

Wikipedia, which aggregated the mainstream, said it was a progressively worsening, whole-body arthritis with long-term inflammation of the spine. It caused chest constriction, lung fibrosis, and a hunched back. In advanced stages, ascending vertebral fusion could form an immobile column called "bamboo spine."

"Maybe I do have AS," said Li at dinner that night. It would explain why his pain was unpredictable and mobile and why yoga, inversion, massage, etc. hadn't helped.

Li's mom praised the rehab doctor for knowing of AS, which affected around 1 in 130 people. Li said they'd also believed the chiropractor. He imagined seeing another health-care professional and changing their minds again.

After dinner, plateauing on cannabis, he brought the apartment's cordless landline into the bathroom. Recording a voice memo with his phone, he dialed the chiropractor on the landline.

"Hello?" said the chiropractor.

"Hello?" said Li.

"Hello?"

"Hi," said Li in English. "It's Li? One of your patients?"

"Hi! How are you?"

"Good. How are you?"

"I'm okay," said the chiropractor.

"I'm calling to . . . cancel Friday's appointment?"

"Okay," said the chiropractor.

"Because my mom and I decided we're going to try a more affordable thing, that we found, first?" The rehab center was the equivalent of six dollars a visit; the chiropractor was sixty times as much. Just the sole cost three hundred dollars.

"Okay," said the chiropractor.

"And if you could call us when the orthopedic comes in."

"When the orthotics come in."

"Okay?" said Li.

The chiropractor was silent.

"Okay," said Li. "Thank you."

"Well, good luck to you. I don't think you'll get anything

better than what I can provide, but that's your choice. I'll call you as soon as your foot orthotics are in."

"Thank you," said Li.

"Bye-bye."

"Bye." Li entered the kitchen grinning uncontrollably. He told his mom what happened, then went to the bathroom, looked in the mirror, and laughed more than he had in months.

In the morning, he felt like settling concrete from the neck down. He tingled with mind-distorting, vaguely psychedelic pain, like a mutant with superpowers gone wrong. After his parents left for a walk, he doddered rigidly toward the bathroom, propping himself against the walls with his arms and hands, feeling sometimes like he was lost or demented.

At the rehab center, he read that a symptom of AS was "alternating buttock pain" and that people with AS died early from strokes and heart attacks. Wikipedia, WebMD, and other front-page results on Google—which Li would supplant years later with DuckDuckGo after reading that Google censored, shadowbanned, and blacklisted natural health sites because its parent corporation since 2015, Alphabet, had ties to pharmaceutical corporations—said it was incurable and had no known cause and that three treatments existed for slowing the deterioration: synthetic drugs, surgery, exercise.

In his room, clicking past the corporate near-internet, Li found articles and videos in which people with AS, doctors, and researchers said the disease could be relieved and/or cured by healing one's gut. He found KickAS.org, a site based on the work of immunologist Alan Ebringer, who had recognized AS as a form of rheumatoid arthritis—an auto-immune disease with microbial factors—and begun to test dietary treatments in 1982. The main advice seemed to be to avoid starches and certain other foods, which one had to identify through experimentation.

At dinner, refraining from rice, Li told his mom and dad, who'd returned from China that day, that starch fed a spe-cies of bacteria called *Klebsiella pneumoniae*. Due to his dam-aged, varyingly permeable gut barrier, the bacterium reached places in his body where it hadn't adapted over millions of years to be. His body attacked the microbes and also itself because three types of collagen (I, III, IV) and a complex of glycoproteins made by some humans resembled something in *Klebsiella p.*

The next day, Li's pain seemed slightly improved. At dinner, Li's mom's hand went to her jaw and she winced. Li asked if her jaw hurt again.

Touching her temple, she said sometimes it hurt up to there and that some mornings her jaw felt like it was going to fall off, which worried Li, who said she should see her dentist because maybe despite the safety measures—coating her mouth in chlorella, suctioning fumes and fragments—mercury had gotten into her gums. "We can go together when you feel better," she said.

It was January 27, and Li had four weeks left in Taiwan. Continuing to avoid rice, he hurt slightly less each of the next three days, during which he said variations of, "If we didn't see the rehab doctor, I would've kept getting treatments that misattributed the pain, which would've kept increasing, because I would've kept eating more rice, steamed and sweetened and fermented, to comfort myself and aid sleep," to his parents four times. It seemed important to remember.

On his fifth day without starch, Li searched Wikipedia's AS page for "starch." It wasn't there. Neither were "diet," "heal," "natural," or "Ebringer." Li's mom canceled the Chinese medicine appointment and went to get the orthotic from the chiropractor.

She told the chiropractor that Li had improved, and the chiropractor was surprised—after two sessions? She said Li had "AS" and had stopped eating starches, and the chiropractor said, "Ankylosing spondylitis," indicating he knew of the disease.

On a train two days later, on the way to a hospital to confirm whether he had AS, Li saw someone wearing a brand of jeans called "Upset." Li's mom said maybe the person equated "up" with good.

They got off the train. It was a rare cloudless day. Li could almost walk at a normal speed. He'd run out of cannabis the previous day after being nearly continuously stoned through the five weeks of increasing pain. He started to feel depressed.

His upper and lower teeth didn't fit snugly, in part because many were missing, and so he was always releasing adrenaline and cortisol, making it hard to sleep or relax, he told his mom. There was a treatment called orthotropics, he said, which widened degenerate jaws, creating larger airways, instead of extracting teeth and root-destroyingly prising the rest into alignment with braces and headgear, as in orthodontics, which he, Mike, and most of their peers had gotten.

"Is your tooth still black?" said Li's mom.

"Yes. But the black part hasn't gotten bigger."

"That's good," said Li's mom.

Li said when he was stoned he felt his mouth more and it felt numb, crowded, and sore. He considered saying that when he was stoned and alone he unconsciously stuck his tongue out a little because his mouth was unnaturally small. Instead, he said something he'd said in an email once: stoned in 4K the past two years, he'd often cried while recalling times he'd been mean to his mom and other people.

He felt better after near-monologuing on degeneration and cannabis.

At the hospital, a doctor asked five questions, diagnosed Li with AS, and ordered a confirmation X-ray.

Walking to radiology, Li's mom said Auntie was coming to the hospital for the results of an ultrasound she'd gotten after noticing blood in her urine, and that Thin Uncle might be coming too, due to chest pain.

Sensing things as somewhat zany, Li began to view life as literature. Life was an extremely long novel, and novels were like dreams, he thought with a gladdening sensation of the mystery, which he hadn't felt in weeks, except sometimes while stoned in bed. Ten millennia of civilization, placing people in high-rises with TVs, computers, walls, and pain, had made the mystery easy to forget. Li suspected that the more he recovered, shedding layers of pain and culture, the closer he'd feel to it.

After getting X-rayed, Li saw Auntie and his mom. The three of them walked through the hospital.

In a sunny hallway, a motorized wheelchair approached Auntie, quiet and fast.

"Li!" said Li's mom to Auntie, who almost always looked down when walking.

Auntie saw and eluded the wheelchair.

"I called Auntie Li," said Li's mom, laughing.

"I heard," said Li, smiling a little.

The doctor looked at Li's X-rays, said he had AS, and prescribed a painkiller and an anti-inflammatant.

"He doesn't want medication," said Li's mom.

"It was pointless for him to have come, then," said the doctor.

On the train home, standing above his seated mom, Li felt alone and doomed, unable to sustain eye contact with her for more than two seconds. It seemed impossible, like doing a split. He hadn't been good at eye contact, maybe especially with his mom, since middle school.

He sat beside her. Beneath AS were darker problems, he thought, looking outside at the sky's steady blue light.

Thyroid

Four days later, twenty tabs of LSD arrived. On LSD at dinner, Li recorded himself telling his parents about the Younger Dryas, a period of time from 12,800 to 11,600 years ago that began and ended with global cataclysms, destroying, he'd read in books by Graham Hancock, at least one advanced civilization.

"People were as advanced as we were in the eighteenth century," said Li, and smiled at his mom, holding eye contact with startling, slightly nervous confidence; on LSD, he could be garrulous and extroverted, sharing thoughts, looking at eyes.

He couldn't remember his mom's pre-surgery eyes. She'd looked perpetually surprised in Barcelona and Florida but

had started to appear normal when he got to Taiwan for his
current visit.

"The same as we were in like 1780," he said, sounding
somewhat accusatory, as, to his rhetorical detriment, he usually did when telling his parents paradigm-changing information.

"Oh," said Li's mom.

"They had ships and had mapped the planet and were
destroyed by pieces of a comet."

"Whole world all destroyed," said Li's mom.

"It hit mostly in North America, and there was almost
no sunlight for a long time," said Li, looking at his dad, who
seemed preoccupied, eating and watching TV.

News was showing security footage of an arcade machine
playing itself—metal claw descending to prizes, stuffed pig
slipping away. They'd seen the segment earlier that day.

"And then, why were there people again?" said Li's mom.

"Because some survived," said Li. "They lived in caves
and underground." He said most people blamed aborigines for extincting mammoths, camels, lions, giant beavers,
and thirty-some other New World megafauna, but it was
the comet. Every June and November, Earth risked another
history-resetting impact by traversing the comet's pieces—
the Taurid meteor storm.

"Modern people look down on aborigines," said Li's mom,
quoting Li.

"Yes," said Li, wondering what his parents understood or
thought about there having been an earlier, deep stumble
into history, with its own technologies, deities, drugs, novels,
and types of pets. To Li, it seemed surprising and illuminat-

ing, showing that history, instead of being linear and unstoppable, was possibly a frequently interrupted thing, requiring two or five or more tries.

"It's good that you have diverse interests," said Li's mom.

Li said his interests were similar in terms of being examples of dominant models being wrong in ways that distorted and simplified and disenchanted reality. With the waning of pain, his attention was drifting back to these interests.

The next morning, Li got an email from his agent saying he'd gained Li a contract for his in-progress novel and proposed nonfiction book. Outlining the latter, Li cast ideas, scenes, stories, goals, and emotions into the future, creating a long, 4D bubble, a new phase, suctioning him ahead. After a few days, he began to feel like the five weeks of pain hadn't happened to him, but to someone in a movie he'd seen.

On his sixth day of outlining his nonfiction book, which he wanted to be about, besides psychedelics, his increasing interests in history and nature, Li went into the kitchen for green tea and saw his dad turned toward him from the sofa, saying, "Mom's weight has been dropping. Why?"

"I don't know," said Li. His dad, seeming rattled, blamed fermented vegetables. Li said his mom, who was out with Auntie and Thin Uncle, would benefit from more, not less, fermented vegetables. His dad told him to research "sudden weight loss" online.

Li entered and exited his room, aimless with worry. Back in his room, he typed "sudden weight loss." Google suggested "in dogs," "in cats," "diabetes," "in elderly," "symptoms," "and hair loss," "in teenager," "without trying," and "in horses." He typed "in women" and clicked "10 reasons why unexplained weight loss is a serious problem."

One was diabetes, two was depression, three was excessive thyroid.

That night, after Chinese New Year dinner with relatives at a Japanese restaurant, Li and his parents and Auntie stood waiting for the train. Auntie told Li it was good he cared so much for his parents. She'd heard Li discussing thyroid with his mom.

Li's mom said it'd be good if Auntie's children cared about her as much, and Auntie agreed. Auntie lived with one of her two sons, her son's wife, and their three children in a small apartment. Her husband had died unexpectedly in 2001 at age fifty-eight.

The previous year, Li's mom had emailed Li asking him to please consider getting a pneumonia vaccine due to his weak heart and lungs. Li had sent her four articles, including "UK Scraps Pneumonia Vaccines Because They Don't Work," and said there were safer ways to increase immunity than with shots containing aluminum, mercury, formaldehyde, neomycin, MSG, polysorbate 80, and other adjuvants, preservatives, stabilizers, and surfactants.

He'd expected a government-and-corporation-trusting reply. Instead, she'd said the flu shot might have killed Auntie's husband, who'd gotten it one day without telling anyone. Rashes had appeared on his neck and face. Auntie had driven him to a hospital. He'd died a day and a half later.

The train arrived to the remixed beginning of the Chopin

nocturne. Li's parents got on. Auntie tried to crowd aboard as the train and platform doors closed. A panicked-looking Li's mom pushed her off.

Li and Auntie were alone on the platform.

"I'm very healthy," said Auntie.

"That's good," said Li.

"I go to sleep and don't wake until morning."

"My mom has problems sleeping," said Li.

"I don't. I close my eyes and it's morning."

"Do you get up to pee?" said Li.

"No. I've always slept well. I eat well and I sleep well."

Li said he and his mom had to pee many times a night. He said they were damaged from living in the States. His mom, doing all the cleaning, laundry, insect control, and yard work, had inhaled Windex, Dawn, Tide, Clorox, Raid, and/or Roundup daily.

"I feel strong and great," said Auntie. "I'm very healthy."

Li thought of breast cancer, which Auntie had gotten two years after her husband died. Her left breast had been removed. She'd continued working, running a night market stand with games for children, until she was jailed for a night because games with prizes were illegal. Since then, Li's mom, who often said Auntie's life was hard due to lack of schooling, had given her money monthly.

"You've always slept well?" said Li.

"Right," said Auntie. "I don't dream, either."

"Hm. Has my mom always not slept well?"

"She's never slept well," said Auntie after a moment. "I've always been healthier than her. My hands are warm. Hers are cold." She held Li's hand with both her hands.

Li felt surprised by how cold his hand felt. His mom had

told him many times that Auntie's hands were warmer than hers, but he'd always viewed her as exaggerating.

Li asked about Auntie's eldest brother, who'd died in 1989 at age forty-nine. Auntie said he'd sprayed DDT on his banana, guava, and orange plants, as Li knew from his mom. Auntie mimed spraying, showing that DDT had fallen onto her brother, who for years had said a fishbone was stuck in his throat. When he learned it was thyroid cancer, he could no longer talk. In the hospital, he'd written notes, begging people to let him die.

Auntie mimed begging. As the train entered the station, she said she was grateful that Li had taught them about organic food.

Li and his mom researched natural thyroid that night. They found WP Thyroid, which didn't require a prescription but entailed making a wire transfer to an individual, which seemed dubious to Li's mom. They found Thyro-Gold—desiccated thyroid glands from grass-fed New Zealand cows—which also didn't require a prescription, but which required that one learn one's dose by tracking temperature and weight daily over weeks. They decided to keep looking.

"It's good we're researching carefully," said Li's mom.

Li agreed it was good, unlike her strategy.

"Huh?" said Li's mom. "What's my strategy?"

"Nexium. You didn't research Nexium."

"Oh," said Li's mom. "Right."

"You didn't even ask me about it. Can you ask me in the future?"

"Of course," said Li's mom.

"If you ask, we can research together."

"I will," said Li's mom.

Around midnight in the park by their building, Li biked in circles around a synthetic hill with a glass pyramid on its flat concrete top, listening to Chopin's funeral march through earphones. He teared as the dulcet, transportive part of the piece began. Biking home, he felt emotional in a hollow-yet-substantial, sponge-shaped way.

Prison

Two days later, Li and his parents went to a hot-pot restaurant for lunch with Li's dad's sisters.

Li's dad, who was three years older and younger than his sisters, said Dudu, who was at home, had refused her chicken earlier because she'd misheard "three" as "four" when he said three people were going to lunch.

"She can understand you," said Li's dad's older sister.

"Yes," said Li's dad, looking at a menu.

"Yes," said Li's mom.

"Du doesn't want these," said Li's dad about dinner-set extras—rice, dessert, beverage.

"You called me Du," said Li.

His dad ignored him.

"Dad called me Du," said Li to his mom, who always acknowledged her nomenclatural mistakes.

"His brain is a little broken," she said.

Li's dad's younger sister said she hadn't known Li was in Taiwan.

"He's been here two weeks," said Li's dad.

"Two months," said Li's mom.

"You've been here two months?" said Li's dad.

"Doesn't know about his own child," said Li's mom.

Li's dad's older sister said Li should get a divorce.

"I know," said Li. "I want to. I will once I'm back in New York." He and his wife had been separated for five years, during which he'd been in one half-year relationship, which had ended thirty-eight months earlier. He'd been celibate for thirty months. It was part of his recovery from everything.

"You don't have money now, but when you do she'll want half," said Li's dad.

"She won't," said Li. "She's not like that."

Li's dad's older sister said something implying it was common knowledge that all of Li's girlfriends had "run away," and Li didn't correct her.

In four of his five relationships, he'd gotten depressed, leading, through general negativity and his blaming habit, to complaints, causing everything he thought or said to seem like a veiled or open insult, as in his parents' relationship. His last relationship had arguably been an improvement— the complaints had been more mutual—but it had still felt dysfunctional.

When the bill arrived, Li's dad said Li was paying, and his sisters laughed. His younger sister said, "Li doesn't make money."

"She doesn't know I make money," said Li quietly to his dad as they stood to leave the restaurant.

It was his nineteenth day without starches. Pain had kept decreasing a little each day. He could almost touch his toes.

At home at dinner that night, Li's mom said, "People from Dad's family only care about themselves."

"Dad's older sister gives us things," said Li reproachfully.

Li's mom said Li's dad's sisters seemed to believe she never cooked. Once, seeing how clean her kitchen was, the older sister had assumed it hadn't ever been used.

Li's dad denied lying to his sisters about Li's mom.

"Do your sisters know you went to prison?" said Li.

"Not my older sister," said Li's dad. In the early aughts, unable to raise sufficient funds for his second company, he'd invested in it himself by laundering money through his younger sister in Taiwan.

"Who else doesn't know?" said Li.

Fat Uncle didn't. Auntie and Thin Uncle did.

"Is this where I came to sell my textbook?" said Li's dad the next day by Taipei Main Station. In the seventies, working as a tutor, he'd written and sold a grad-school physics textbook to a bookstore for a one-time fee.

"He says this every time we're here," said Li's mom, who'd typed and formatted the textbook.

"How old were you?" said Li, who'd heard the story two or three times that year.

"Twenty-eight or twenty-nine," said Li's dad.

"When I was that age, I'd published six books," said Li. Earlier, his dad had non sequitured that each of the four papers he'd written that year would be more influential than any of Li's books.

"I've published almost two hundred papers," said Li's dad.

"When I'm your age, I'll have twenty books," said Li.

"You don't make money off them," said Li's dad.

"I'm making fifty thousand per book now," said Li, exaggerating. "And I still get royalties from every book."

"You two are funny," said Li's mom.

"I made two children," said Li's dad. "You haven't made any children."

"I can make children," said Li.

"Sometimes, you make two children and get four," said Li's dad, referring to Alan and a second grandchild whom he seemed to think was forthcoming from Mike. "When you have children, you can leave them in Taiwan. We'll take care of them."

Li's mom said she'd end up caring for them, as with Mike, Li, Binky, Tabby, and Dudu.

Around midnight, Li's parents sat in Li's dad's office with the TV off. Li's dad used a magnifying glass to read his semi-illegible notes on his time at Coleman, a low-security prison complex in Central Florida. Li's mom typed what he said into her computer.

"Blow job," he said in English. "One hundred dollars."

Li's mom made a disapproving noise.

"This is real," said Li's dad.

Li was drawing in his room. He'd said he'd read the notes

in the future and maybe use them to write a book. He started a voice memo, put his phone on the piano in the hall, and returned to his room, moved by his parents' activity, which seemed like the most intimate thing they'd done together in years.

"Mr. Fat," said Li's dad.

In 2003, on his dad's sentencing day, Li was a sophomore at New York University. At the courthouse in Brooklyn, he sat with his mom and brother. His dad, who'd been offered a six-month sentence if he pleaded guilty, read a prepared letter. "In prison I cannot make further contributions to society. In prison I am useless. I will fight to the end for my reputation, innocence, and name."

The judge said seventy-one months. Three months later, in July, Li's mom drove Li's dad to prison. His first cellmate, Mr. Fat, was a four-hundred-pound high school English teacher in prison for possessing child pornography. He wanted the top bunk. Li's dad said he should have the bottom, and Mr. Fat agreed. They played Ping-Pong, even though other inmates told Li's dad not to talk to Mr. Fat.

In August, Li's dad paid a man twenty dollars a month in stamps and ice cream to be his bodyguard. Cell phones cost five thousand dollars from officers. An inmate with prison blueprints offered Li's dad a helicopter escape for four million. Some inmates had paid servants, who made their beds, folded their clothes, cleaned their rooms.

In September, Li's mom said in an email to Li that his dad had written her "a real letter, the first one in twenty years," saying he'd gotten too focused on business and forgotten to care for his family. "This is the real Dad I knew a long time ago," said Li's mom. "I was so moved that I cried for a long time." Li cried too, reading her email in a computer lab where he often teared up while working on short stories about loneliness and resignation.

In November, Li's dad was locked in a windowless cell for twenty-three hours a day for three days for his own protection after he told on someone for stealing eggs from the kitchen. Li and his mom didn't understand why Li's dad had cared, and told him not to do it again, and he didn't.

Li's mom visited twice a week, driving west for an hour. Li visited around ten times when home from college. Mike visited once. The cafeteria-like visitation room had rows of vending machines and microwaves. Li's mom snuck in food in her waistband. Once, she and Li were caught transferring peanuts, Li's dad's favorite food, into microwaved fried rice, and had to leave early. Officers began to call Li's dad Mr. Peanut.

He worked outside (mowing grass, picking up cigarettes) and in the library and the kitchen. He played poker, watched TV, and wrote papers, which he mailed to Li's mom, who typed and mailed them back for edits and submitted them to journals. He gained two patents, used statins (which at home he often forgot to take) daily, and began to gain weight.

In 2004, Li and his mom gave a woman two hundred thousand dollars in gold bars in a parking lot. The woman's husband, an inmate at Coleman, had lied to Li's dad, saying he'd graduated from MIT, had connections, and could get Li's dad out early. Efforts to recover the gold were unsuccessful.

In 2005, Li's dad sometimes leaned back in his chair and said life in prison was good. In 2006, he moved to a halfway house. In 2007, Li's parents sold their Florida house and returned to Taiwan, and in 2008 they bought a four-month-old Dudu.

Li visited his parents for a week in 2008; three weeks in 2009; four weeks, with his wife, in 2010; and six weeks in 2013, spending most of his time away from them, in his room or the city, private and preoccupied.

On his fifth visit, in the Year of Mercury, from November 2014 to January 2015, he suddenly started to spend most of his time with his parents, writing about them and involving them in recovery, leading to intimacy and conflict.

Now it was February 2016, and he was near the end of his sixth visit.

Conflict

Tidying his room, then washing a cup in the kitchen, Li heard his mom tell his dad four times to finish working so that they could go on a walk. Li quietly told her excessive pressure could make his dad refuse out of spite.

"That's how she is," said Li's dad, and began to mutter that all Li's mom did, day and night, was niànjīng—a term for chanting Buddhist scriptures that Li's parents often used on each other pejoratively.

Li stood by his dad, feeling wary of himself. He'd used LSD thirty minutes earlier. He'd learned to be alone for ninety minutes post-LSD, as he became more emotional and contentious, but sometimes he didn't time it right, wanted to test it, or got confused.

"No one told me when we were leaving," said Li's dad, randomly moving files around his computer screen.

"Next time we'll tell you," said Li. On the time problem, which went back decades, he'd sometimes sided with his dad, but mostly he'd sided with his mom.

"You think he'll listen if we tell him?" said Li's mom, looking down at her hand, wiping piano keys with a cloth.

Li shut his dad's computer.

"Don't hit me," said his dad.

Li looked helplessly at his mom.

"Did you hit him?" said Li's mom.

"No. I closed his computer."

Li's dad blamed Li's mom for Li's behavior.

"I copied *you*," said Li, pointing at his dad with his right forefinger, which he for some reason touched with his left forefinger, confused and overwhelmed. When he was seven, he'd blamed his parents for making his LEGO structure fall by vibrating the air with their voices—a story his parents often amusedly refreshed.

"You always blame others!" said Li, feeling suddenly out of control and near tears. "I copied *you*. My life is ruined because of you," he said, unsure what he meant. As a teenager, he'd blamed his mom for ruining his life (by spoiling him), but this was the first time he'd blamed his dad for this.

"Since you came back, we've been bickering half the days," said Li's dad, putting on his jacket. He criticized Li and his mom for fomenting an atmosphere of constant bickering.

"It's because of you two!" said Li. "Since I've been born, every day, I've heard you two bicker."

"Can only one person bicker?" said Li's dad.

"I said *you two*," said Li. "You're both to blame. You're the only one out of us who has hit anyone; you hit Brother. You say not to *throw* things. But you *hit* people."

Li's mom stood between them, telling them to stop.

Li's dad said every child in Taiwan had been hit, that it was right for children to be hit. He said Li needed to stop throwing and destroying things.

Li said he and his mom agreed it wasn't good to throw things, but his dad kept defending hitting Mike. He picked up his dad's decrepit laptop, disconnecting a cord.

"There's important things in there," said Li's dad.

Li's mom reached for the computer.

"Didn't you say throwing things is good?" shouted Li incoherently.

Li's mom pulled Li's arm down.

Li put the computer on the table.

Li's dad walked away, picked up an umbrella.

"How did it get like this?" said Li's mom.

"Isn't hitting things good?" shouted Li, cheeks and lips quivering. "Five seconds ago you said hitting things is good. One minute ago you said it was right to beat Brother." He grabbed the umbrella from his dad. They pulled it back and forth. Li gained control of it as its handle broke.

"Mike deserved to be hit," said Li's dad.

"If hitting people is good, I should hit you, since you don't listen," said Li.

"You dare hit me?" said Li's dad.

"You're so fat," said Li. "Of course I do."

Li's mom was shouting at them to stop.

Li's dad picked up Dudu and moved toward the front

door. "We're scaring Du," he said, looking down to put on shoes. "This kind of child is useless," he said, and left.

"I'm not going for a walk," said Li, legs shaking.

Li's mom took the broken umbrella.

Li entered his sunny room. He closed his door to his empty luggage's extended handle. When he'd gotten to Taiwan, he'd kept his door shut for at least two hours a day, saying he needed privacy because he was normally alone all the time. Four weeks earlier, after pushing his dad's machines off the table, he'd begun to keep his door ajar with the luggage handle. The change had made him feel less curmudgeonly. Working on his nonfiction book the past two weeks, he'd been friendly and cheerful and calm. He was returning to New York City in ten days.

Li lay supine on his bed with his crura—his legs below his knees—extended horizontally off the mattress. He was wearing shoes. He'd put them on for the walk. He heard his mom softly crying in her office. His closed eyes watered.

An osmotic, oval, pastel form grew and shrank on his personal screen as he sloshed in and out of consciousness.

He remembered Kathleen Harrison saying there was a phase near the end of her psychedelic trips when she practiced "mending"—thinking about people close to her, trying to understand them a bit more, considering what she could do for them, what she could say that she'd never said before.

Li's dad entered the apartment. The TV bloomed on. Li heard his parents berate each other at a restrained volume. His dad said, "Bickering for an entire lifetime." His mom began to prepare dinner.

"Li?" she said at his door.

"Ng," said Li, who'd been motionless for around fifty minutes. His crura and shoed feet were still horizontal off the bed. His room had darkened.

"We'll eat at 6:30. Okay?"

"Okay." Wondering where his phone was, Li felt it in his pants pocket. His mom had emailed: "I am sorry I kept pushing Dad and let you feel bad. I know it must be annoying. From now on, we just set a time and everybody follows it. You yelled at Dad, I understand your stress, but as soon as you calm down, apologize and let it pass. Dad loves you the most, try not to be so mad. We are all responsible for this kind of thing. We must try using other methods to settle disagreements and love one another more."

Li began typing a reply.

"We're eating now," said Li's mom.

"I'll come at 6:30," said Li.

"Okay," said Li's mom.

It was 6:26. Li stood at 6:29, still typing. Leaving his room, he pushed send: "I shouldn't have closed Dad's computer and yelled. But you shouldn't have said he won't listen even if we set a time. He does listen sometimes, and we can wait when he doesn't. He isn't as strict with time as us, and work can be disrupted but a walk can wait. I am not criticizing you. I like being on time, like you. Dad should be more considerate of others' time. He shouldn't have blamed you for me closing his computer."

"I shouldn't have closed your computer," said Li, approaching his dad.

"It's okay," said Li's dad. "Nothing was lost."

"Sorry. I don't want to close your computer in the future."

Li's dad apologized to Li in a general way, seeming unupset.

Li's mom told Li's dad to apologize to Li.

"I just did," said Li's dad.

"I'm getting better," said Li. "I haven't done that in a long time."

"Don't throw things," said Li's dad in a friendly tone.

"I know," said Li. "I'm trying to stop being like this."

At dinner, Li's mom nudged Li's dad after he said for the tenth or so time that Li needed to control himself, shouldn't break things. Li's dad made a little noise.

"When Dad says I need control, I don't feel not good," said Li. "I agree. It's good to keep reminding me. It's like me reminding you two all the time about health things."

"When I hit Mike . . . ," said Li's dad, trailing off.

"What about it?" said Li.

Li's dad said every child in Taiwan had been hit, that it was okay for adults to hit their children but not okay for adults to hit anyone else.

Li said Mike had been "old," sixteen. Teenage Mike had rarely been home. He'd broken his curfew sometimes, sneaking out his window to skateboard with friends. One night, as Mike and his mom shouted at each other, his dad had emerged from work with a thin, metal clothes hanger, muttering loudly.

"I hit Mike in the garage," said Li's dad.

"You hit him in his room," said Li, who'd been ten and had stood crying in front of their unyielding dad, hitting him with the plastic end of a foam Nerf baseball bat as he left and returned once or twice to continue to hit Mike, who was bigger than he was.

Mike had cowered floorward, screaming.

Li's mom said Binky had attacked Mike.

"He bit the wrong person," said Li's dad.

"He bit whomever was loudest," said Li's mom.

"I made Mike listen to Mom," said Li's dad.

Li's mom expressed sympathy for Mike.

"It's so far in the past," said Li. "We shouldn't talk about it." He said he normally never brought it up, even though Li's dad often referenced Li and his mom's disreputable behaviors.

"He always says I throw things," said Li's mom. "Actually, I haven't thrown anything in seven years."

"Brother isn't as close to Dad as I am due to being hit," said Li.

"That probably has something to do with it," said Li's mom.

"I've never hit you," said Li's dad.

"So I care for you two," said Li. "I'm here. I'm here so much."

"Mike has his own family now," said Li's dad.

"Li really loves you, right?" said Li's mom.

"Right," said Li's dad.

"Dad counts as a good dad, right?" said Li's mom.

"Ng," said Li. "Right."

Li's mom said Li's dad's dad hadn't cared about his children at all. He'd left home for ten years when Li's dad was five; when he returned, Li's dad's mom hadn't let him in the house; he'd lived with his younger brother the last seven years of his life.

Li's dad said they should get soft things to hit.

"We should be alone when upset," said Li's mom.

Li said one had to increase self-control over years, and that no matter how much one tried to heal one's mind, if one didn't also heal one's body, change wouldn't happen.

"Is that so?" said Li's mom.

"I think so," said Li, and remembered the saddest thing he'd ever owned—a set of twenty tapes for reducing social anxiety through self-directed cognitive-behavioral therapy. He'd found the tapes on a message board late in high school, after the lung collapses; they'd helped a little. "Or the change won't be as much. Everything I do now is to try to change. Even writing."

"You can also write about our clashes," said Li's dad.

"I know," said Li. "I am."

Li's mom said she'd learned in college that novels needed "conflict."

"It's because we bicker that I can write about us," said Li. Years later, he'd turn against this belief, thinking instead that conflict wasn't necessary for art, as it didn't seem to be for culture. Megaliths, agriculture, pottery, metallurgy, textiles, writing, and probably books had been invented when peace was mainstream, he'd read. Riane Eisler called this "one of the best-kept historical secrets"—conflict wasn't necessary for cultural or technological advancement.

"Do you sometimes bicker on purpose, then?" said Li's mom.

"No," said Li honestly. "I'm always trying to not bicker." It was probably impossible, though, to not be influenced by his wavering belief that maybe conflict was good for his novel.

"That's good," said Li's mom.

"Du, you're the most obedient," said Li's dad, petting Dudu.

"After yoga, I have less control," said Li, offering some explanation for his outburst. He'd done yoga that day for the first time in eight weeks, causing pain that seemed expected and beneficial, microtears that'd mend stronger.

After dinner, Li and his parents agreed to walk in an hour.

An hour later, at 8:15 p.m., Li left his room.

"You're always right on time," said his mom.

"I'm still writing. Can we go at eight forty?"

"We don't need to walk if you're tired from yoga."

"I want to," said Li. "Let's go at eight forty-five."

"You can write for longer if you want."

"I like time limits. They help me focus."

At 8:45, Li felt amused and endeared, seeing his dad, wearing magnifying glasses and carrying machine parts, rush from the kitchen, where he stored some of his stuff, to his office, saying, "Two minutes, two minutes."

On the unusually late walk, Li said he'd written 4,100 words in ninety minutes.

"What did you write about?" said Li's dad.

"Fighting and dinner," said Li.

"Bickering," said Li's mom, correcting him, as she had many times over decades. They'd disputed verbally (chǎojià), not physically (dǎjià).

"Did you write about picking up my computer?" said Li's dad.

"Yes," said Li.

"Did you write about Du hiding in the corner with her tail down?"

"No," said Li. "I didn't see that."

"Maybe you shouldn't write about Dad hitting Mike," said Li's mom. "Child abuse," she said in English.

"Wasn't everyone in your generation hit?" said Li.

"I wasn't," said Li's mom. "Only teachers hit me." Teachers had hit students with a sticklike tool made from rattan, a palm plant, until 2006, when physical punishment was banned in schools. Laughing a little, Li's mom said her eldest, DDT-using brother—her only sibling out of eight who'd died—had hit her once, but she couldn't remember why.

"Did your dad hit his children?" said Li to his mom, who sometimes said her mom had loved her more than anyone else in the world.

"No, but he was always yelling," said Li's mom. "He had a very not-good temper. I was lucky; he didn't yell at me. He yelled at Auntie all the time."

"Were you hit?" Li asked his dad.

"My mom hit me with a stick. She made me kneel on the abacus." Li's dad rarely mentioned his mom except to say that after his dad gambled away all their money when he was two, she'd supported the whole family by selling fish.

Li's mom said Li's dad always automatically blamed others, even blaming Dudu (in a kind voice) when he couldn't find the TV remote, because his mom had hit him.

"In other people's novels, people get murdered," said Li.

Li's mom laughed.

"And it's fine," said Li. "People like it a lot."

Li's dad began to intermittently stop walking to use his phone with an engrossed expression, standing motionless for increasing amounts of time as the others waited at a distance.

"Let's just keep walking," said Li. "He'll run to catch up."

"Du will stand in the middle," said Li's mom.

"That's okay," said Li, and they walked toward home.

They stared at Li's dad from around forty feet away.

"Use your phone at home," said Li's mom in a low voice. "Du is waiting. Everyone is waiting."

Dudu stood in between, looking at one side, then the other.

At two a.m. Li's dad entered Li's room and said, "I'm going to sleep; you're not going to sleep?"

"Ng," said Li, browsing his notes on his computer.

Li's dad picked up a book of tweets by Li and Li's friend and read one of Li's tweets from his drug phase aloud: "Urge to leave society upon losing cards/keys."

"Don't be so fierce!" said Li's dad the next night after dinner as Dudu barked and howled at a dog in an apartment across the hall. "Du. Ayo. This kind of child is too powerful."

Li was clearing the table, plateauing on LSD. He entered the bathroom and laughed uncontrollably, remembering his dad saying, "This kind of child is useless," the previous night.

Li swept the floor, calm and focused.

"Sweeping is good, you can think while doing it," said Li's dad from bed.

"You should sweep, then," said Li.

"I'm thinking while lying here," said Li's dad, who was

known to push trash or food under furniture even when watched, grunting noncommittally when censured.

"The new mop is better, right?" said Li's mom as Li scrubbed the floor with peppermint oil and water.

"Yes," said Li, happy to bond with his mom over the long-handled pad mop with 360-degree rotation.

Li felt scared the next morning when he looked in his mom's mouth. She seemed to have barely any gums left. Parts of her jawbone seemed visible in a way that made Li picture her skull. The earliest her dentist could see her was in three weeks. She made an appointment with the dentist whose office they'd stormed out of the previous year.

The next day, Li walked for three minutes to Taipei's largest farmers market, which was open on weekends. He bought turmeric root and made turmeric-ginger-honey drinks for his parents and himself. He theorized his mom's pain was like his, and she began to refrain from eating rice.

Three days later, she said it was her second painless day. She canceled her appointment with the Huggins-trained dentist and bought turmeric for Auntie and Thin Uncle, but at dinner Li saw her touch her jaw, and she said it felt "cramped." They affirmed she'd see her dentist in two weeks.

On the bus to the airport the next day, they looked at photos from Barcelona, Florida, and the past eleven weeks. Li's dad's neck had reemerged through weight loss. Li's mom was concerned that she, like Li's dad, had lost six pounds. Li was more worried about her jaw; he feared cancer.

"When I get home and see that your room is empty, it will be very not good," she said.

Microfireflies

Back in apartment 4K at one a.m., Li scratched his eyes with his knuckles. He sneezed repeatedly. His nose bled twice before he slept. In the morning, he cleaned rodent poop along his walls, then inhaled cannabis from the device he'd made from a Dr. Bronner's soap bottle to smoke DMT. Despite suspecting he was inhaling aluminum and plastic, he used it for two more days, until one of the potent hits empowered him to discard it by catalyzing, among other thoughts, "It will be too bleak to return to the plastic bottle."

On the same hit, he realized language was his metaphysical microbiome. As the trillions of microbes in his gut, brain, eyes, and other parts modulated his feelings, thoughts, and behavior with electrons and molecules, the billions of words

he'd thought, said, read, heard, dreamed, and written, his
internal literature, influenced him from the other direction.
Li suspected his newer, superstratal symbiosis, with meaning, ideas, and stories, was as damaged as his primeval one.

In March, stoned on a lunch break from jury duty, he
bought purple potato chips at Union Square farmers market. On the train back to city hall, he realized he'd missed
his stop and that he seemed to have blacked out for a few
minutes. Ascending to street level with gooey chest pain, he
felt paranormal and bemused. His only memory of the train
ride was of sustaining mutually blank-faced eye contact with
a seated, elderly woman while chain-eating chips—his first
starch in two months.

In Brooklyn six days later, he got his mailbox key from
his friend who'd gotten his mail while he was in Taiwan. His
friend gave him modafinil, a drug he hadn't tried. On modafinil
that night, drinking 250 percent as much coffee as planned,
he wrote for five hours and masturbated to online porn, which
he hadn't looked at in five months, for four hours, alternating sessions. "You terrible fucking piece of shit," he thought
throughout the night, sometimes while grinning manically.
His inner voice became profane on strong stimulants. "You
absolute piece of shit. Jesus." He blamed modafinil for the
regressive binge.

The next day, still awake, he found himself earnestly considering returning to his drug phase's last third, which had
featured the solitary polydrug binge—a late-historical activity with probably millions of practitioners—but by night he
didn't want to anymore.

In the morning, chip-induced pain, which had fluctuated
for a week, decreased to almost nothing, and he felt himself

trying to attribute the redress to modafinil in what seemed to be a last-ditch effort to lure himself back to the drug phase. He felt more amused than unnerved. Each time, in the past two years, he'd felt like returning to centering his life around the vice-generating use of corporate drugs, the urge had left after minutes to days.

That night, Li's mom emailed saying her dentist hadn't found any problems with her jaw, which, with turmeric usage and continued rice abstinence, rarely hurt anymore.

"Got out of it," sang Li one night after canceling a social interaction. His old hermitude, lacking a contracted, long-term art project, had often felt lonely and demoralizing. His new one, working on his nonfiction book around seven hours a day, felt meaningful and satisfying and sustainable, as if it were his natural lifestyle—scrupulously matched with his DNA over millions of years—which he'd learned was actually to be embedded in nature with five generations of kin.

Life was a novel that he was allowed to read a page per day, and that described a day per page, he thought in bed. If the novel of life began at conception, Li was on page 12,200-something of *Li*. Some people believed the soul entered the body on page 49. Maybe Li's soul had browsed *Li* in a metacosmic library, flipping through it and other novels, before deciding on *Li*, but he couldn't remember the reasons for his decision. Maybe he could remember by writing about himself, he thought, falling asleep.

In April, Li went to Mike's for Alan's fourth birthday. Alan gregariously showed Li his toys, including Transformers and a fire engine. Li gave him a helicopter LEGO and, while building it together, asked if he remembered reeling in a fish in Florida five months earlier. He did.

On the train back to Manhattan, Li imagined Alan remembering a sentence from page 1,600-something of *Alan*. The earliest Li remembered of *Li* was around page 1,470, where he saw a spider in a basement in Taiwan and cried himself to sleep in his mom's lap, repeatedly moaning, "I don't want to sleep here."

In May, in upstate New York with his parents, who were visiting for four days, and his brother, Li learned his mom's prediabetes had worsened. To improve her general health, they decided to try switching from Levoxyl (pills made from seven toxins) to Thyro-Gold (vegetable capsules of five natural ingredients). Levoxyl, Li had read, provided a molecule one-thousandth the size of the molecule complex that thyroid glands made and that Thyro-Gold contained—an example of modern medicine crudely simplifying natural complexity.

At night in a B & B, Li read an essay by Merlin Stone in which she suggested moving the "church-imposed division" of BC/AD to the start of agriculture to reclaim eight millennia of Goddess worship as part of "our era." Counting backward at BC took tricky energy, Li had learned, encountering phrases like "last quarter of the third millennium BC" while researching history for his nonfiction book. Considering Stone's time-repair idea, Li imagined he was in 11617 AR, after (the Younger Dryas) reset.

On the drive back to the city, Li's mom miscalled Mike "Du," which made Li smile. Mike said he was driving to Yale, his graduate alma mater, to attend a graphic design conference. He asked his parents if they wanted to go. They declined. Thinking that their parents would go somewhere with him if he asked, Li empathized with Mike.

The next night, walking to Mike's on a third of a tab of LSD, faraway things seemed easily examinable, as if small and near.

After dinner in an Italian restaurant, Li, Mike, and their parents walked to a Foot Locker. Mike bought shoes for his dad's sixty-eighth birthday, which was that day.

"We're going to Whole Foods," said Li outside about himself and his mom.

"What?" said Mike. "It's really far."

"It's twenty minutes away," said Li.

"It's really far," said Mike.

"I looked it up. It's a twenty-minute walk."

"It's going to rain," said Mike.

"You don't have to go," said Li.

"I know. I'm not. But you need to get an umbrella."

It didn't seem to Li like it was going to rain.

At Whole Foods, Li said other older brothers didn't act like Mike. Li's mom said Li didn't know how other brothers related. She said she and Auntie had bickered often when they were younger.

Walking back to Mike's, where his parents were staying, Li said when he and Auntie had been alone on the train platform three months earlier, he'd asked her about her DDT-using brother.

"How did you choose what to ask?" said Li's mom.

"All I talk about with you all is health," said Li, smiling. "So I chose that." He said Auntie's hands had been warm. He asked if his mom's hands were still cold. She said they were. She held his hand; cold on cold, the hands felt normal.

Li said a doctor had installed a defibrillator in Terence McKenna's eighty-something-year-old dad without asking his family. On his deathbed, revived repeatedly by the machine, he'd died many times.

Li's mom said Auntie's husband, ribs broken from CPR, swollen body and head filled with tubes, had looked ghastly when he died.

"There's no need to worry about death," said Li, who as a child had habitually feared it, dreading cancer when his dad coughed too much, believing his mom had AIDS, pressuring them to see Dr. Chan, who'd put Li's dad on statins.

"I'm not worried. I'm just shēbudé to leave you."

"What is shēbudé?" said Li, thinking it meant "reluctant."

"It just means I don't want to be apart from you."

"We might be together in a new way after we both die," said Li.

"Dead people can't return to say what happened," said Li's mom.

Li said scientists at NYU had given mushrooms to people with terminal cancer to decrease their fear of death, and that it had worked.

"Are you still eating mushrooms?" said Li's mom.

Li said they were tools, which he wanted to use.

"That's fine. As long as you don't overdose."

Li said he viewed nothing as off-limits.

"Just stay away from heroin," said Li's mom.

Li said he'd gotten heroin when his lung collapsed. Li's mom uncertainly said he'd gotten opium. Li admitted he'd gotten morphine, which had nine fewer atoms than heroin, which was called diamorphine. He said millions of American children used amphetamines, which Taiwanese news viewed as a deadly menace, daily in the form of Adderall.

"Too much of anything is not good," said Li's mom.

"You should ask me about drugs," said Li. "Dad knows a lot about lasers, so I wouldn't give him laser advice. I'd ask questions."

"Then why don't you ask Dad about lasers?"

"I don't know," said Li after a moment.

"How do you buy weed?" said Li's mom.

Li said he texted a number, causing someone, usually a different person each time, to ring his doorbell one to six hours later. Imagining his mom viewed dealers as nihilistic killers, Li said he had a friend who became a dealer and liked it, got tipped well.

Li's mom advised against tipping.

Suppressing mild annoyance, Li said the cannabis he'd smoked since 2013 was probably pesticide-ridden and that he looked forward to buying organic cannabis from stores when he moved to California in four months, after drafting his nonfiction book.

Approaching Mike's apartment, Li felt moved and a little surreal that part of him wanted to stay outside to keep talking. His parents were going to Chicago for an eye conference the next day.

Li said psychedelics made one closer to people. Li's mom said she'd noticed him smiling and laughing more—a theme, a valuable one, Li felt, that they seemed to regularly refresh.

They entered the house and walked upstairs. Alan was at the top, behind a gate, which he opened.

"He can open it," said Li's mom.

"Of course he can," said Li.

Li's mom went to tell Mike.

Li and Alan played catch with an avocado. Li focused entirely on the activity—speaking encouragement, watching the avocado fly, making sound effects—and felt impressed by Alan's easy delight, giggling after almost every toss, catch, or miss.

In bed on his floor in 4K, Li thought positive thoughts about Mike. In restaurants, Mike gave Alan new foods and asked Alan what he thought about them. Mike prepared Alan's food carefully, providing varied, whole foods when home, Li had noticed.

Two-year-old Mike had played for hours with other toddlers in his dad's grad school dorm when he got to the United States, speaking only Taiwanese. Adolescent Mike had excelled at soccer, Li thought uncertainly, vaguely recalling a photo of Mike smiling with a soccer ball. Teenage Mike's main interests had been drawing and skateboarding.

Li remembered Mike skating in their empty garage with the garage door down, sounding troublingly upset when he fell, yelling "God!" or "Oh my God!" Li hadn't understood back then why Mike was so frustrated, why he didn't practice calmly, as he seemed to do with drawing. He'd drawn fish and horses, Li remembered with effort.

Mike disliked car-honking, viewed it as belligerent and unnecessary; Li, too. Li had learned of punk music by buying a CD by the Descendents because he recognized the band's name from one of Mike's T-shirts, which Li had worn as a nightie after Mike left for college when Li was eleven. Mike had listened to A Tribe Called Quest and Wu-Tang Clan on cassette tape.

Mike might've been Li's first source of doubt against society. Around 1992, he'd begun, whenever he saw Li drinking milk, to say it came from diseased cows filled with antibiotics and growth hormones. Their mom had stopped buying milk, which previously had seemed obviously good. Celebrities on TV had said, "Milk: it does a body good" and "Got milk?," and at school everyone had gotten milk.

Mike seemed like a good friend. Secretly listening in on Mike's landline conversation, nine-year-old Li had heard Mike's skater friend say he'd woken drunk in the driver's seat of his car at a green light at an intersection to a police car honking behind him—again. "You've got to stop doing that," Mike had said in a concerned yet somewhat detached, maybe slightly amused tone.

In college, Li had emailed Mike one of his short stories, and Mike had given generous praise, seeming to get Li's writing and to be impressed, which had moved Li. In emails, Mike was remarkably friendly. Except for verbal speech to nuclear kin when not in a good mood, the four of them (Li, Mike, their parents) seemed to be this way—courteous, considerate, positive, sensitive.

Once, Mike had emailed Li asking what he should read. On Li's recommendation, he'd bought *The Quick and the Dead* by Joy Williams and the Richard Zenith translation of *The Book of Disquiet*. Li remembered an attentive, solitary Mike at the release events for his three novels—at a tiny bookstore deep in Brooklyn, a Barnes & Noble near Wall Street, power-House Arena in DUMBO.

In 2008, a year after his first novel was published, Li had

lived with Mike and his French bulldog for two months in 4K, which their parents had helped Mike buy. Li had slept on a mattress pad. Late one night, Mike had said, "You think they care about you?" about Li's part-time job at an organic vegan restaurant. An incensed Li had walked half an hour to NYU's twenty-four-hour Bobst Library, staying there until Mike, a graphic designer, was at work the next day. A week later, Li had moved to a place off the Lorimer L station. They'd stayed unfriendly for months or years, during which Mike had met his wife and moved to Brooklyn.

In 2011, at Mike's offer, Li had returned to 4K to live alone for seven hundred dollars a month—the building's maintenance fee. They'd been friends, or at least friendly, for two years, until the London vacation, when he slapped Mike, Li realized with surprise.

Remembering they'd once recovered was like learning that the culture leading to world wars, nuclear weapon hoarding, and U.S. patriarchy had begun with at least five millennia of partnership civilizations—gylanies—in which black signified soil, life, fertility, mystery, and the womb; snakes denoted wisdom and regeneration; and deities were compassionate, in control of their emotions, and resonant with nature.

It seemed egregious to have forgotten and auspicious to have remembered, changing the story's theme from "confused struggle in a grim world" to "recovery toward a former harmony."

In June, 4K started to feel claustrophobic and bleak, so Li began to work in Bobst Library for five hours each morning, then spend time reading in parks, before going home.

Supine in Washington Square Park one day, he saw flitting, ephemeral, glowing dots that seemed not in the air, the sky, his mind, or his eyes. They weren't the wormy question-mark shapes he suspected were microbes, or the tadpole-like shadows, drifting past in tugs of movement belying their inter-eyeball nearness; the semi-translucent dots seemed to be in every area of empty space but were only visible against sky. They appeared, squiggled rapidly, and vanished, like densely packed fireflies in fast-forward.

Li could see two to four microfireflies, as he termed them, into their world, as if looking into murky water. He saw them focusing five feet above himself, on a cloud, and on nothing. Blowing air at them and waving his hand through them didn't seem to affect them. He searched "glowing dots in air" and other phrases online but found nothing. He observed them daily in the park.

Maybe microfireflies were the other-dimensional flickerings of a personal, specieal, or global emergent property. Had humans achieved a sufficient density of interconnection for an overmind to emerge? Individual minds couldn't exist in the imagination except vaguely and fleetingly, as visitors or observers, but maybe eight billion minds on one planet couldn't *not* be volitional and participatory there.

Maybe an infant overmind, made of minds as animals were made of cells, was self-preservationally downloading partnership ideas into society, in part by sprinkling them over urban parks.

In late June and early July, Li spent a week in Northern California for his nonfiction book. He met Kathleen Harrison, whom he'd learned of through Terence McKenna, her ex-husband, and she showed him her garden, which included cannabis, tobacco, peaches, and lemon balm. At night, the rural sky's latticed, everywhere stars seemed like a structure for generating or reaching other worlds.

Back in the starless city, Li learned his mom weighed less than ever. Her heart had been beating scarily fast. She'd gotten her lungs X-rayed; intestines colonoscopied; pancreas, liver, stomach, and kidneys ultrasounded. Doctors couldn't find any problems. Li felt guilty and emotional, thinking he'd neglected his mom while in California, even lashing out at her once in an email when he got defensive after she seemed disapproving when he revealed he'd lost his phone.

Telling himself not to transfer his worry about all the tests (medical errors were the third leading cause of death in the States) to his mom, he researched and drafted an email to her over three days.

On the second day, his friend Kay emailed saying she wanted to rent an apartment in his building, which was near her office, but didn't want him to think she was "stalking" him. Li encouraged her to move in, said she wouldn't be stalking him because he was moving soon, had a one-way ticket to San Francisco for September.

On the third day, Li left bed at six a.m. after a sleepless night of rampant worry. He drank coffee, smoked cannabis, and tweaked and sent his mom the email, sharing a strategically simple plan of intermittent fasting, staggered Thyro-Gold, raw eggs, and more animal fats. That night, he began to regularly go to sleep before ten p.m. for the first time since grade school.

He became more social for a month, seeing Kay three times.

1. In East River Park, he told her about convincing his parents to get their fillings replaced. Kay said her mom lived on the Upper West Side with three elderly cats, filled her bathtub each day to monitor the water quality, and suspected people entered her apartment when she wasn't home to steal her documents and poison her cats with mercury. After confirming that neither Kay nor her mom was joking, Li said he related to her mom. He avoided tap water, felt heavy-metal poisoning was a major problem, and had once been framed by his superintendent.

2. In Kay's 39th Street apartment, where she'd moved a year earlier from London, where her husband still lived, to start a job editing a new online literary magazine, Li bought hash from her dealer and lent her *Cure Tooth Decay*.

3. Two weeks later, in August, Kay moved into his 29th Street building. They smoked hash and talked in her new home, 3A, a floor down from 4K. She said *Cure Tooth Decay* had made her feel hopeful and that two of her mom's cats had died.

Li withdrew back into his world. He began to FaceTime his parents—on a new iPhone that he kept on Airplane Mode most of the time—once a week, in part to better discuss his mom's health. Tracking her temperature, weight, and thyroid usage daily together in a shared file, they discerned she'd been taking too much Thyro-Gold. They titrated her dose over weeks. She grew warmer and heavier, her heart stopped pounding, and she started sleeping better.

Reading *The Art of Seeing* by Aldous Huxley, Li realized he'd forgotten, since maybe middle school, how to look at faces. He was prone to staring at one eye, as if the eye were the whole face, leading usually to him looking away. Staring was a greedy, self-defeating attempt to see more than possible, wrote Huxley. A repression of natural movement, it caused mental strain. Vision wanted to glide and dart and skip from nose to cheek, brow to mouth, collecting new data. When one looked in this naturally analytic way, one seemed calmly alert, eyes gleaming from light-reflecting motion.

Li learned of flashing (closing one's eyes to study one's memory of a glanced-at image) and sunning (looking near or at the sun with one or both eyes). The sun looked color-shiftingly metallic, like in the Nintendo game *Metroid* when the protagonist becomes a flashing ball when jumping. Sunning was easier after eating raw liver and when stoned and well rested. The sun appeared to be the same size as the moon because, in an impressive coincidence, it was four hundred times larger and four hundred times farther away.

It could always be the last time anyone clearly saw the sun, Li knew. An impact or supervolcano eruption anywhere could block sunlight for decades everywhere. Li would freeze or starve to death in Manhattan. The global culture would die fast. History would restart millennia later, as it seemed to have at least once before, from the stable, undegenerate substrate of wild humans, who were like a backup team and living library as the others ventured out of nature, into buildings, books, and screens.

"Please do not poop in the stairway, people can slip" notices from Li's super, typed on computer paper, appeared on each floor. Li invented a practice called chestfeel, putting his hands on his upper body while deep-breathing. He made a broccoli-garlic-cilantro fermentation. He ordered liver capsules for his parents and bought animal organs—the most prized food of his aboriginal ancestors, inexpensive because Americans shunned them—for himself.

Since stopping starches, he'd continued to experiment with diet. Pain had returned after the chips and various other foods, like dried figs, in non-debilitating ways—brief, informative visits from an old acquaintance. Beneath the pain were smaller, more diffuse pains, which he viewed as aches and cramps. He was probably unreachably far from full recovery for any of his problems, which seemed good because, compared to his first three decades, he already felt energetic and powerful.

He learned from a 2015 study that, out of awe, amusement, compassion, contentment, joy, love, and pride, it was awe, somewhat surprisingly, that had the strongest correlation with lower inflammation levels. He decided to feel and note awe or its intellect-grasped variation, wonder, at least once a day, which, with cannabis supplied and pain mostly gone, was easy.

His body had become a reliable source of wonder. Many motions—torquing his hips, turning his neck, rising from supine—surprised him by not hurting. With less pain and inflammation, he seemed to move more effeminately. He used his hips more, rotating his upper body and looking around while walking to and from the library, leveraging his torso by pushing a hip with one hand, alternating sides, half-akimbo, amused.

Resting on his back on grass in the park, he felt like a sheet of paper—thoughtless, two-dimensional, pleased by the sporadic breeze. He fell asleep, became a moxic red energy, rising and fast. When he woke, he kept his lids down and saw dark microfireflies, pinpricks of shadow that seemed slower and sparser than when backdropped by sky.

In bed, he examined different areas of his private screen, looking far left and right to see what was there, and remembered exploring and testing reality with his senses as a child. He'd stopped at some point because public education had taught him that everything was already discovered, that new discoveries would be on the news, and that objective experts were working together to find and spread truth. In his own education, he'd learned things weren't that simple.

Walking to the library, he noticed he'd unconsciously channeled nail biting into nail cleaning. He danced in a drunken style one night, seeming to mimic Jackie Chan, falling and catching himself repeatedly. Waking from a world of stilts, he realized dreams exercised far vision and that his eyes, staring at screens so much that year, seemed to have been allotted dream time to heal.

Returning from a YG while smoking from a one-hitter south of the library, he saw ". . . ime Lan . . ." (the sign for Time Landscape, a strip of land with precolonial plants), felt surprised by the floating image, realized it was the center of his vision, and intuited it was possible to see places on other planets.

Partially YGing in the park while deep-breathing and reading, he watched a printed, stapled paper on *Salvia divinorum* become transparent for four seconds.

With drugs, he traveled in various metaphysical directions and returned automatically, through his body's homeostaticity, with new thoughts and feelings, bending his reality, allowing him to sense and do new things. With nutrition and detoxification, he traveled slowly in one direction without returning. With YGs, he teleported away and back.

Post-YG in 4K, he invented "squid arms," an exercise in which he flung his arms out horizontally with loose fingers. He self-quenched many YGs—instinctively sitting up in a panic, afraid to leave concrete reality. When he YGed while standing or sitting, he lowered himself to the floor to avoid hitting his head.

YGing while flapping on his fire escape, he maneuvered semiconsciously through his window, back into 4K, imagining people blaming his accidental death on suicide.

In late August, Li began using Thyro-Gold, which made him almost frantically energetic all day while deepening his sleep, decreasing the bobbleheadish stiffness of his neck, and dilating his macular and peripheral vision.

On his seventh day on it, walking home listening to Chopin's fourth ballade for around the hundredth time, he noticed a haunting midsong bass passage for seemingly the first time—entrancing, echo-y near-glissandos beneath the melody.

"Hi," he said, approaching his super at their building's entrance. "I left my keys upstairs. Can you let me in?"

The super showed no response.

"This is the first time in a long time," said Li, who'd locked himself out often during his drug phase. "My brain is getting better."

"That's good," said the super, smiling.

"Yes," said Li, smiling. In 2012, his bathroom had flooded, water had dripped into the floor below, and the super had knocked on his door and angrily tossed his towel into the ankle-level water. Weeks later, the super had scattered Li's discarded mail and other trash in the hall, photographed it, and put a note on Li's door saying if it happened again he could be evicted. Li had ignored the note. Their relationship had improved gradually since that nadir.

The super opened the door.

"Thank you," said Li.

"Do you need your room key?"

"Huh?" said Li.

"Your key. To your room."

"No," said Li. "It's not locked." He ran up the leaden, noxious, paint-peeled stairway, through a musty hall, into 4K. Usually, he took a deep breath outside and held it until he was in his room, which he didn't lock because the doorknob sometimes fell off, he didn't want to risk lockouts, and he disliked carrying too many things.

He worked on his divorce. He and his wife had separated in fall 2011 after an eleven-month marriage. In 2013, unable to remember (a typical drug-phase malfunction), he'd emailed her asking if they'd divorced. She'd said no, reminding him she'd researched it and seen it would cost "~$2,600."

In 2015, Li's mom, who did Li's taxes, had asked Li for around the tenth time in four years to divorce to avoid tax problems. Li had said his wife had been filing as "single." Nineteen more months had passed.

It was September 2016. Li had delayed moving until December to finish his nonfiction book and the divorce. The money from his two-book contract was almost gone, but he'd learned he was getting fifty thousand dollars, minus agent fee, soon because his third novel was being made into a movie.

He found a website with $399 divorces, learned he'd already paid $299 for an account at some point, and emailed his wife, who lived in Baltimore, saying he was "finally moving forward with divorce."

In October, he spent six days in and around San Francisco with his parents. Walking through Berkeley, he said maybe he'd live in the distant hills. He'd delayed moving again—until after visiting Taiwan from January to April.

At their hotel room, he learned his dad was back on statins. He reminded his dad the drug broke the body's ability to synthesize cholesterol, which was vital in mood regulation, brain functioning, hormone production, and tissue repair, and his dad berated his doctor.

At night, in bed on a sofa, Li read Karen Wetmore's memoir *Surviving Evil*, which he'd found by searching "MKULTRA"—the CIA mind-control program that lasted from 1950 to 1972 and stayed covered up until 1975—on Amazon and checking every result. In 1965, when Wetmore was thirteen, she threatened to kill herself or her mom if she was sent home from school. Months later, at Vermont State

Hospital, she was given a psychological test called Personality Assessment System; the results, she learned forty years later, were sent to CIA headquarters. "PAS objectives are to control, exploit or neutralize," said an internal CIA document that she quoted. "These objectives are innately anti-ethical."

When Wetmore was eighteen, she was locked in near-continuous, straitjacketed seclusion without a mattress or toilet for eight months, during which, according to hospital records, she was denied food and water for up to three days at a time, put on eight drugs simultaneously, and subjected to abnormally intensive, memory-erasing electroconvulsive therapy. A week after the seclusion, she was given 1,800 milligrams of Metrazol, a drug used on POWs in Soviet gulags to "produce overwhelming terror and doom," said a CIA document. She was released from the hospital a year later, in 1972.

The next twenty-five years, in and out of hospitals, she continued to be monitored and experimented upon. During an allergic reaction to Haldol, she was seemingly dosed with LSD. She blacked out in a clinic in a room with a dozen men in suits seated in a circle. Doctors continually tried to label her schizophrenic ("schizophrenic rehabilitation" was a cover for MKULTRA research), and she repeatedly attempted suicide. In the late eighties, compelled by a "strange compulsion," she rented a car, bought a gun, checked into a motel, held the loaded gun against her temple, and called her psychotherapist.

Li and his parents walked for two hours to the Golden Gate Bridge, where they saw ducks with red faces. Li felt energetic and talkative on Thyro-Gold and half a tab of LSD. His mom began to talk about death, as she seemed to do whenever Li was in especially good moods. She said "if" she died, she wanted her ashes scattered on her mom's grave. Li would need to contact Thin Uncle's son to learn how to get there. Li imagined emailing his cousin in fifteen years.

In 1997, Wetmore's therapist suggested she write a narrative of her life, Li read in the hotel. Wetmore requested her medical records from the state of Vermont and was denied. Her lawyer was also denied. When they finally got the incomplete records, they realized she'd survived MKULTRA and sued the state. The lawsuit ended after Wetmore's second heart attack, when her doctor said she'd die if she continued.

Continuing her research alone (filing Freedom of Information Act requests, contacting researchers, reading books), she uncovered that the CIA seemed to have killed around 1,200 mental patients at Vermont State Hospital, mostly or all women, in three decades of terminal experiments.

As his parents slept, Li felt tantalizingly scared, mulling over how in modern dominator societies one could at any moment find oneself trapped in abject pain, without memories or other frames of reference, unsure where or who one was— a counter-possibility to being suddenly, after dying or crossing history, in an eternal dream with its own dreamworlds.

In November, back in Manhattan, Li weaned himself off Thyro-Gold, drafted his nonfiction book's Goddess chapter, and FaceTimed his parents and Dudu for the seventeenth to nineteenth times; they'd talked for twelve, seven, six, ten, thirteen, thirteen, fourteen, fourteen, sixteen, fifteen, eighteen, fourteen, fourteen, fifteen, eighteen, twenty, twenty-two, seventeen, and seventeen minutes.

In bed, gazing into closed-lid darkness, Li saw a distant, bluish, holographic bucranium—a symbol of a cow's head and horns. As it whooshed through him, he felt a light wind on his neck. Bucrania, he knew from Marija Gimbutas, had been Goddess symbols in pre-dominator Europe and Anatolia because the horns modeled the waxing and waning moon, and the head and horns resembled the uterus and fallopian tubes. Anatomy had been known, Gimbutas theorized, through excarnation—placing corpses on wood platforms to be defleshed by birds and insects.

Born in Lithuania in 1921, Gimbutas emigrated to the United States in 1949 with a doctorate in archaeology. At Harvard, she translated archaeology texts and wrote books on European prehistory. In the sixties, excavating Neolithic sites in southeast Europe, she realized a culture existed in "prehistory"—the BC/AD-like mental partitional term for before 6,000 years ago—that was the opposite of all that came after. In 1968, she named that culture, which lasted from 8,500 to 5,500 years ago, Old Europe.

The most respected members of Old European society, which was organized around multistory temples in communal towns of up to ten thousand people, seemed to have been elder women. Old Europeans invented writing two millennia before the Sumerians, argued Gimbutas. Their writing appeared 7,500 years ago; looked to Li like a more naturalistic, somehow psychedelic Chinese; and may have been inspired by worship of the Goddess, whom Gimbutas called "nature—nature herself."

The untranslated script was based on a core of thirty abstract symbols. The vulva-derived V had at least twenty-five variations, made through repetition, rotation, strokes, crosses, and dots. "The main theme of Goddess symbolism is the mystery of birth and death and the renewal of life," wrote Gimbutas in *The Language of the Goddess*. The symbolism went back at least four hundred thousand years to the Acheulean culture of *Homo erectus*, who'd sculpted pubic triangles, mother images, and women birthing.

Awe seemed somewhat elusive in urban America, where it had gotten strongly associated with "shock and awe," the military tactic used in the 2003 televised invasion of Iraq. Li felt it by learning and thinking. He felt it most at night, when, after accumulating cannabinoids all day, he was least culture-bound. He felt it musing on life, which seemed to be a purposeful transition context; death, which was possibly a subtle, dimensional teleportation to a realer place; and increasing complexity.

He felt it by thinking about how a fetus who predicted nothing existed beyond the womb would be wrong, how a character who believed its eighty-thousand-word world was everything would also be woefully incorrect, how there might be places as unknowable to people as dreams were to electrons, and how entities probably existed who synchronized hundreds of ontologies, not just body and mind.

He felt it watching an animation on YouTube called "The Central Dogma of Biology," which showed life building itself in real time—the equivalent of a star using a planet-sized microscope to see hands piecing together LEGOs. Giant, fist-shaped machines called ribosomes, millions of which were in each of his trillions of cells, were intaking small molecules called amino acids and linking them into one-dimensional sequences, which, ticker-taping out, were folding and jiggling and crunching down into three-dimensional, globular objects (receptors, enzymes, and other proteins), which were rushing off to begin their work.

Researching his physical beginnings online, Li absorbed a two-threaded chapter of backstory in which half of him won a blind race against hundreds of millions of others. Butting into his larger half, he'd gone furiouser ahead, unwittingly completing a genetic dyad. His mitochondriated, elder, spherical half, the self-sustaining imagination to the sputtering, dying universe of his sperm half, had won a longer race through patience and self-preservation, outsurviving millions of other oocytes since 1982.

Weeks later, Li felt more awe when he read "The Egg and the Sperm," a paper by Emily Martin on how sperm didn't race toward and penetrate the egg, as he'd gleaned from memory and brief, Wikipedic research; they were more guided there in feedback-looped partnership. Most accounts of fertilization in pop culture, college textbooks, and medical journals were egregiously inaccurate; dominator ideas on "passive females and heroic males" had been written in at the level of the cell, making them "seem so natural as to be beyond alteration."

Sperm wanted to escape. As they shook their heads back and forth, their sideways motion had ten times the force of their forward motion. They proceeded eggward in part through quantity, as an amoebic glob. Thousands reached the fallopian tubes. Hundreds found themselves near the egg, which attracted them with chemicals and trapped one in its coat—"a sophisticated biological security system that screens incoming sperm," Martin quoted a researcher. The wriggling sperm, still trying to get away, released stored enzymes—millions of long words, a clustered spell—dissolving the zona pellucida to begin a forward escape with the egg into the world.

Li sometimes felt a bleak, almost discouraging awe while reading, like when, researching the mainstream model of history, he realized that Yuval Noah Harari's 2014 book *Sapiens*, an international bestseller recommended by Bill Gates and Mark Zuckerberg, didn't mention the Younger Dryas impact theory, which had emerged in *Proceedings of the National Academy of Sciences* in 2007. The lacuna allowed Harari, in his 443-page argument that humans have always been violent, cruel, and male dominated, to confidently promote the "overkill theory," blaming Native Americans for exterminating billions of megafauna in decades for no reason. "Don't believe tree-huggers who claim that our ancestors lived in harmony with nature," wrote Harari.

From *Tending the Wild*, a book by M. Kat Anderson on native management of California's natural resources, Li knew, though, that Native Americans had followed harmony-promoting rules when hunting and gathering, including *Do not needlessly kill* and *Leave some for other animals*, and that when Yahweh worshippers reached California in the sixteenth century, they'd found a massive, parklike garden in which flora and fauna seemed unnaturally abundant. Over eleven millennia, the natives had "knit themselves to nature through their vast knowledge base," wrote Anderson. It was the same, Li knew from other books, when Europeans reached Australia. Aborigines seemed to naturally steward their environments into fecund forest-gardens, in which they lived in optimized symbiosis with thousands of life-forms, catalytically nourishing themselves over tens of millennia, as if to prepare for hundreds of generations of J-curved decline in the one-way trip of history.

Harari also didn't mention the thousands of female figurines that had been found across Eurasia from 40,000 to 12,000 years ago, a period with no explicitly male figurines, and to the years 12,000 to 6,000 years ago he devoted only around 250 nonconsecutive words (less than a page), not enough to say that every culture known from then had been egalitarian and Goddess worshipping. He concluded "patriarchy is so universal, it cannot be the product of some vicious cycle" and that there was "some universal biological reason why almost all cultures valued manhood over womanhood"—the opposite of what researchers who seemed to Li better informed on the past argued: for most of human history, mainstream culture had revered women as the ultimate metaphor for nature due to their ability to birth and nourish new life.

In early December, when the European Union announced mercury fillings would be banned in July 2018 for pregnant/nursing women and children under fifteen, Li visited the set of the movie of his third novel in a Chinatown café. He watched a scene, in which newlyweds MacBook-record themselves on MDMA in Taipei acting in a mockumentary, get filmed ten times.

The director was a friendly young man. Li was finding it easier to like people. He was auto-shit-talking—half-consciously cathecting disapproving thoughts about himself, his family, his friends, and his acquaintances—much less than he had one, two, or three years earlier. "Stop shit-talking [person] and focus on [productive activity]," he'd been saying aloud whenever he became aware of himself doing it.

Walking home, the urge to return to his drug phase's first, social half, which had given him social skills while withering his already weak coping and relationship skills, wandered toward his core and loitered there, attracting attention. He felt familiarly heartened as, editing his nonfiction book's DMT chapter in his room, the urge left.

Drawing, he considered how he probably wouldn't smoke DMT again for a long time—it didn't seem good for stably working on books—and realized millions of people had smoked DMT, but probably no one had read the set of books he'd read. As he walked to a bodega for mineral water, falling snow reminded him of microfireflies.

Supine in the park the next day, he couldn't see them at first. After he blurred his vision a little and stopped thinking, translucent, vibrating, meshed hexagons appeared and changed into a teeming layer of curlicuing, light-trailing specks.

Maybe microfireflies would coalesce into a holographic overlay cognizable into 3D meaning. Already immersed in layered visuals, people would integrate visual language quickly.

It could be a transitional ability, something to practice on Earth and take into the imagination.

In *An Electronic Silent Spring*, Li read about the effects of electromagnetic radiation—the spectrum of frequencies of photons—from CT scans, Wi-Fi, smartphones, cell towers, and smart meters: cancer, diabetes, arthritis, inflammation, rashes, headaches, leaky blood-brain barrier, DNA and ion-channel damage, raised stress hormones, impaired memory and sleep.

Life had evolved in Earth's electromagnetic field, the invisible glow made by the fifty or so lightning bolts that occurred globally every second. The field's main frequency was 7.83 hertz—oscillations per second—with weaker harmonics up to 45 hertz and spikes to more than 100 hertz. Human brain waves oscillated in the same range, except during sleep, when they slowed to below 7.83 hertz, as if to resonate with a different world. The U.S. power grid operated at 60 hertz. Phones and Wi-Fi used microwaves from 0.8 to 2.4 billion hertz. Waves from 400 to 800 trillion hertz were visible to humans as color. CT scans used X-rays, which exceeded 30 quadrillion hertz.

Li realized the waveringly transauditory buzzing he sometimes heard or felt might be unnatural frequencies and amplitudes of light. He noticed he could parse language, feel emotions, sustain thoughts, discern tone, and remember things better in parks than in 4K, and better in 4K, despite the seventy-plus Wi-Fi routers his MacBook detected, than in the library, where, amid computers and phones, he seemed to regularly go brain-dead.

One night, Li bought six capsules of cayenne pepper from a tea shop. He'd never used cayenne on a headache and was eager to try.

In the library, he swallowed two capsules at a time with chamomile tea. At 5:52 p.m., minutes after ingesting all six capsules, he stood with increasingly troubling pain. He entered a bathroom, sat on a toilet, put his glasses on the floor, and held his head, moaning. He vomited reddish water. Hacking loudly, he unsuccessfully tried to vomit more. He noticed with surprise that his jacket, over two shirts and a sweater, was sweat soaked.

He put on his glasses and left the bathroom. Ascending stairs to the first floor, he felt hunchbacked and near-unconscious with pain. He seemed to only have peripheral vision. He staggered outside. It was snowing.

He crossed the street to Washington Square Park and fell onto a bench into a position he remained in for twenty minutes, grasping his hair with his right hand, groaning.

He walked elsewhere and dropped onto a bench by NYU's business school with his right forearm as a pillow and his left hand between his thighs. Deep-breathing, he began to shiver uncontrollably.

After a while, he stood and walked into a slow jog. It was 6:43 p.m. Stomach pain and headache were gone. No one seemed to have noticed his problem. He liked Manhattan's anonymity, allowing him to allow his body to heal itself.

Strolling home, he felt heightenedly comfortable. He noticed the conspicuous fractalness of naked trees for seemingly the first time. The city's artificial lights, zooming by on cars, floating past on lamps, seemed pretty and affecting as near, teary stars.

The library, where he'd been standing in the eighth-floor fiction stacks, hand-editing in relatively low-radiation privacy, closed for Christmas, so Li switched to working in his room and in nearby Bellevue South Park. He enjoyed working most on holidays, when people were doing things that alienated him, making him feel closer to himself.

The first two weeks of 2017, his cannabis intake climaxed. He worked on a mandala for his mom's birthday and stayed in the world of his book ten to thirteen hours a day, finalizing a first draft with myriad small edits. After sending the draft to his agent and editor, he indulgently reread parts of it at random, then went to visit Mike's family.

On Mike's front steps, Li and a weak, coughing Alan discussed a stair-handle-entwined vine, reminding Li of the tiny leaf they'd discussed on Tom Sawyer Island. Their conversation fell apart after forty seconds. Alan faced the door, waiting for his parents.

At a Mexican restaurant, Li asked Mike's wife, Julie, about her pregnancy—her second son was due in April. It was harder this time, she said, because she was older. She gave Li chia-flax-peanut bars she'd made from dates that Li had ordered for her family.

Mike seemed happy and tired. Li imagined he'd been grumpier the past few years due to worrying about Alan, who, Li knew from their parents, had seen a speech therapist for a while but now seemed, when not sick, to be garrulous and articulate.

Mike asked Li about 4K. Li told him about the poop notices. Mike asked about the movie of Li's third novel. Li said the director's dad had directed *Commando*. Julie joked Arnold Schwarzenegger should play Li's dad, and Li felt a little defensive.

Li asked Alan if he liked school. Alan didn't respond, even after his mom asked him to, but later he began to whisper phrases like "eyebrow butt" and "face butt" to his parents and giggling. He walked to Li, whispered "glasses butt," and laughed.

Mike grinned and asked Li if he wanted clothes. Whenever Li visited, Mike gave him some clothes, which comprised most of Li's wardrobe. Li said yes.

Walking to the N train, he ate two date bars and praised them, though he knew the peanuts would probably cause days of pain. He told Mike he'd get clothes next time.

Julie photographed Li with Mike and Alan. Mike smiled at Li and, for the first time in their adult life that Li could remember, moved toward him to hug him.

Year of Mountains

Mediation

When Li arrived in Taiwan on January 17, 2017, for a twelve-week visit, his longest yet, his parents seemed startlingly averse to each other. His presence inflected their bitter rapport into a faintly comical disgruntledness, like on day four, when his mom, napping in the TV room, said, "Can you help me cover my legs?" about a blanket.

"Help me cover," she repeated sternly.

Li's dad seemed to silently help.

Li was drawing tiny circles in his room.

"Give me some," said Li's mom a minute later.

Li's dad gave her probably two or three peanuts.

"Why are you so selfish?" said Li's mom. "So weird."

"Should have bought more," said Li's dad.

"In the whole world, I've never met anyone as selfish as you," said Li's mom.

"Give Du one," said Li's dad.

The next morning, Li's dad asked Dudu to bring him toilet paper. "Dad is weird—even though I'm here, he asks Du," said Li's mom, and asked Li to bring his dad toilet paper. Li told his parents they'd be fucked—bù xíng le—without him and Dudu, through whom they could speak, think, and feel in friendly, loving tones to themselves and each other, and his parents agreed.

Switchbacking up a paved trail on Flamingo Mountain that day, Dudu ran ahead, stopping regularly to watch and wait for the others. "Mountain-climbing dog," said Li's dad, listening to music from his phone without earphones. Descending the mountain, Li piqued with interest, hearing his parents bondingly criticize a seventies Chinese singer together.

"You started going with me your first year of college?" said Li's dad, suddenly contemplative.

"*Going with you* what," said Li's mom.

"Started being with me," said Li's dad.

Li's mom didn't respond, but they stayed in a good mood, praising Dudu's exploratory curiosity, protective leadership, and biophilia.

That night, researching for his novel, Li emailed his mom asking if she'd ever seen his dad cry. She said she'd seen it once, before they wed, when he talked about his parents dying when he was a college freshman. "I felt sad seeing him cry so I made a promise in my heart that I would help and take care of him all my life. I have kept my promise so far."

The next day, Li emailed his mom asking how she met his dad. She said in 1971, after her first year of college, while teaching high school English and caring for her stroke-weakened mom, five of Fat Uncle's friends, including Li's dad, had visited. Days later, she'd gotten a letter from Li's dad, asking if they could write to each other to improve their English.

They married in 1976. Half a year later, Li's dad left for the United States for his doctorate. Li's mom joined him a year later. "The first time Dad said he was going, my heart ached," she said in her email to Li. "I did not want to leave my family. My mother cried. She was worried she might not see me again. At the airport, I gave Mike to Auntie and cried all the way to America."

In 1979, she returned to Taiwan and brought Mike to the States. Two months later, she got a telegraph from Thin Uncle. Mike started crying before she read it: "Mother passed away peacefully."

At a waterfall at the bottom of Carp Mountain, Li learned of phytoncides (antimicrobial compounds given off by plants) and anions (molecules with extra electrons) from a dual-language sign calling them "air vitamins crucial to mental and physical health."

In his room that night, he read that forests, mountains, seashores, and waterfalls had tens of thousands of anions per cubic centimeter, countrysides had a thousand, city parks five hundred, city streets fifty, air-conditioned rooms zero to twenty-five, and that below a thousand impaired cognition and slowed physical recovery.

At dinner the next night, Li told his parents a Japanese study had found that cancer-killing lymphocytes and intracellular anticancer proteins showed increased activity for a week after trips to forests, or "forest-bathing," as it was called in Japan. The study was more evidence that the broken human—nature symbiosis caused cancer and other diseases.

"Then we should keep climbing mountains," said Li's mom.

Li didn't get visibly upset with a parent until day eleven. They were underground on a train platform in transit to lunch with six relatives. Li's dad's younger sister called, unable to find the restaurant. Li's dad began to blame Li's mom with an anguished expression, as if something terrible had happened.

On the train, Li criticized his dad for overreacting and habitually blaming others. Li was on LSD. He'd been alternating days of LSD and cannabis. They alighted after two stops to transfer trains.

As they waited on the platform, Li's dad's sister called again, and Li's dad became upset again. Li took his dad's phone, gave it back, said he was leaving, escalated up and away, turned around, escalated back to his parents, and continued to lecture his dad, who walked away. The jazzy, laidback remix of the Chopin nocturne played in the station.

On the train, Li began to assign some blame to his mom. She'd pressured his dad too much, hounding him to finish work. Pressure could build. Spite could emerge.

At Ximen Station, they couldn't find Li's dad. Li found him and called him "stupid," feeling strange and mean. He seemed to be trying to give his dad, who compulsively called people, including sometimes Li, stupid, "a taste of his own medicine."

At the restaurant, Li gave Thin Uncle a bottle of liver capsules, rich in vitamin B12, for his hand tremor, which had returned in the past year, and got up twice to reconciliatorily share food with his dad, who was seated with his younger sister's family.

Near the end of lunch, Li's dad briefly massaged a seated Li's shoulders from behind. "Don't be so mean to me," he said. "Okay?"

"You were mean first," said Li. "To Mom." While waiting on edits from his editor, he'd been putting his energy into parent mediation, which until that day had felt calm and gameful and productive. The first ten days, he'd increasingly thought he'd just be lighthearted and composed with his parents from then on—a sagacious, Zen presence.

Outside, they seemed happy again, glad to have recovered, but at Cotton Field, an organic grocery store, Li's mom got overcharged for the third time in a year, and Li's dad began to berate the employees, seeming troublingly distraught.

On the busy sidewalk outside the store, Li lectured his dad, who, aware his son was currently shameless and would employ cheap tactics, like increased volume, became quiet and agreeable. "Criticizing employees will *obviously* only make them make more mistakes—the opposite of what you want," said Li, and felt self-conscious and unruly but kept talking, finally even quizzing his dad on three reasons why his behavior was unhelpful.

Walking to the train station, Li felt like he'd woken from a fluctuatingly nightmarish dream. Li's mom, probably wanting to be apart from an unstable Li, said she was going to go get her watch fixed.

On the train, Li apologized to his dad and said he shouldn't raise his voice, especially in public. His dad agreed and called him out of control. Li agreed and berated himself.

The next day, on the way to a movie, they passed where Li had escalated away from, then back to, his parents. "Remember when I left yesterday?" he said with a grin.

"You would've lost if you left, missing lunch," said Li's dad.

"No. Lunch was unhealthy. I'd rather eat at home."

"Leaving is not good," said Li's mom. "It's better to talk."

"I've only yelled at you two once this year. Next year, I'll yell even less."

After the movie, they went home and went on a walk.

"In the past, I never wanted to walk," said Li.

"You used to not want to do anything with us," said Li's mom.

"You used to be angry all the time—heh," said Li's dad. "What was there to be angry about?"

"I wasn't angry," said Li. "I was uncomfortable."

After dinner, Li's dad said, "Du! Hair child. It's time. To lie down and rest." Dudu followed him to bed, twirling and yapping. She liked when he slept. It was when he was least likely to go anywhere.

Li washed dishes, as he'd begun doing that year. Entering

his room, he heard his mom call herself "Mi Mi" to Dudu. "Heh—I'm Mi Mi," she repeated, seeming manic and zany.

Li felt comically uneased. His parents had been adding spoken, stoned-seeming laughs—"Heh" or "Heheh"—to the beginnings, ends, and middles of their sentences.

In his notes, Li listed some reasons why they were all getting more stoned over years—increased DHA, EPA, AA, and other endocannabinoid precursors; less glyphosate and other enzyme-inhibiting pesticides; more exercise and sleep.

In the morning, Li said he felt unwell due to eating frozen, unripe pineapple before bed, and had vomited in the middle of the night, so wasn't hiking that day.

"What color was the vomit?" said Li's mom.

"Black," said Li, which seemed to scare her. "Not black. Brown."

"We need to go to the emergency room if there was blood," said Li's mom.

"There wasn't," said Li. He measured cold coffee, brought it into his room, put it on his desk, and lay on his floor bed. In the past, he'd gotten defensive when his mom told him not to eat pineapple on its own; pineapple had become a sensitive topic.

Li's mom knocked on Li's ajar door. "Did your stomach hurt when you vomited?"

"No," said Li, thinking the question seemed hard to answer.

"If you shit blood, you need to tell us," said Li's mom.

Li was silent.

"If there's blood, we need to go to a hospital now."

"There wasn't blood," said Li.

As his mom left the room, she said, "And you shouldn't drink coffee now," which frustrated Li because it seemed like bad advice and because he felt like it meant, "You're so addicted to coffee that you're even going to drink it now."

Li left his room and told his mom he'd get a headache without caffeine. He emailed her an article on caffeine withdrawal, then went to tell her to read it. She was wearing earphones, washing dishes.

"We can't talk when you wear earphones," said Li. He returned to his room, chugged coffee, and lay in bed.

He got up and emailed his mom, apologizing for getting defensive about her concern, then went outside and felt better while biking and collecting orange flowers. He'd been gathering plant parts and posting photos of them online.

Biking home, he began to feel nauseated and negative again. His parents had said they bickered "even more" when he wasn't there, which made him feel pressure to be there more. He felt overwhelmed by vicarious misery sometimes, imagining his parents hardening in his absence into the coral reef of resentment they'd grown over decades.

"You're feeling a lot better," said his mom when he got home.

Annoyed by the assertion, Li entered his room and lay frowning in bed. He felt disappointed and frustrated that he'd fallen so hard into hostile despair again—twice in three days, against his dad and now his mom. He felt infected by his parents' bickering.

"Li," said Li's dad, pushing the door open. "Do you want to eat?"

"No. Can you buy mineral water for me?"

"Yes, after dinner," said Li's dad.

"Thank you," said Li.

"If your stomach hurts too much, you should say something."

"Of course I will," said Li, who wasn't bothered by his dad's concern because, as he'd told his parents, it wasn't overwhelming, unlike his mom's sometimes.

Li's mom entered and asked if she could touch Li's forehead to check for fever. Li left his room, asked his dad to tell his mom to stop bothering him, went in his room, hit the dresser, closed his door in a last-second-softened slam, lay in bed, felt his heart grimacing, and emailed his mom another apology.

He felt better by that night. Before bed, he printed and read a paper that said buildings, besides lacking anions, which were neutralized by metal ducting, electronic screens, and Wi-Fi, had high levels of cations—molecules that lacked electrons and so absorbed them from people, suppressing immunity and muddling thought.

On a pre-dinner walk, Li said he'd shat blood two nights earlier. His mom calmly listened as he said the unripe pineapple's enzymes had gotten deep into his gut, causing bleeding sores, and that if they'd gone to a hospital he probably would've gotten recovery-impeding procedures and/or drugs.

Li's mom said she'd shat black for five days while alone in Florida in 2004. Finally, she'd gone to Dr. Chan, who'd sent her to a hospital, where she'd gotten a transfusion of three bags of blood.

They entered a public rose garden. Li and his dad filmed Dudu as she tumbled vigorously through a rosemary bush with her mouth open, stretching and squirming like a giant, short worm, inhaling phytoncides, anions, and microbes.

Li lifted Dudu to a *Rosa multiflora*—or Japanese rose—flower, which she sniffed. Many plants in parks in Taiwan were labeled with their scientific and common names.

Li's mom said that except for fighting politicians, physically attacking one another in bleak displays regularly covered by international media, Taiwan was actually pretty good.

"They haven't fought recently, right?" said Li.

"They still fight," said Li's mom.

The next night, Li was in the kitchen making chamomile tea when he heard his dad telling him from the TV room that his mom, who was on a walk, was brainwashed.

Li didn't respond. He'd recently learned his dad supported a liberal party in Taiwan and a conservative party in the States, and that his mom preferred the opposite in both countries.

In his room, Li emailed his dad, "When you think Mom is brainwashed, remember that I think you're brainwashed, but I don't try to make you feel bad about it. Don't call her brainwashed. Everyone is brainwashed. If you have to talk about it, talk to me."

"Okay," replied Li's dad. "Good point. I need to have someone. Maybe you. To talk to when I need to comment on KMT." His receptivity surprised Li.

On Carp Mountain the next day, Li carried Dudu while ascending steep stairs. Twice, Li's dad sat, told the others to go without him, and continued climbing after encouragement. They reached a Daoist temple called Whole Epiphany Temple.

Li's dad asked Li if it was good that monks meditated and chanted all day. Li said monks showed there were other ways to live. Monks didn't "contribute to society," said Li's dad in English. Li said they contributed to their own society.

Li's dad said with five employees he turned one day into five days, and Li said with recovery he was able to do and think five times more new things a day than before 2014.

He walked away and stood in place, flapping for five minutes. He couldn't see microfireflies, or they weren't there. The sky seemed empty, lucid, uncharged.

Maybe the swarming dots of light were an urban phenomenon. One cubic centimeter of urban air contained probably hundreds to millions of molecules of glyphosate, Earth's most used pesticide, because gasoline, as per the 1990 Clean Air Act, was partly made from glyphosate-filled corn or sugarcane, Li had read. Maybe microfireflies were pesticides, flashing as they got buffeted and interpenetrated by municipal intensities of synthetic electromagnetic radiation—electrosmog—or maybe the overmind was helpfully disassembling toxins into atoms and light.

Li and his mom smiled while observing Li's dad, who was seated on the temple stairs with Dudu on his lap, talking angrily into his phone with a grievously exasperated, extra-twitchy face, which often appeared during business calls.

They descended the mountain and rested at the waterfall with the phytoncide-anion sign, eating cookies that Li and

his mom had made from almonds, ghee, honey, ginger, turmeric, black pepper, and sea salt.

On the train home, Li's dad asked if the movie of Li's third
novel, which was about the first half of his three-year drug
phase, would have fighting sequences.

"I don't know," said Li. "I only read half the screenplay."

"It's good we're going to be in a movie," said Li's dad.

"You'll be in more movies in the future," said Li.

"Can you write more about Du?" said Li's dad.

"Yes," said Li.

"Can you write more about me?" said Li's dad.

"I'm already writing a lot about you."

"Can you write about me writing papers?" said Li's dad.

"The more I see you writing papers, the more I'll write
about it."

At Daan Park Station, a man got on the train wearing a
jacket that said "Antisoclal"—a typo, it seemed, for "Antiso-
cial." Li and his parents laughed.

Li asked his parents how they'd first heard of the stock
market. They said a man named Johnny told them about it
in 1991. They'd given their money to a stockbroker, who'd
lost most of it. Later, when Li's dad was in prison, Li's mom
had excelled at stocks.

"Without Mom, we'd have no money," said Li's dad.

"It's true," said Li's mom.

Li's parents discussed China for a while. Li's dad was trying to get government approval to sell his lasers in China.

At Taipei Main Station, Li's dad said he needed to buy

batteries and got off the train. Dudu, in her enclosed container, squeaked in an almost inaudibly high-pitched tone for the remaining two stops, looking out her mesh window for Li's dad.

"Don't worry," said Li's mom. "Dad went to buy batteries."

Two days later, on a train to Elephant Mountain, Li's dad wrote notes on a thrice-folded piece of paper. Noticing Li photograph him, he proposed sending Li an equation a day to post online. Li declined and encouraged his dad to do it himself.

On the mountain, Li's mom said, "We should let Dad bring his phone next time, so he can listen to music." They'd forbidden him to bring his phone that day.

Li said he related to his dad's phone addiction.

"I've never had that problem," said Li's mom.

"Because you don't do business," said Li's dad.

"I do half your business," said Li's mom.

After hiking, they walked through a dense cityscape toward the train station, passing bakeries, cafés, a KFC, a Hi-Life, a FamilyMart, and other stores.

"Is Chiang Kai-shek good or not good?" said Li's dad to Li.

Li didn't respond. His dad asked twice more.

"I don't care," said Li. "Don't talk about that."

"Mom thinks he's good," said Li's dad, and began to tell Li in a strangely serious voice, as if he were telling a scary story, that his mom had been brainwashed.

Li's mom's face flushed with irritation.

"Try not to be too affected by him," said Li.

"She's too affected," said Li's dad. "She's threatened divorce over politics." But then instead of getting increasingly riled, as in the past, he laughed self-consciously, as if stoned, and said, "I've been trying to say political things less around her."

"Then keep trying," said Li. Ostensibly changing topics, he said he'd realized his personality was influenced by his health; he'd been taciturn, monotone, and withdrawn for most of his life because that was what his body could muster.

Li's mom said that once, when she was in middle school, she'd hidden when Fat Uncle brought home one of his friends because she'd been too shy to meet anyone new.

Li's dad said something Li didn't hear.

"Don't talk," said Li's mom.

"What's the matter?" said Li, frustrated his parents kept falling into bickering.

Li's mom looked gravely distraught.

"What happened when you hid?" said Li.

"Nothing. I was just embarrassed."

"What happened just now? Why did you get upset?"

"Dad was going to comment," said Li's mom, "comment" in English.

"He might say something good," said Li, escalating down into a train station. "You assume he'll say something bad. I want to hear what Dad says too. It's a conversation."

"Why did Fat Uncle hide?" said Li's dad.

"He didn't," said Li. "Mom hid."

Li's dad said Li's mom had been so afraid in college that she had to be taken around by people. She never went anywhere alone.

Li felt closer to his mom. For most of his life he'd viewed

her as confident and well-adjusted—a strong mom raising a weak, tortured child. He was realizing she'd changed over decades.

It was Li's dad's job, after hiking and walks, to wash Dudu's feet and put newspaper and a soup-pot mat on the dinner table. Usually, Li's mom reminded him repeatedly to do his tasks, sometimes more than ten times, but that night he did everything before being told, even moving the one-seat sofa that Li used at dinner nearer the table—a task from the previous year, when Li had had debilitating pain—then went into the kitchen to help some more.

Li's mom was sautéing pork.

"It's good you didn't grind the pork," said Li's dad.

"If someone cooked for me, I wouldn't complain," said Li's mom.

"Dad is just stating his preference for non-ground meat," said Li.

Li's mom said Li was good at [a word Li didn't understand].

"What is that?" said Li.

"Mediating," said his mom in English.

Li said he felt unhappy when his parents bickered.

Li's mom said their bickering never led to anything.

Li said bickering itself was something.

At dinner, Taiwan's president appeared on TV. Li liked her—she was one-fourth Paiwan, Taiwan's second-largest aboriginal group, and had issued Taiwan's first apology to its indigenous people, saying their rights had been brutally violated by every regime who'd gone to Taiwan in the past four centuries—but he changed the channel to deter parental tension.

"Did you like this one?" said Li's mom about a pigskin dish in a surprisingly, almost confrontationally friendly voice, looking at Li's dad, who quietly said he did, seeming discomfited by the rare tone, then non sequitured, "Don't grind the pork," which visibly annoyed Li's mom, but Li smiled at her—her bangs, cut that day, made her seem childlike—and she smiled back.

Li's dad began squeezing her thigh, and she uncharacteristically did not move his hand away. "Look at Binky—Tabby—Dudu," she said, smiling at her original mistake, grace-noting "Dudu" with a poodle recap—they'd gotten Binky in 1988, Tabby in 1993, Dudu in 2008. "After dinner, when she doesn't need us, she looks away."

Dudu was on the sofa in a Sphinx position, facing no one.

Later that night, when Li returned from taking trash/recycling to the basement, his mom, supine on a sofa with her eyes closed, said he'd been in Taiwan for almost three weeks. "Only nine more weeks until you go back," she said. "Time goes too fast."

An hour later, she emailed Li, "Sorry we have not been a good role model as a couple and let you feel sad. I have always been upset by Dad's wrong accusations, but I always get over it and still love and take care of him, no matter what."

"You misunderstand me," replied Li. "I don't care if you take care of Dad or not. I actually think it could be good if you two lived separately. Bickering and fighting all the time is what I don't like. It makes it unenjoyable and stressful to be here."

"All couples fight and argue from time to time. It is normal. It is impossible for two people to live together and have the same way of doing things. The most important thing is to compromise and forgive. That is the way of life."

"I will visit less then. I can't be around this all the time. I'm trying to help but it feels like constant tension. You and Dad need to keep trying or I won't visit."

"I will try my best. We like you to visit as often as you can."

"Okay, good. I am trying also."

The next day, Li woke to his mom's exasperated voice. He emailed her, "Feels terrible to wake to bickering. You already nagged Dad yesterday about his employee. I am serious about going back. When my editor sends me edits, I'm going to work on my book and I may want to go back to NYC."

He lay staring out the window, past an elevated train track, at the placid sky, seeing no microfireflies. The clouds seemed feeling-shaped, amorphously morphing.

He went to his computer. His mom had replied, "I was not angry, just suggested to Dad instead of complaining what the employee wrote, why not just write it himself. Maybe I used the improper tone."

"You did," replied Li. "And when dad responded (saying the same things as yesterday) you told him to stop talking. It was rude."

"I did not realize that I used the wrong tone, thanks for pointing that out to me again. It has been this way for such a long time, it is hard to change, but I will try."

"Be nice to Mom," Li emailed his dad. "If you and Mom keep doing this, I will come back less each year. You were good last night, washing Dudu's feet and putting newspaper on the table. Thank you."

The next day, on the way to a movie, Li had his first nosebleed in months. His parents noticed. He blamed it on being upset due to their bickering. His mom said upsetness didn't cause nosebleeds. Li said it could.

Stoned during the movie, he imagined the characters frantically researching the mystery in between the on-screen scenes. Every part of the mystery—every atom, cell, dream, and dimension—seemed to lead to more of itself. The more one learned about the everywhere-portal of it, the more of it there was. Maybe it had no end.

A cantankerous character in the movie suddenly reminded Li of how much his parents had seemed to hate each other when he got to Taiwan three weeks earlier. He realized they'd definitely gotten friendlier to each other since then. His mediation efforts were working. He felt heartened and encouraged.

After the movie, Li and his mom mimed the arm motion his dad, who was in the bathroom, used to do, in which it seemed like his arm was paralyzed and he had to shake it to regain control.

Li's mom's laughter sounded purer than Li had ever heard from her, almost performative with inflection. "Actually, Dad isn't a not-good dad," she said. "He just doesn't know how to talk sometimes."

On the way home, Li admitted his nosebleed had probably been due to excessive fish liver oil. He told his parents he'd been recording them for his novel.

"Then we need to be careful of what we say," said Li's mom, smiling. She'd read all of Li's published writing, online and in print.

Catatonia

Two days later, on the train home after seeing *Split*, a movie about a man with twenty-four personalities, Li said society put children and elders with problems into hospitals, where they became bù xíng le. "You two are lucky," he said. "You don't have to fear me putting you in a hospital. Even if you were insane, I wouldn't."

"You care about us," said Li's mom, and Li said people who brought their relatives to hospitals also cared, which made it complex and tragic and hard to discuss.

At home, Li's parents seemed on the verge of sustained, active bickering. "Five more minutes," said Li's dad. Five minutes later, he still wasn't ready. He began to mutter that all Li's mom did was nag him. Li's mom retreated to her office and dejectedly said they'd go someplace nearer to walk instead of Daan Park since it was getting late.

Li asked his dad when he'd be ready, told his mom ("Five minutes"), mounted the inversion table, began a voice memo, and said that as he got more limber and less inflamed he could crack more of his bones, including, while inverted, ones in his sacrum.

Li's dad stood, finally ready to go, and asked if Dudu could use the table. Li's mom said she was too short. In the elevator, Dudu did Downward-Facing Dog and other stretches, and Li said she didn't need the table.

Outside, Li realized his parents had been bickering about a FedEx issue for two days. He decided to distract them with questions. He asked his mom what she'd thought in July, seven months earlier, when she weighed less than ever.

"I thought I had cancer. Cancer causes sudden weight drop."

"Were you very scared?" said Li.

"Very worried. Not scared. If I had cancer, it would be very inconvenient, needing to do this, do that."

"Did you tell Dad?"

"No. Telling him would be of no use."

Dudu chased Li's dad as he jogged ahead, saying, "Run, run, run, run!" Each morning, she guarded him from inside or outside the bathroom as he sat on the toilet with two phones—emailing, messaging, checking stock prices, watching videos.

"He doesn't know what's going on with me," said Li's mom.

"He knows," said Li accusatorily. "One day when you

weren't home, Dad told me to check the internet for what it meant that you lost two kilograms."

"I only tell Auntie," said Li's mom. "And Thin Uncle and Mike."

"In the past, have you told Dad before?"

"I've said, 'Ayo! I only weigh such-and-such.'"

"When your weight only went down a little, he knew. He looked very worried, and it had only been two kilograms. It was before you lost even more weight."

"It could be there's worry, but he won't say it," Li's mom relented.

Li's dad was ahead in the crowded plaza, carrying Dudu, who'd gotten scared and stopped walking.

Dudu seemed to favor Li's dad mainly because he didn't rub fish oil on her gums or clean her. Whenever Li's mom approached her to retrieve her for cleaning, Dudu huddled in place, growling with increasing ferocity until becoming abruptly docile once held.

"Did you tell Auntie why you lost weight?" said Li.

"I told her it could be, if not cancer, a thyroid problem."

A plane flying to an airport two miles away lumbered past, fuming and low, muting the Sunday crowd, maybe half of whom were there for the farmers market.

"When I was switching medications . . . ," said Li's mom about Thyro-Gold.

"What about that?" said Li.

"It could be that, switching."

"It was," said Li, surprised by her uncertainty. He explained thyroid's connection to weight, then said, "The director of *Split* directed *The Sixth Sense*. Have you seen it?"

"I have," said Li's mom. "The child, who sees . . . I must have seen it with you."

"Child who sees what?" said Li's dad.

"Ghosts," said Li in English.

"Most of the movies I've seen, I've seen with Li," said Li's mom. They'd seen many movies together when Li was a tween and teenager. Mike had been at college. Their dad had usually been away on business.

"Ayo—you haven't seen any movies, Du," said Li's dad, setting Dudu on the sidewalk. "Li saw so many movies as a child and he forgot them all. Children watching movies isn't much use."

"I haven't forgotten," said Li quietly.

As Li's mom told a story involving Li and jumping, Li's dad interrupted her, saying, "Hey, are they digging something here? Look. Are they building something here?"

Li's parents seemed to be vying for Li's attention. Li's mom continued reminiscing: The two of them had often gone to restaurants—Steak and Ale, Olive Garden, Yae Sushi. "Once we sat, you'd say, 'Do you believe there is a God?'"

"What would you say?" said Li, surprised.

"I would just say there was," said Li's mom.

"I don't remember asking that," said Li.

"You often asked it. At that time, you believed there was."

"What was one reason I gave for there being a God?"

"Reasons, I can't say," said Li's mom. "Don't remember."

Dudu pooped, and Li's dad wrapped the poop in a paper towel, then wiped Dudu's butt.

Li thought that how his parents treated Dudu, with attentive patience, enduring curiosity, and unconditional love, was probably how they'd treated him when he was small and maybe how they still treated him.

Minutes later, they saw Dudu forty feet behind them, standing motionless, looking at them with her blank gaze.

"Du, come," shouted Li's mom, and clapped thrice.

"She hasn't walked here before," offered Li.

"Has," said Li's mom.

Dudu sat. Li's dad took a business call. Li and his mom discussed the ten or so wild dogs who lived in the parks by their building. "If we see wild dogs, we should pick up Du," said Li's mom. "Du would be dead in an instant. A wild dog bit Thin Uncle's Mianmian. Mianmian was hospitalized many days."

"Come, child," shouted Li's dad after his call.

"A moment ago, she walked a little," said Li.

"Walked two steps," said Li's mom.

"Hasn't used that technique before—walking a little," said Li.

"She's thinking, 'Do I want to or not?'" said Li's mom. "Du, come!" She clapped seventeen times as a train passed on the elevated track parallel to the sidewalk. "Haven't seen a dog like this before."

They walked ten feet farther from Dudu.

"Du, come, Du, come," shouted Li's dad.

"People are noticing her," said Li.

Before Dudu, Li's parents had tried two other poodles. The first had been quiet until suddenly yowling at two a.m. They'd returned her. The second had been silent for three days. They'd returned him. At the store, they'd watched siblings play with a box. The sister, Dudu, had mouthed open a door that her brother hadn't seemed to notice.

"Go pick her up," said Li's dad, and hid behind a bush.

"When she can't see you, she'll panic," Li predicted.

"Is she coming?" whispered Li's dad.

Dudu stood but didn't walk.

"Still not coming," said Li with a laugh. "She knows we've waited a very long time before."

Sometimes she seemed to want to go home or elsewhere. Sometimes she seemed to be resting. Sometimes she seemed depressed or brain-dead. Usually, after a minute or so, Li or his parents would follow her elsewhere, walk in small steps behind her to mobilize her, or, most often, carry her.

Li's dad whistled. Dudu sat.

"Sits down!" said Li's mom.

"Sits down," said Li's dad.

"She knows we won't leave her," said Li. "She trusts us a lot."

"Normally, when she can't see me, she panics," said Li's dad. "I'll come out of hiding, then." He got on the sidewalk. "Du, let's go."

Dudu looked surreally wild or recently abandoned. She most feared being alone, without companions, Li's mom had said once. Except for sitting, standing, taking two steps, sitting, standing, and sitting again, she hadn't moved in six minutes.

"We've waited so long today," said Li. "We must not let her win."

"Is she sitting?" said Li's dad. "If she's sitting, someone will take her."

Dudu ignored a group of six passersby.

"They're pointing," said Li's mom. "Go get her. A wild dog might run out."

Li jogged to Dudu, picked her up, jogged back.

"If you didn't go to her, she'd have no dignity," said Li's mom. "If we ignored her, she'd have no dignity. And because you went to get her, she was like, 'Okay, you've come, so I will walk.'"

"This time she's very happy," said Li. "We waited so long."

"This way, she has more dignity," said Li's mom.

"Next time, we'll need to wait even longer," said Li.

"Someone will steal her," said Li's dad.

"Next time, we'll need to wait *too* long," said Li.

"Longer and longer each time," said Li's dad.

"I heard one of those people say, 'There is a dog . . . that no one wants,'" said Li's mom.

"Her hair is cut so short, she'll be cold," said a passerby, a woman in her fifties.

"She's not scared of the cold," said Li's dad about Dudu.

"How do you know?" said the woman.

"When she wears clothes, she refuses to walk," said Li's dad after a pause. In winter in Taipei, most small dogs wore clothes. Many wore shoes.

"Is that so?" said the woman.

"Dogs: let them run a bit and they won't be cold," said Li's dad.

"It's because she's young. If she was old—"

"Young?" said Li's dad. "She's nine."

"Nine counts as young," said the woman.

"Mountain-climbing dog," said Li's dad. "She climbs mountains. Started when she was one." From 2007, when she was born, to 2016 she'd only climbed once or twice, but it was only February 8, 2017, and she'd already climbed six times that year.

As they approached a ramp that bikers sometimes careened down, Li's dad picked up Dudu while saying, "Hug, hug."

"That person asked how we knew Du wasn't cold," said Li.

"How would you respond?" said Li's dad.

"We don't know," said Li's mom.

"I do know," said Li. "Wild dogs didn't used to wear clothes."

"Ah," said Li's mom. "Dogs of the past."

"It's healthier that way," said Li. "If Du is a little cold, she'll move. Wild dogs in the past all had to experience winter. They were cold every winter. Every year."

"Pet dogs are overprotected," said Li's mom.

"She said, 'How do you know she's not cold?' and I suddenly didn't know what to say," said Li's dad.

Li's mom brought up *Zhuangzi*—a 2,300-year-old book by Zhuangzi in which a character named Zhuangzi, seeing minnows in a stream, said they were happy, and his friend said, "You're not a fish; how do you know they're happy?"

"Then what?" said Li's dad, who'd told Li the story many times over decades. "Fish are happy, then what? Li, let Li say it. What was the response?"

"I'm thinking," said Li. "Zhuangzi said the fish were happy, and the other person said, 'How do you know they're happy; you aren't them,' and Zhuangzi said, 'You aren't me; how do you know that I don't know that they're happy?'"

"Ehh. Right, right!" said Li's dad. "This is logic. Then what? If you add more?"

"If you aren't me, how do you know I don't know the fish are very happy," said Li's mom.

"And then what?" said Li's dad. "You're not me, so you don't know. Then what?"

"Then it's endless!" said Li's mom.

"Then—no, no! Then you say, 'You aren't me. How do you know I don't know you don't know the fish are very happy,'" said Li's dad, seeming to mangle it a bit, laughing.

"I'm trying to think of a better answer," said Li. "What you said, everyone knows."

"Just keep adding," said Li's dad.

As Li tried to think of how to transcend the loop, he looked to his right and saw his dad looking at him with a self-conscious, vaguely vulnerable face, saying, "Because I've been a fish." Startled and moved by the mystical answer, Li made no response.

It began to rain. They turned toward home. Li's dad said something about fishing, and Li's mom said, "Why do you have to mix up everything with fishing?" and Li felt like they were in a Raymond Carver story about a quarrelsome couple.

Li told his parents he'd recorded their walk. "I've written a lot about fighting," he said. "I want to balance it with good things."

"So, today was good?" said Li's mom.

"Yes. I've recorded more than enough fighting already."

"Bickering." Li's mom corrected with a smile.

Two minutes later, Li's dad dropped Dudu while picking her up—she yelped loudly but seemed unhurt—and Li's mom told Li about Dudu's childhood trauma. When Dudu was one or two, Li's dad had lifted her container without closing it. She'd fallen on her head and vomited.

"But the worst was . . . ," said Li's mom, and told of how,

on their way to the States in 2008, they left a five-month-old Dudu in a cage outside a boarding kennel, which they hadn't anticipated being closed in the morning. In the cab to the airport, they'd called Auntie, who'd found Dudu by following her continuous screams.

Falling

Four days later, they went to Fairy Story Organic Farm, a B & B in Yilan County. They put their luggage in their room and went outside.

Li's dad stood in place talking on his phone. Dudu walked away with her tail down, then Li and his mom smelled what seemed to be pesticides. Walking away from the chemical scent, they reached a grade school's outdoor area.

Minutes later, Li noticed his mom looking at her phone in a Dad-like manner—stationary, facedown. He realized she rarely zoomed into photos of her face anymore. She seemed to have stopped the previous year, when his pain returned.

That night, at dinner in a large room with one other table occupied, Li and his dad cooked meat and vegetables in a pot of simmering soup. Li's mom fed lamb to Dudu. "Du likes to drink water after eating," she said.

Li, who was stoned, went to their room, got Dudu's water, began a voice memo, returned to the table, and sat opposite Dudu, who was on her own chair between Li's parents.

"Is that good? Satisfied?" said Li's mom to Dudu.

"Tell her to obediently stay on the chair," said a woman at the other table.

"Du, you're full," said Li's dad.

"Hasn't eaten any vegetables yet," said Li about his dad.

"At buffets, you can't see green on his plate," said Li's mom.

Li left for more mulberry sauce, returned grinning, and said he'd forgotten how to get someone's attention in Mandarin so had tapped the counter and said, "Eh."

Li's mom laughed.

"How should I have said it? 'Hello'?"

"If not 'hello,' then 'embarrassed,'" said Li's mom. In Taiwan, "embarrassed"—"bù hǎo yìsi," literally "not good meaning"—meant "excuse me."

Li's mom said when she left Taiwan in the seventies, people had said "sorry" for "excuse me," and that it had taken her a long time to learn to use "embarrassed." She said people used to reply "don't thank" to "thank you" but now they said "will not."

"People get it from TV," said Li's dad. "If the TV says something—"

"He finally gets a vegetable," said Li's mom, laughing a little.

"—if the TV says something, everybody starts saying it."

"It came from Taiwanese," said Li's mom.

"Taiwanese," agreed Li's dad.

Li's mom explained that in Taiwanese when people said "thank you," you replied "no need," which translated in Mandarin to "will not," as if to say, "You will not thank me."

Li asked what Dudu was doing.

"Lying there," said Li's mom.

After a while, Dudu was standing.

"Tell her standing there is dangerous," said Li's dad. "She's too close. The hot plate is too hot. Come here."

"Come," said Li's mom. "Come here."

Dudu fell on the floor.

"Aiyo!" said Li's mom in an anguished, disturbed voice.

"Wah," said Li's dad, a noise of regret.

Li laughed quietly.

"Why did you . . . ," said Li's mom, seeming to want to blame someone.

"Nothing's wrong," said Li emphatically, worried about imminent bickering.

"Child was standing on the edge," said Li's dad. "Slipped."

"Nothing's wrong," said Li. "I laughed. Because I knew nothing would happen. She—"

"She fell but has four legs to stand on," said Li's mom.

"Right," said Li. "She didn't even yelp."

"She only went, Ng!—like that," said Li's mom.

"Her four legs prop her up," said Li's dad, and got Dudu a wider chair.

"She shouldn't fall off that," said Li.

They ate quietly for a while.

"When you were small, at Fat Uncle's home, you fell off the sink," said Li's mom.

"Who?" said Li.

"You," said Li's mom.

"Where?" said Li.

"The sink in the bathroom at Fat Uncle's home."

"Fell from where?" said Li's dad.

"Sink," said Li's mom.

"When?" said Li.

"When you were a baby," said Li's mom.

Li laughed strangely, with air leaving his nose, then laughed more, causing his mom to laugh. "From sink . . . to where," he said, glad he was amused. Part of him seemed to feel vaguely resentful, but it was a small part that felt automatic and fleeting.

"Fell while bathing?" said Li's dad.

"Not bathing. Cleaning . . . his butt, or something."

"Didn't hold him well, huh?" said Li's dad. "What was the floor?"

"Fell from the top to the floor," said Li.

"Did he cry?" said Li's dad.

"Of course he cried. How would he not cry?"

"Didn't hit his head, right?" said Li's dad.

"What hit what?" said Li.

Li's mom made a small, withdrawn noise. "The floor was very hard," she said.

"Tile?" said Li.

"Ng," confirmed Li's mom.

"Ng," said Li, looking down.

"Hadn't known how to take care of a child yet," said Li's dad.

"It's good nothing happened," said Li's mom.

"Not too knowledgeable about taking care of a child," said Li's dad.

"At least I took care of him," said Li's mom.

"Can't let him stand on the sink—it's slippery," said Li's dad.

"Feet very slippery," said Li's mom.

"How old was I?" said Li.

"You were a baby," said Li's mom.

"Fell from so high," said Li's dad.

"Like one?" said Li.

"Around that," said Li's mom.

Li's dad mumbled something that was inaudible in the recording, in which he sounded muffled and distant because he was the farthest from Li's phone.

"At least I took care of them," said Li's mom. "Right?" she said to Li.

"Right," said Li. "If Dad had taken care of me, he also would've done something to me," he said, and laughed.

"Because he never took care, he never had accidents," said Li's mom.

"Regardless of who is caretaking, there will always be mistakes," said Li.

"The Greatest Love of All," sung by Whitney Houston, was playing in the room.

"Taking care of Du, you dropped her twice," said Li's mom. "And I don't talk about it."

"It's just that *everyone* will make mistakes," said Li.

"Right," said Li's mom.

"If you want to be productive, you need to try to forgive," said Li.

"When Dad does anything, I don't keep talking about it," said Li's mom as Li's dad, looking at Li, said, "Once, we were going somewhere. From her container, she fell out."

"Right, and I don't talk about that," said Li's mom.

"We dropped you when you were so small," said Li's dad to Dudu.

"*Dad* dropped." Li's mom corrected.

"Everyone will—" said Li.

"Accidentally," said Li's mom. "It's not like . . ."

"If I took care of someone, I'd also drop them," said Li.

"The most important thing is that nothing happened," said Li's mom, which somewhat amused Li because part of him was viewing the fall as possibly another factor, among thousands, in his various problems.

"Four-leg dog," sang Li's dad. "Animals are very smart. Use their legs when they fall."

"Lamb tastes better, right?" said Li's mom to Dudu, who ate chicken at home. "In the future, Du will bicker with us about wanting to come stay here."

"She has wolf genes," said Li's dad. "Right?"

"Hm?" said Li.

"DNA is wolf," said Li's dad. "When she smells lamb: 'Ayooo!'"

Li's mom had fallen down stairs when she was seven, hitting her head on a lead bucket, Li knew. Her four-foot-nine mom had carried her a mile to a doctor, who'd sewn a flap of her forehead back on. She'd stayed home a month; sometimes the house had seemed to spin. Fearing brain damage, her mom had fed her pig brains and bone marrow.

"This food has no flavor," said Li's dad.

"It has flavor," said Li. "This sauce has no flavor to you, because normally you eat artificial flavor. So this food really has no flavor for Dad. This makes sense, right?"

"Right," said Li's mom. "Look, I ate all my vegetables."

"I didn't eat my vegetables," said Li's dad. "Me and Du are animals. We eat meat."

"She likes meat more than you," said Li. "You mostly like rice."

"We are animals," said Li's dad to Dudu.

After dinner, they walked on a dark, narrow road, between fields of rice plants in shallow water.

"Walking after eating, my blood sugar won't rise as much," said Li's mom.

"Right," said Li. "Because. Because . . ."

"Why?" said Li's mom.

"Because when you're moving, your body will use more sugar."

"There was a big dog earlier, who Du scared," said Li's mom.

"Why do you tohk others?" said Li's dad to Dudu. "On others' land. Still wants to tohk others."

"She doesn't respect others," said Li's mom.

"The big dog was frightened," said Li's dad.

"How do you say that in English?" said Li's mom.

"Look down," said Li's dad.

"This," said Li's mom, miming a snapping motion with her hand.

"Snap," said Li.

"Snap," said Li's mom.

"Snack," said Li's dad.

"Snapped at," said Li.

"In Taiwanese, it's 'tohk'!" said Li's dad. "Tohk-tohk-tohk."

Li's mom laughed quietly and cheerfully.

"Snap," said Li. "And then you need to write a little more."

"Snap at . . . something?" said Li's mom.

"Need to write, like, 'in a bitelike manner,'" said Li.

"Hoh," Li's mom understood and laughed a little.

"Need to write more to make it accurate," said Li.

Li's dad said it'd be good if his employee sold ten lasers by June. Li walked ahead and listened to his parents amicably discuss business. His dad was going to China soon, possibly to bribe their government into letting him sell his lasers there. Li's mom, to Li's surprise, had seemed supportive, telling Li that bribery was necessary in China.

After his parents and Dudu went inside, Li walked around thinking about his nonfiction book. His editor had emailed him edits the previous day, encouraging him to write more about himself and to delete the last three chapters.

In the distance, two garbage trucks syncopatedly and repeatedly broadcast an electronic, stiff-sounding version of the first eight bars of "Für Elise."

"I recorded parents confessing," Li emailed himself, walking on the dark road. "I forgave happily."

"Don't walk into water like Binky," he thought. In Florida, a very old, deaf-blind Binky had fallen into the swimming pool, making a surprisingly loud splash.

Li stood flapping in moonlight, thinking that his mom's forehead scar was like a burned-off eyebrow to an invisible eye, then watched TV with his parents, laughing when people got electrocuted by eels in a *Survivor*-like show.

Novels crystallized dreams into prose, made them share-able through matter, he thought in bed. Like dreams, they could be disruptive and unhelpful, fomenting fear and bit-terness and confusion, or calming and uplifting, connecting disparate elements from history and memory into holistic stories with natural resonance.

Statins and Coffee

Two days later, clearing the table after dinner, Li found a pink fragment of round tablet. He felt disturbed, challenged, and calmingly self-conscious. On PillIdentifier.com, he learned the fragment was a brand of statin called Crestor.

He dreaded discussing statins with his parents again. He was only mildly stoned. He was out of LSD and had reduced his daily cannabis to half a capsule per day to ration his supply. He only had twenty-seven capsules left for sixty-three days, which somewhat worried him.

After washing dishes and taking out the trash, he emailed his dad, "The drug you take, statin, causes many problems and may be why your eye twitches," with a link to an article on nerve damage.

It was 8:32 p.m. He'd agreed to wake his dad, who was napping, at nine. He went in his mom's office (she was looking at stock prices), said he'd found a statin on the newspaper, and asked where the newspaper came from.

"Auntie's," said Li's mom.

"Does Auntie use statins?" said Li.

"She used to, but hasn't for a long time."

Li realized he knew that. "I think Dad's doctor pressured him into taking statins again," he said, unsure if it was the second, third, or fourth relapse.

"I don't think so," said Li's mom. "I haven't gotten any statins." She did all the doctor-related things that didn't require Li's dad's presence.

"Can I send you the email I sent Dad?"

"Of course," said Li's mom.

At nine, Li woke his dad, who said to wake him in ten minutes. Li went to his room, returned to his dad, and said he was going to focus on writing, so wasn't going to wake him—he could set an alarm, like other people—and so wanted to ask him something first: "Are you using statins?"

"No," said Li's dad, and began to criticize the drug.

"Why did I find a piece of statin on the table?"

"It must have come from elsewhere," said Li's dad.

It was possible, Li knew, that it was an errant fragment, left over from decades of use, or unwittingly transported from Auntie's or elsewhere—statins, like heavy metals, pesticides, cations, amphetamines, and benzodiazepines, seemed ubiquitous in society.

"Tell him about the nerve damage," said Li's mom, cleaning a toilet.

Statin users were fourteen times more likely to develop

nerve problems, including muscle twitching, Danish scientists had found.

"Then how does one lower one's cholesterol?" said Li's dad.

Li reminded his dad that it was a lie that low cholesterol was good. Studies had shown that the lower one's cholesterol, the higher the risk of death.

Li's dad criticized his doctor and said it was all about money. Li said statins were a thirty-six-billion-dollar industry. Li's mom said Li should write a book on statins.

Li said people already had, and he could just promote their books. If he wrote a whole book on statins or certain other topics, billions to trillions of dollars of aversion could flow toward him, leading potentially to injury or death.

Biking an hour later, Li considered how civilly the rereturn of statins had gone. His left eye quivered in a distinct but minor way that was probably unnoticeable to others, reminding him it did that sometimes—a private sign of emergent damage.

After a movie the next day, on the brief walk home from the train station, Li's mom said she was going to buy toilet paper. "The store is there," she said, pointing. "Li, you can go there in the future if you notice we're out of toilet paper."

"Should we help you carry it?" said Li's dad.

"No," said Li's mom. "I'll carry one in each hand."

Li and his dad walked toward home.

At the gate, they realized they didn't have keys.

"When Mom asked if you had a key, why didn't you say anything?" said Li's dad.

"I didn't hear her," said Li, who'd been distracted by his own paranoid suspicion that his mom had passive-aggressively wanted him, not her, to go buy toilet paper.

They turned around and walked toward Li's mom.

"If Mom bought coffee, don't say anything," said Li's dad.

Li had 90 percent believed his mom had stopped buying store coffee. It had toxic forms of sugar and milk, detrimental to blood sugar, as they'd discussed many times.

She was across the street, buying coffee.

"Let's walk back, then," said Li, turning around.

"Just pretend we didn't see her," said Li's dad, laughing a little.

"Why doesn't she drink what we have at home? It's the best quality."

"She wants hot coffee," said Li's dad.

"We can heat it," said Li.

"She wants store coffee. When she said she was buying toilet paper, I knew she was buying coffee. Just pretend we didn't see her. You can't control us too much."

"When your and Mom's brains are bù xíng le, it will be my problem."

"We'll hire people to care for us," said Li's dad.

"No you won't," said Li. "It will be me. I already said that."

"When our brains break, we'll have no worries."

"You'll *only* have worries," said Li. "You and people around you."

"We'll be pushed around in wheelchairs. We won't have to walk."

"Mom is addicted to buying coffee from stores," said Li. "I used to be addicted too."

"My legs go soft when I don't buy red bean soup," said Li's dad. "Mom needs store coffee or else her legs will go soft."

"I know," said Li. "Everyone needs things."

"When you're old, you'll be even more yāoguǐ than me," said Li's dad. "Yāoguǐ," literally "starving ghost," was a Taiwanese term for people with insatiable appetites.

"I was like you in the past," said Li.

"In the past, you were like me?"

"Of course. I ate a lot of candy as a child."

They sat across the street from their building. Li said he'd posted a video online of his dad cutting his feet skin with big scissors. Li's dad seemed delighted. He said he'd make a video explaining himself for Li to post. Li said it was better unexplained.

Li's mom appeared in the distance with one bag of toilet paper.

"There she is," said Li. "How did she drink it so fast?"

Li's dad repeated that they should pretend they hadn't seen her buy coffee. Li felt heartened and impressed that his dad was sympathetically mediating.

An hour later, on a pre-dinner walk, Li's mom said Dudu was like Li—she liked nature, exploration, and novelty—which led to discussion about moving out of Taipei.

Li's dad said Li's mom couldn't leave Taipei—unlike him, who wanted to live in Taichung, a smaller city—because she needed coffee, Auntie, and friends.

"What friends?" she said. She had a college friend in Chicago and a friend at Sun Moon Lake in central Taiwan, but no friends, except for family, in Taipei.

"You need coffee, Auntie, and friends," repeated Li's dad.

Li felt disappointed that his dad seemed to be trying to provoke him into mentioning the coffee. The change seemed unstable in a way that Li felt he knew well.

But then Li's dad's attitude seemed to fade. Setting down Dudu, he walked ahead and began to eat single-wrapped candy that he got as free samples from various places and seemed to always have in his pockets. He was going to China in the morning.

That night, Li finished transcribing his voice memo of the walk when Dudu went catatonic for six minutes, then browsed his notes. He was amassing too many notes—thirty-five thousand words so far that visit, plus thirty-six recordings totaling around fifty hours. He heard his mom outside his room.

"What did you say?" he asked her in the hall.

"Heheh—I was talking to Du. I said, 'Mi Mi is going to exercise.'" She laughed. "I am Mi Mi. Mi Mi."

Friendship

The next day, Dudu seemed unfazed by Li's dad's absence. She startled Li and Li's mom at the elevator by putting her front paws on Li's leg, as he'd tried for years to entice her to do by excitedly patting his thighs while saying her name.

That night, Dudu lay surreally with Li as he read in his room, where she'd previously gone only when Li had sufficiently desirable food, like pork or beef. Li's mom entered, and Dudu hid behind Li, who handed her to his mom, who carried her away to brush her teeth and clean her face.

In the morning, Dudu sentried a Li-containing bathroom. Li felt moved by his new friendship in a shriveled way due to what seemed like an unrelated situation: he'd begun to feel depressed for vague reasons, causing tension with his mom that was extra frustrating because they were, he sensed they both thought, supposed to be enjoying their rare time alone together.

"I need friends," thought Li, lying on his back in his room with Dudu on his chest in Sphinx position. He had friends, but he rarely communicated with them. He was a loner. A loner who felt lonely. Loneliness was unhealthy, he knew. Talking only to his parents in a stunted vernacular seemed adverse to mental health.

"Thought 'I need friends' while feeling unhappy," he emailed himself, and, gaining some distance, felt a little better. He stared at Dudu's thin black lips. Her mouth looked like how his might've looked without orthodontics: ghastly, comical. Her fangish bottom teeth jutted away from her face, pointing at nothing.

At dinner, Li's mom said she'd called Fat Uncle, who lived in south Taiwan, that day because he'd lamented weeks earlier to Auntie that she, Li's mom, hadn't called him in a long time. On the phone, Li's mom had said they'd talked on Line, a messaging app that was popular in East Asia, and he'd said Line wasn't the same as voice, then had complained about their eighty-one-year-old sister, their eldest sibling, not attending sǎo mù—an annual event in which people visited their parents' graves—in recent years.

"When did she last go?" said Li, who'd never gone to sǎo mù, literally "sweep grave," because he'd never been to Taiwan in spring. As a child, he and his parents had visited Taiwan almost every summer.

"Before the car crash," said Li's mom about an accident in which her sister's right crus had been torn off. "Five years ago."

"That long ago?" said Li.

Li's mom said women normally weren't allowed to attend sǎo mù because people absorbed energy from their ancestors during it, and men hadn't wanted to share, but Fat Uncle had said that in their family women could and should attend.

Li's view of Fat Uncle changed a little. The few times he'd told his mom that male dominance was an aberrational declension, he'd felt shy and unconvincing, even though she seemed to believe him. He considered saying it again. "Goddess," "partnership," and other relevant words felt weird to say in English, and he didn't know them in Mandarin.

"Everyone listens to Fat Uncle," said Li's mom.

"Is he older than Thin Uncle?"

"Three years younger," said Li's mom.

"Then why does everyone listen to him?"

"Because his temper is not good. You're like him."

Li felt closer to Fat Uncle again. He began to emit monosyllabic responses to his mom's questions and comments, sounding distracted and far away.

He'd read in *The Chalice and the Blade in Chinese Culture*, a Chinese anthology inspired by Riane Eisler's suggestion in *The Chalice and the Blade* that non-Western cultures also research their full histories, that Chinese civilization also began with millennia of Goddess-worshipping partnership societies. The Zhaobaogou, Yangshao, Hongshan, and other cultures had sculpted nude and pregnant female figurines that resembled those from the same period in the West, including in Old Europe.

The Hongshan, which archaeologist Guo Dashun called "the dawn of Chinese civilization," existed from 6,700 to 4,900 years ago in an Arizona-sized area west of North

Korea. They lived in river valleys, grew millet, raised pigs, carved jade, and built ceremonial complexes, one of which, excavated in 1983, had a pyramidal artificial hill, a ten-acre walled platform, and what Chinese archaeologists called the "Goddess Temple," a semi-subterranean structure containing fragments of female figurines up to three times life size, including a life-size, jade-eyed head.

The first Chinese dynasty, the Xia, began around 4,100 years ago. They initiated the male hereditary principle, in which the ruler's eldest son became the next ruler, and replaced "All things belong to the public" with "All things belong to the ruling family," but were still influenced by their partnership ancestors. The Xia government and people, according to ancient texts, favored the color black, the most modest, inclusive color; promoted compassion and benevolence; and seemed to have practiced an early form of Daoism, which valued nature and viewed a mysterious force called Dao as the mother of the world.

After the Xia Dynasty, things deteriorated further. In the Shang Dynasty, from 3,600 to 3,050 years ago, female infanticide, the drowning of baby girls, began. To "make people forget goddesses and the partnership between the sexes," wrote Min Jiayin in *The Chalice and the Blade in Chinese Culture*, "a religious myth of a god in the form of a male" was promoted in the West while "a philosophy of exalting *yang* and degrading *yin*" spread in China. In the Zhou Dynasty, from 3,050 to 2,250 years ago, the government instituted the Rites, a set of rules that said women belonged to men and were banned from politics.

There was a partnership revival in the Tang Dynasty,

from 1,400 to 1,100 years ago—Wu Zetian, the only Chinese female emperor, reigned for fifteen years, and emperor Li Shimin promoted Daoism—but in the Song Dynasty, which began 1,000 years ago, Zetian was viewed as "evil" and foot-binding became customary, and in the Ming and Qing Dynasties, from 650 to 100 years ago, women weren't allowed to leave home, husbands striking wives was "generally accepted" as "required for good housekeeping," and, for a time, "literary works with love as the theme" were banned.

The Chinese Communist Party, founded in 1921, affirmed that there should be equality in law, marriage, wages, education, property inheritance, and social issues, but male domination continued through habit and momentum, with, among other imbalances, males doing little to no household chores and only 12 percent of the National People's Congress being women in 1954, up to 24 percent by 2017.

News was reporting on a politician who'd accepted a corporate bribe. A segment began on the toxicity of oil sticks—fried dough that people ate for breakfast.

"In China, they add detergent to oil sticks," said Li's mom.

"Not everywhere in China," said Li.

"Some places in China," said Li's mom.

After dinner and chores, Li carried Dudu into his room and lay thinking for an hour, falling asleep sometimes, then left his room, Dudu in tow, surprising his mom in the hall.

"Du wants to see you," said Li.

"Come," said Li's mom.

Dudu walked to Li.

"Eh?" he said, self-conscious that he was smiling more than he had in two or three days, during which he'd smiled at his mom only once or twice, weakly.

"Why did you change?" said Li's mom to Dudu, sounding tired and unenthusiastic. "Huh? She only wants to be with you."

"No," said Li. "She wants . . ."

"Right?" said Li's mom.

"Ng," said Li inaudibly, distracted by thoughts on how they were supposed to be learning from and enjoying Dudu's change together, how he'd ruined it with his glumness and surliness, which had given his mom a perpetual slight frown.

"Ever since I hit her by accident yesterday," said Li's mom, who'd walked into Dudu the previous day.

Li entered the kitchen.

"You don't care about Mom anymore?" said Li's mom. "Wah, wah, wah. Look, sitting in your room."

Dudu jogged to Li.

"She goes again!" said Li's mom, finally sounding unself-conscious and cheerful. "Look!"

Li laughed quietly.

"Hurry and hold her!"

Li kneeled and petted Dudu.

"Why did she change to like this?" said Li's mom. "She's a very sensitive kind of human."

"She really likes me," said Li, holding Dudu. "Once Dad is back, she won't like me."

"Will," said Li's mom.

Li put down Dudu, got a handful of almonds from the refrigerator, put sea salt on them, and heard his mom talking to Dudu.

"I said, 'Mom hug-hug,' and she went to you," said Li's mom, entering the kitchen.

Li saw Dudu looking at his eyes.

"Do you want to hug-hug?" said Li's mom.

After a moment, Dudu walked to her.

"See, she also wants you," said Li.

"I told you Mom did it by accident," said Li's mom. "She doesn't believe me."

Li went in his room and typed some notes, then crossed the hall to his mom and asked if she had extra earphones that he could use. She did.

He apologized for having sometimes seemed against her earphones, getting annoyed when she kept them in while talking, and she smiled and said it was okay.

"You're going out?" she said.

"Yes," said Li. "I'm going to bike."

"Wah. Then Du is worried. She's afraid I'll hit her again."

"Feed her ghee," said Li. "Keep saying sorry."

"Keeps looking at you," said Li's mom. "Look."

"Why is it like this?" said Li, smiling widely, happy he and his mom were friendly and lighthearted again.

The next morning, Li's dad returned from China with small bags of snacks, a beyond-hacking cough, and a rapidly twitching right eye. His trip had gone well. He'd met with a government agent, who'd said bribes weren't being accepted anymore, so the application to sell his lasers in China should be submitted as normal.

In a movie theater that day, Li's dad ate a mochi and wiped his mouth with a paper towel, then stretched his neck, touched his face and hair, moved his shoulders, scuffed his pants, grunted, and coughed for half an hour before falling asleep open-mouthed—seeming in Li's peripheral vision like one long sleepward convulsion.

On a pre-dinner walk, Li approached a catatonic Dudu. Instead of avoiding him, or begrudgingly, without eye contact, allowing him to carry her, like every previous time, she strolled agreeably into his embrace.

At dinner, Li asked his parents if they'd heard of pig-dragons—the earliest depictions of dragons in China, jade Hongshan sculptures with the head of a pig and the ouroboric body of a snake. They hadn't.

"I'm going to sleep," Li, who was born in a pig year, announced at ten p.m. "Good night."

"Good night," said Li's mom, who was born in a dragon year. "Are you saying good night to Du?"

Li sat with his dad and Dudu on the sofa. Now that they were friends, Dudu seemed calm and happy and affectionate. Before, she'd seemed worried, defensive, even paranoid.

Li patted his lap. Dudu walked onto it.

"Du," said Li's dad, typing on his computer. "You don't love me. You're not obedient."

"Dad is being jealous," said Li's mom.

Daoism

Four days later, on February 22, Li emailed his editor, thanking him for the three-chapter-deletion edit, which he'd gotten increasingly excited about over seven days after three days of internal resistance; the excised chapters—"Goddess," "Younger Dryas," "End of History"—would eventually be absorbed into his novel.

Working on his nonfiction book's second draft for five hours each morning after a brief jog and two hours each night after dinner, Li entered a flow state, which he viewed as whenever life felt enjoyable, he wasn't idle or bored, and he didn't seem to be ignoring his problems but addressing them in a long-term, premeditated manner—times when, easing into resonance with nature, minutes to weeks passed in a novelty-clouded, calmly emotional, deathward trance.

On a walk one day, Dudu stared at a man holding a large sign with three blinking lights on it. She circled him, looking at the sign, which promoted a new bank.

"She sees something strange," said Li's mom.

"This kind of child is too smart," said Li's dad. "Hair child is both smart and beautiful."

"So, everyone in our family is smart," said Li's mom.

"Yeah, didn't you, in school . . . ," said Li, not remembering the details.

Li's mom had been ranked first in middle school, second in high school, fourth in college. Li's dad, who'd also excelled academically, said school, in which they'd memorized things, had been useless, though.

Li's parents, flanking Li, bumped into him repeatedly, from both sides, as if continuously nudging him, while reminiscing about memorizing data on hundreds of emperors.

Li moved out of it, overwhelmed.

"We memorized Confucius's *Analects* in high school," said Li's mom.

"What did he write?" said Li, who'd read in *The Chalice and the Blade in Chinese Culture* that Confucius "despised women indiscriminately" and that his writings had "played a role similar to that of the Bible in the Indo-European culture in setting up an irrational, unequal gender relation." Society's unfairness, destructiveness, and amnesia could only be changed by amending those same tendencies in oneself and one's relationships, argued the anthology.

"Can't remember," said Li's dad after a moment.

"He had finicky rules on how to cut meat," said Li's mom.

"Had to cut it straight—not at angles. Had to cut it into cubes."

"What was his main message?" said Li.

Li's parents seemed stumped.

"What was one of his messages?"

Li's parents still weren't sure.

"Didn't he not like women?" said Li.

"Don't know," said Li's dad. "No."

Li's mom laughed, looked at Li's dad, and said Confucius, who was born five centuries before Jesus, had said xiǎo rén (villains) and women were the same.

Despite four millennia of autocratic patriarchy, China hadn't fallen as deep into domination as the West, though, it seemed to Li. Confucianism hadn't violently spread across the planet. After Confucius, Daoist texts had revived archaic partnership ideas. *Zhuangzi* referred longingly to a time when people cared for their mothers, weren't aware they had fathers, and didn't think of harming one another. *Daodejing*, a five-thousand-word, poetry-collection-like book by Laozi, promoted the return to a former egalitarian society; viewed de, nature, as the most faithful expression of Dao; and called Dao, which seemed to be synonymous with change, the underlying creative, maternal source of everything.

A huge, giraffish dog approached Dudu, sniffing and calm. Dudu bared her teeth, stiffened, and leapt at the dog's face with her mouth open, emitting a cackled bark. The dog twisted away, surprised.

Li's parents remembered driving for seven hours in 1982 from New York to Virginia with their possessions, a five-year-old Mike, and a cat Li's dad had brought home from the University of Rochester.

"Du wasn't born yet," said Li's dad. "Li. Li wasn't born yet." He said Li's mom had had three abortions between Mike and Li.

"And now we've had three dogs," said Li's mom.

"Look," said Li. "We're walking as a square." He moved right, toward Dudu, and everyone shifted a space, counter-clockwise, continuing ahead in the same shape.

"Can you stay in Taiwan for six months instead of three?" said Li's dad.

"No," said Li, smiling. "I have to do things. I have to write."

"You can write here," said Li's dad.

"I have to have my own life," said Li.

"Dad is happy when you're home," said Li's mom. "It's like he has a friend."

On Round Mountain the next day, Li's dad got a call from India. He was organizing an eye conference in Beijing. He was in demand, he'd said, because he was becoming "most senior" in his field.

"Look, Du wants to walk to the edge to look," said Li's mom.

Dudu patrolled or explored whenever the others idled.

"When I was a baby, when I fell off the sink, did I hit my head?" said Li somewhat unexpectedly. That morning, tran-scribing his recording of the dinner at Fairy Story Organic Farm, he'd noticed his mom hadn't answered the first "what" in his question "What hit what?"

"Don't know," said Li's mom, laughing a little. "I was very scared, picked you up."

"What noise did it make?"

"It's forgotten. It must not have been your head, because nothing was the matter."

"Was something the matter with my arm or leg?"

"No. Not at all. Maybe when you fell, I quickly caught you."

Walking the next day to Ximen Station after seeing the movie *Moonlight*, Li and his parents passed a beggar whose forehead seemed glued to the ground in a sustained kowtow.

"Nothing is wrong with him," said Li's mom. "He could get a job."

"You don't know what's wrong with him," said Li.

"Looks like nothing's the matter."

"If you didn't have family or friends, you could be him."

Li's mom argued against Li again, and Li began to criticize her to his dad, who said little things in agreement.

Li continued muttering about his mom as they boarded a train, then moved away to stand alone, feeling more upset than he'd felt in weeks.

Li's mom touched Li's shoulder as they got off the train. She began to say something reconciliatory, but Li callously turned away, and she went home.

Li and his dad walked toward the farmers market. Li's dad said Li's mom's family had had money—her dad had been a Chinese medicine doctor—and that she only cared about her own family.

"Caring for family is good," said Li.

Li's dad said Li's mom had donated money annually to a Buddhist group until their leader disappeared with everyone's money. "We shouldn't give money to Buddhists," he said, eyeing Li.

"I don't care about that at all," said Li.

Li's dad sort of snorted a little, smiling.

"I just felt not good that she criticized the beggar," said Li.

"You're right that it's not easy to beg," said Li's dad.

At home, Li said he was going to set up the printer they'd bought the previous day, and do work, and not go on a walk.

In his room, he felt terrible. He heard his mom tell his dad to walk Dudu alone. As he set up the printer, the cannabis he'd ingested during the movie began to work.

He went into the kitchen, loitered there, and, without saying he'd changed his mind about the walk, left the apartment with his parents and Dudu.

In the elevator, Li and his mom apologized to each other at the same time. They patted each other's backs.

Outside, Li was friendly and garrulous. He said he was currently extra-defensive of beggars because he'd written in his nonfiction book about listening in high school to punk bands that extolled panhandling as monkish and ideal.

After the walk, Li washed Dudu's feet—a Dad task he'd taken on to reduce parental tension—then read an email his mom had sent before the walk: "I have been feeling good that we have been able to communicate and reach an understanding when we have different points of view. But it hurt me so much when I tried to talk to you outside the station. You turned away with abhorrence on your face. Please, can we go back to how we have been?"

Li read an email she'd sent two minutes earlier: "I feel so happy now."

The flow state resumed. Li began to spend an hour in bed each night before sleep mentally reviewing his day's edits. Li's dad's weight and Li's mom's blood sugar reached new lows. Li proofread one of his dad's papers that kept getting returned due to deficient English. Li's mom made a dish called Lion Head—small pork burgers over stewed cabbage—and said a phrase that meant, she taught Li, "success." Li read that in oracle bone script—the oldest known Chinese writing—a character that resembled the pig-dragon meant "to recover."

In an email, he asked his mom about the word xuán (玄), and she said it meant "too mysterious to explain." Ellen Marie Chen translated xuán in *In Praise of Nothing: An Exploration of Daoist Fundamental Ontology* as "inscrutable" or "dark." Dao, according to the *Daodejing*, was xuán. It was "dark, dark and darker again, the way to mystery"—which seemed to Li like an earlier, positive form of Lorrie Moore's "she was gone, gone out the window, gone, gone."

Reading in Chen's book that Daoism was "a repository of all Chinese religious beliefs and practices from the earliest animistic, shamanistic origins down," and gleaning from various sources that Laozi didn't invent Daoism but found it in ancient texts while working as a government librarian in the Zhou Dynasty, Li realized Daoist ideas may have appeared in Old Europe on pottery, pendants, walls, and possibly cloth or felt books five millennia before emerging in China on bamboo strips threaded together like miniature picket fences.

Maybe, thought Li in bed, history would end when Earth

was coated in enough time-collapsing minds, holding sufficiently detailed eons in emotioned awareness, to invoke a wheel-like property, making the planet roll out of its ontology. Emergent properties were unpredictable and weird, he knew. Everything, he'd realized, was an emergent property, had once been a strange surprise. When he was in two places at once, as brainless gametes, his future had been beyond impossible to anticipate.

One day, Li's dad answered a call and talked in a detached voice. "Hang up," said Li, loud enough for the caller— a solicitor, it seemed—to hear. "Just hang up." Li's dad had a growing tea hoard and various unused appliances, like a noodle maker, due to his susceptibility to sellers. After Li's dad hung up, Li learned the caller was his dad's older sister, laughed for a while, and apologized.

One night, Li's mom entered Li's room and said her college friend who lived in Chicago had bought a house in Hawaii, in Honolulu, and was moving there with her husband. Li said Hawaii had no nuclear power plants and that Terence McKenna and Kathleen Harrison had moved there in the seventies and started an ethnobotanical forest-garden and that maybe he'd move there.

In mid-March, Li and his parents went to central Taiwan for são mù. At dinner with thirteen relatives, everyone held up tea or water for a toast. "Du," said Li's dad, clinking Li's cup. "Yes, Du is you. Du is the one we love most. When you're home, you're Du."

At a Buddhist temple the next day, Li photographed photos of his dad's parents on urns containing their ashes. Afterward, walking by Sun Moon Lake, which was shaped like a conjoined sun and waning crescent moon, Li's dad told Li to stand by two boys looking at the lake and say, "Clear water, no fish." Li laughed and said, "No. Not today."

The next morning, they visited Li's mom's parents' mountainside grave. Li and around ten of his relatives swept leaves, branches, and vines off the oval, concrete tomb. Fat Uncle, the last living kin who remembered what to do, directed the loose, easy rituals—putting down fruit and paper, verbally thanking their ancestors.

Sweating, Li realized it must've gotten grueling for the eldest sibling to attend. He reconceived Fat Uncle's complaint of her absence as encouragement.

Back in Taipei, Li's mom said she feared Li and Mike would discard everything in her office after she and their dad died. Li briefly tried to say it wouldn't matter—after death, which Chen called "change's most drastic form," they might be where lives were as explorable and secondary as novels—then asked what was in there.

Under Li's dad's cardboard-box hoard were birth certificates and other documents; family photo books; Mike and Li's art, awards, and school yearbooks; Li's childhood collections (pogs, coins, Magic and sports cards); and other things from their three decades in the States.

On Round Mountain, Li confused a parent with Dudu for the first time, saying, "Du forgot phone today," about his dad. On the way down, he asked his dad about his inventions, and his dad said that besides LASIK, in which the stroma was ablated with lasers, he'd also invented a way to correct presbyopia by lasering eight lines outside the limbus.

Li's parents fell into political bickering one night. Standing by one of his machines, Li's dad touched it repetitively, seeming frustrated to have gotten upset. It seemed to Li that his dad had entered the kitchen and said something political, but Li's dad said Li's mom had entered the TV room and told him to stop talking to the TV. "What you two did was not good," said Li. "I'm going to work on my book."

But they recovered quickly—by that night instead of after one or more days, as in previous years—and Li viewed the conflict as an expectable resonance of decades of habit, a piece of experiential evidence of improvement.

Reading his notes before bed, he thought of a way to end his novel. Within the nested fluctuations of gradual, fractal change—rising, falling; rising, falling, like in a stock market for life—he could end on an uptick.

Momo

On a walk six days later, they encountered Momo's owner, a woman in her sixties. She removed Momo, her Dudu-sized dog, from a spacious pram stroller.

"No shoes today?" said Li's dad. "Oh—haven't put them on yet."

"How old is yours?" said Momo's owner after shoeing Momo.

"Nine," said Li's mom. "Yours?"

"Seven. Any problems with her heart?"

"No," said Li's mom. "How about Momo?"

"Today he got X-rayed. The vet said his heart was too big."

"They always say that," said Li's mom.

"They do?" said Momo's owner, who seemed quieter than normal. Usually, her greeting began with bellicose criticisms of Dudu's hair—dirty, yellow, too long, too sparse. Once, when Li's mom had lost weight due to excessive Thyro-Gold, Momo's owner had said, "Ayooo! You became so skinny! So frightening!"

"Heart too big—that's nonsense," said Li's dad. "They lie! They want your money!"

Momo stood unsteadily in place, seeming so far away from making eye contact with anyone that it was like he had no eyes. The effect reminded Li of his teenage self.

It was April 10, and he was returning to New York in six days. Three days earlier, he'd finished his nonfiction book's second draft, which was 24.1 percent shorter than the first draft. To conserve his cannabis, he'd reduced his daily dose again, this time by two-thirds. His dreams, previously siphoned into life, had become vivid and riveting—in one, as cars fell from the sky, he told his mom he was willing to kill people to save them; then she was gone and he was teleporting into a series of airborne planes, calmly amazed—but concrete reality had gotten duller and bleaker.

"They're small," said Li's mom. "Of course their hearts are crowded."

Li's dad said when Dudu was five a vet had said her heart was too big. Li's dad had asked what size it should be, and the vet had produced a diagram of a big dog. Li's dad had berated the vet, questioning his understanding of proportionality.

"I spent five thousand NT today," said Momo's owner, around 140 dollars.

"Heart too big, liver too big, everything is too big," said Li's mom.

"They say things to scare us," said Momo's owner. "Today, Momo got a shot, an X-ray, a new medication, and his blood taken."

Momo took a few stiff steps, looking down.

"Can still walk," said Li's dad positively.

In one dream, Li had repeatedly time-traveled backward to stay in the same day, catalyzing an incoherent-seeming protest on a college campus with notes-assisted feedback loops until many people had special powers, were levitating and telekinesing in a library.

Momo peed a red puddle.

Dudu walked toward it.

"Du," said Li's mom jitterily.

"That's dirty," said Momo's owner. "Don't."

Li's mom picked up Dudu with a nervous laugh.

"Medication is no use, medication and whatever," said Li's dad, seeming to restrain himself because he knew Momo was on multiple drugs.

Momo's owner put Momo in the stroller and left.

"The color wasn't right," said Li's mom.

"Reddish," said Li's dad.

Dudu sneezed twice, snapping her head.

"Momo's mom was quiet today," said Li.

"She was worried about her dog," said Li's mom.

"She didn't criticize Du this time," said Li.

"Her dog is sick, so she doesn't criticize ours," said Li's dad.

"She just loves Momo a lot," said Li's mom.

In a dream that night, Li's mom, Auntie, and Thin Uncle ate Reese's Pieces while watching TV. Li's dad showed Li his mom's notebook; she'd drawn two heads connected, meaning she was getting surgery for cancer. Li threw something heavy through an open window, dimly aware he could hurt someone. Police arrived. Li jumped away in frustratingly slow, tall, wide arcs; his dream jumps were wonky and unrealistic like this, maybe because most of the jumps he'd seen as a child had been in video games.

He woke sweating. He removed his wet shirt, dried himself with it, and put on a different shirt. It was 4:42 a.m. Did the sweat wake him or the nightmare? Were nightmares interrupted dreams? Most stories could seem nightmarish if they ended too early. Maybe night sweats and nightmares were mutually causative. Intermittently researching night sweats over the past decade, Li hadn't been able to learn much about them. They seemed to be one of the body's more desperate ways to detoxify itself.

Five days later, Li and his parents rode a train and two buses to Yangmingshan National Park. The entrance was dominated by eight people repeatedly hitting tennis balls connected to elastic strings and stable bases in continuous demonstration of their product, but Li felt only theoretically amused. He'd run out of cannabis the previous day. He feebly asked his dad if tennis had anything to do with Yangmingshan.

"No," said Li's dad. "Heh."

Walking past beautiful mosses, grasses, ferns, herbs, trees, and vines, Li couldn't stop frowning. He felt anguished in an undefinable, helpless way that he knew indicated complex problems with his psyche. Previously, Yangmingshan had been a fun topic; it was the site of one of the earliest known instances of cannabis use by humans; for weeks, Li and his parents had discussed finding cannabis, harvesting some, and photographing the location for future harvests, but now they were there and hadn't mentioned cannabis at all.

Li privately berated himself for running out of cannabis and LSD for the third consecutive visit. In the Year of Mercury, he'd only brought LSD and had run out twice. In the Year of Pain, he'd run out of both cannabis and LSD due to pain but had ordered more LSD. That year, which he'd begun to think of as the Year of Mountains, he'd run out due to miscalculation and to prioritizing his nonfiction book: he could've started to use less earlier but had wanted to stay on the same, stable dose while working on it.

At an especially lush area by a river, Li started a timer on his phone and breathed while standing in place flapping. He thought about the millions of anions he was inhaling. He thought about Dao, which the *Daodejing* likened to water—gentle, yielding, humble, persistent, and powerful, nourishing and smoothing all things. If Dao was change, was it part of the mystery, since the mystery was everything besides what humans—and other life-forms—made? Or did Dao, which was sometimes translated as "the way," create the mystery?

Li remembered feeling deeply moved by an epic dream in which he was a neuron trying to reach a neuron-friend in another brain. Lately, dream-emotions—the kind he might feel all the time after he died or history ended, whichever came first—seemed more affecting and substantial than life-emotions.

Leaving Yangmingshan, Li apologized to his mom for his bad mood. He considered and rejected saying he was quiet and irritable due to cannabis mismanagement. His parents had asked him ten to fifteen times in the past two and a half years if he'd brought cannabis to Taiwan. Not wanting to spread worry, he'd always said no.

The next day, despite having warned himself in his notes not to get upset on the last day, he got upset when his mom made him hard-boiled eggs to bring onto the plane.

That night, on the train to the airport, accompanied by his parents and Dudu, Li felt distant and troubled in a self-loathing, fluctuatingly ashamed way. At the airport, he hugged his parents and Dudu bye.

"The visit passed quickly," he typed on the plane. "I spent every night with parents for the first time. They laughed a lot and seemed stoned sometimes. We mountain-climbed a lot. Dudu became my friend."

He began to draft an email to his mom that he hoped would shift the focus away from the bleak last week to the unprecedentedly happy eleven weeks before that.

Resonance

Back in 4K, Li smoked cannabis, lay on his floor, and realized what might've been a major factor in his mom's decision to get cosmetic surgery in the Year of Mercury: dietary changes he'd introduced that year. She was the only family member until Li was in college who'd promoted health—without it and family, there was nothing, she'd often said. She was like Schopenhauer, who wrote "the greatest of follies is to sacrifice health for any other kind of happiness." Li cried, imagining how she must have felt, learning from him and other sources that she'd unwittingly fed her family less-than-ideal and toxic food.

In the morning, he sent her a six-paragraph email titled "Thank you," saying that her family was lucky to have her (his dad's post-China cough always healed at home, as he ate her healthy, varied food, for example); that she and her husband's mutual harshness had softened over months into something friendlier, which made him happy; and that in 2014 when he got to Taiwan for his Year of Mercury visit he wouldn't have predicted that by 2017 he'd look forward to eating dinner with his parents every night.

"I cried reading your email," replied Li's mom. "I must have done something good in my last life to have a son so good in this life. Yes, we did so many good things. Ate healthy, exercised, climbed mountains, and most importantly we were together, we communicated, shared our thoughts and feelings. You have become so mature and knowledgeable. Stay calm, open your heart. I have learned a lot from you."

The next day, on his way to Mike's for Alan's fifth birthday, Li heard the subway intercom say, "Assaulting an MTA employee is punishable by up to seven years in prison," and it sounded, after three months away, like a non sequitur. New Yorkers boarded trains in impatient groups, bumping into alighters, instead of queuing calmly as people did in Taipei. Alan spoke rapidly, showing Li his abstractly vehicular LEGO creations. Li gifted him more LEGOs. Alan's parents were at the hospital with his new brother, born days earlier.

In late April, after finishing the third, 4.5 percent pruned draft of his book, Li remembered microfireflies. In Washington Square Park, he saw the tiny, lumine orbs, which hadn't been in Taiwan. Maybe the new property would start in the States, where consciousness had been moiled by decades of larger witting and unwitting doses and mixtures of pesticides, psychedelics, and pharmaceuticals than in any other country. Ten percent of Americans were polypharmaconic, taking five or more psychiatric drugs a day, Li had been surprised to learn from *Anatomy of an Epidemic*.

Two weeks later, in May, Li's parents visited for five days, staying at Mike's. Mike drove Li and their parents to his wife Julie's parents' home in New Jersey. Alan slept in a rear-facing child seat in the SUV's front passenger seat because he'd wanted to be near his dad. "Is it normal for kids his age to snore?" said Mike, scrunching his face. No one responded.

In New Jersey, Li grinned widely at Mike and Julie's new son, who stared at Li with a stunned expression. Mike said Julie's family was ordering pizza but that he'd drive Li and their parents to Whole Foods. Li thanked him. That night, sleeping in a guest room with his parents, Li recorded them both snoring.

Three days later, after their parents left for an eye conference in New Orleans, Li emailed Mike saying that Alan's snoring was maybe caused by his jaw and nasal cavity being undersized, like most people, due to deficiencies in vitamins K2, A, and D. "I was deficient too, so I had buckteeth, as you used to say," said Li. "You were too (we got headgear and braces), but less than me, maybe because you were in Taiwan until you were two." He recommended fish liver oil and ghee, and Mike thanked him.

A week later, Li visited Kay in 3A, where she'd lived for nine months, during which they'd seen each other twice—before going to Taiwan, he'd given her his mailbox key and gifted her a green mandala; when he returned, five weeks earlier, he'd gotten his key and bong, which she'd been using on Friday nights to get stoned before reading.

Li asked if he could have her large cardboard box for his forthcoming move. He'd been researching Santa Cruz and other places in Northern California. Kay said yes and gave him a novel from 2000 that she was reissuing. She'd recently become editor in chief of a small publishing company.

They carried the box to 4K, which seemed to Kay like a Montessori school, with its pull-up bar, mattresslessness, and tables—drawing, writing, inversion, fermentation. Li lent her *The Twenty-Four Hour Mind* by Rosalind Cartwright, a sleep researcher who called sleep "a built-in physician" and dreams "an internal psychotherapist."

In June, after finishing the fourth, 2.4 percent trimmed draft of his book, Li began to feel overwhelmed despite having no social commitments, non-self-directed responsibilities, or job with a boss. He emailed his mom, whom he'd been emailing many times per day, saying he felt overwhelmed by her emails. "If you notice I email less, it's because I'm not used to emailing so much and it doesn't feel good sometimes, feels like constantly checking in, but then I feel restricted when I want to stop because I feel you'll worry."

"I am sorry I let you feel pressure," she replied.

"You have no need to apologize, you didn't give me pressure, I gave myself pressure," said Li. "My email was, in a way, unnecessary."

Walking home from the library, he felt troubled by "in a way." Had the email been necessary or not?

That night, he unexpectedly scrawled a crude, schematic,

scary-looking face ruiningly over the intricate patterns of a near-finished mandala, then sobbed while drawing the face repeatedly over itself, pushing down hard with a brown-colored pencil. He walked three steps to his computer, sat, and typed what had happened, briefly wondering what would've happened if he hadn't stopped to type.

Other signs of "insanity," as he thought of it, that week: He kept feeling his leg touched at night, making him twitch fractionally awake. He found himself involuntarily sighing and closing his eyes while engaged in mundane tasks, like checking his email. He couldn't, in a way that felt somehow psychological, seem to sate his breath. His glasses made him feel insectile and like he needed to whimper or scream. He attributed the disturbances to four main reasons.

1. Toxins in the city and his body. He was eating one meal a day, so maybe his body, given the time and energy to clean itself, was unstoring, metabolizing, and trying to excrete plastics, pesticides, phthalates, PFOAs (surfactants he'd learned were in 99 percent of Americans), flame retardants, heavy metals, brake dust, and other toxins. Evidence for this: one night he got a headache that peaked over three hours and was gone two hours later, like a dose of poison.

2. Insomnia due to caffeine (climaxing that month), pain (which returned some nights in a way that he often forgot by morning), computers (whose screens emitted sleep-disrupting blue light), mosquitos (around ten had flown down from the ceiling

for two nights, biting him seemingly in tandem, before he noticed them, having misattributed his itchiness to rashes and/or bedbugs), and a probably barely functioning pineal gland: glyphosate, aluminum, fluoridated water, Wi-Fi, artificial light, and sunlight deficiency confused and damaged the gland, which made melatonin, DMT, beta-carbolines, and other sleep-related compounds. Disturbed sleep meant disturbed dreams.

Normally, Li knew from *The Twenty-Four Hour Mind*, one's mood reliably improved from night to morning. The mind accomplished this by telling itself around two hours of stories in the form of three to five dreams, which contained difficult information but grew increasingly positive, dream to dream, so that the overall effect was calming and enlivening. Cartwright and other researchers had found this by waking and interviewing sleepers in labs. Minds, like bodies, were self-healing systems that urban society seemed almost designed to break.

3. Unstable mood. He often felt bloblike and doomed, prostrate on his floor. He'd drink coffee and/or smoke cannabis, hang on his pull-up bar, and still felt bleak and uninspired; then, noticing he was unconsciously stretching in new ways, he'd realize with chagrined relief that he'd toggled, again, from sluggish despair to energetic creativity in less than ten minutes.

4. Isolation. When not immersed in book-writing, he functioned better, he knew, when he was in one social situation per five to eight days, but he was letting himself go longer. Since visiting Kay seven weeks earlier, he'd been in two social situations, after ten and sixteen days alone. He'd begun to feel isolated even virtually because of an old problem he had where he fantasized about sending an email, mentally drafted it, and lost interest.

But he didn't go insane. He bought new glasses lenses; reduced his daily caffeine; killed the mosquitos, standing on furniture and hitting them with books; and continued having his most wonder-filled, least inflamed, fullest yet quickest-passing days ever, though not without near-constant inner conflict: as he removed his broken AC from his window one day, surprised that procrastination on the task was ending after two years, doubling his view of his fire escape, four tall trees, and the side of a brick building, he could hear a disquietingly clear voice in his mind say, "You can't do it. You lack energy. Stop. Do it later. Later!"

He laughed one night from delight at his low inflammation, flapping so intensely that it felt unseemly and almost spooky. He tracked inflammation daily by timing how long he stayed aloft on his pull-up bar, hanging by various combinations of his arms and legs, using his hands, chelidons, and houghs. Hanging upside down one day, he unconsciously cracked his thumbs for the first time, noticing the novelty as it ingressed.

He read a nonfiction poem by Starr Goode in which Goode visited Marija Gimbutas at her home in the Santa Monica

Mountains and asked, "What were they, our ancestors?" and Gimbutas said, "They were like us, only happy."

Rereading his notes, he realized, not for the first time, that a problem with only noting happy times was that it would always seem like he used to be happier. He was more prone to dwelling on sadness and conflict, making life seem somewhat nightmarish, which had been comforting in his previous worldview, in which despair and confusion were romanticized and so could be amusing and affirming, but was an error, he felt, in his new worldview, in which his goal, in terms of his memory, notes, nonfiction, and model of history, seemed to be to maximize accuracy, while in his novel he seemed to want, not counting its nonfiction parts, to strive for a kind of dream accuracy.

Besides improving mood, dreams rehearsed coping strategies, reviewed new learning and experiences, and maintained and updated one's identity, he'd read. The mind's main technique in dreams, which grew longer and weirder and more complicated each night over an average of four narratives, seemed to be to make connections. It seemed to save the strangest connections for last, easing into them so that they did not startle the person awake and interrupt the process.

Late in June, Li had his first social interaction in nineteen days, walking to the East River with Kay. Notices had appeared in their building from their super that said, "Please refrain from urinating in the stairway, it is very dangerous," but neither of them had noticed urine.

They discussed their parents. Kay's mom's last cat had

died. Kay's parents had divorced in 2005. Her dad had returned to Japan. Li said his mom had been doing well since switching to natural thyroid, and that he'd noticed from photos that his dad seemed to have visibly aged in the past two and a half years (whiter hair, wrinklier face, droopier eyelids), maybe due to mercury contamination from the second dentist's interrupted removal, but he seemed younger in other ways—stoned laughter, hiking energy.

They discussed a study in *The Twenty-Four Hour Mind* on people with post-divorce clinical depression who didn't get treatment. The dreams of those who didn't recover after five months were brief and simple; the dreams of those who recovered had complex plots, many different scenes and emotions, and a blending of images from past, present, and future.

"I like viewing dreams as healing," said Kay. "It seems new and good."

"I like how, this way, I can just enjoy my dreams instead of analyzing them."

"I like what it's doing to my brain," said Kay.

"Imagination-bathing," thought Li in bed that night. Maybe spending time in the imagination—dreaming, wondering, remembering, reading, making art—was inherently healing, like being in forests and other natural environments.

Three weeks later, they walked and talked again. Rain forest destruction was in the news. Li explained McKenna's view of history as a natural, inevitable process—the culmination of billions of years of acceleratingly increasing complexity—which like childbirth was painful but purposeful.

"So he's not saying all the destruction is bad," said Kay.

"No. That was what I first liked about him. He seems positive in a convincing way."

Kay wondered if history had to be fast. Maybe it was fraught due to speed. Li resisted the idea, thinking he'd explained history wrong, before remembering that, though their history was violent, chaotic, amnesic, and rushed, there were probably species on other planets who were wending slowly and safely toward discarnation.

Kay asked Li how he'd been preparing to move. Li said he'd been working on his divorce. He'd triplicately printed fifteen forms, notarized twelve, mailed eleven to his wife with an SASE, gotten them back, and was turning them in soon.

Li learned Kay was also divorcing. She'd met her husband in 2004 in Brooklyn, moved to London and married in 2010, and moved to Manhattan alone two years earlier in 2015.

At city hall the next day, Li learned double-sided forms were verboten. He had to redo the forms and remail them to his wife to sign again, but he couldn't notarize forms without his passport, which he'd lost in May, or his ID card, which had been missing for a decade, and he couldn't get either without his birth certificate, which was in Taiwan.

He emailed his mom about the certificate. In another email, he said he was almost out of money—the movie money was gone—and asked if she'd financially support him while he worked on his novel and until he got paid again the next year, when his nonfiction book would be published. As expected, she said yes.

Li's parents had paid for his undergrad tuition, but he'd otherwise refused their money until then. Now that he had meaningful-seeming tasks—recovery, his two books, caring for his parents—he was glad to accept their money.

On July 24, the day Li finished his book's final, 1 percent buffered draft, his mom asked him when he was visiting Taiwan and for how long. He said he'd think about it for a week.

The next day, he returned to working in the library—for the first time since it had closed for Christmas the previous year—despite the radiation because his room had begun to feel bleak again. With his nonfiction book done, he resumed work on his novel. He decided to rewrite the draft he'd sent his editor two years earlier (a hundred pages on his Year of Mercury parent visit) and printed his 123,001 words of notes from that year.

On July 31, he emailed his mom, proposing that he visit Taiwan for ten weeks, from early November to late December. His mom suggested eleven weeks. He felt frustrated that she'd replied almost immediately after he'd thought about it for a week.

Part of him felt he should spend more time with his parents now that they were financing his life. Another part of him, aware he'd been living with and writing about them for years, felt he was already paying them a good, balanced amount of attention.

In the library the next morning, he emailed his mom saying ten and a half weeks. His mom asked if he could stay longer—around twelve weeks. Li said no, and they emailed twenty-something times. "I will think about staying longer but I feel upset now so I will email you my decision tomorrow," typed Li in a crazed-feeling rush.

The next three hours—circling parts of his Year of Mercury notes to potentially use in his novel, browsing months-to-years-old email drafts, compiling a third round of divorce forms (the post office had lost the second)—he couldn't stop worrying about how long to visit Taiwan.

His worry scattered that afternoon in Tompkins Square Park, where he talked to his friend Rainbow, who was writing a poetry book titled *I Fell in Love Today* and had recently begun a relationship with an urban farmer, but recondensed that night in 4K.

In bed failing to sleep, eyeballs pulsing against closed lids, Li helplessly cognized recursive, mom-related irrationalia. He felt she was being belligerent, but he knew not to trust his feelings—two nights earlier, he'd noted, "Remember: Mom isn't the insane, paranoid one. I am!" and had even said aloud, "*I'm* the one whose brain is broken!"—but he didn't always know. Sometimes his knowledge was a dreadful mess, which he had to goad into storage, as the body stored toxins in fat, to deal with gradually, before he could think or feel clearly. He punched the wood floor, which he'd never done before.

Probably there'd been histories even crueler than theirs—grisly ones with no partnership past, surviving aborigines, public parks, legal books, pacifist philosophies, holistic healers, or awareness of psychedelics, just four to six millennia of technology-driven, self-destructing carnage. Doomed histories. Maybe the post–Younger Dryas history was doomed.

Maybe a dominator overmind had emerged around 4500 BC, or maybe Yahweh had disqualified the species. The imagination probably kept insane species out, as eggs kept most sperm out.

Maybe only a few species per eon per galaxy made it through history, and so histories were platforms mainly for individuals to transcend matter. Maybe only people with keen interests in invisible realities would become immaterial beings. Possibly, civilization was a dead end transcendence-wise, and only aborigines with millennia of animism (believing every stream, plant, and animal had a spiritual counterpart) and shamanism (routinely exploring the intangible half of the mystery with psychedelic plants and fungi) would drift imaginationward at death, in which case for most people life really was it—the only thing.

At six a.m., Li woke sweating from a nightmare in which people didn't believe him on glyphosate toxicity. He felt even more worried than the previous night. His eyes and face seemed sprained. He ate half a gram of dried psilocybin mushroom, a gift from Rainbow; went downstairs; saw rain; and returned to 4K, hearing thunder. Seated cross-legged on his floor, he drifted away from the crude home he'd built around his mind and saw how derangingly small it was.

Finally viewing his finally lapsing despair not as a distressing, random outburst, but as evidence of partial recovery from June's week-length episode, when he told his mom he felt overwhelmed by her emails, Li teared with relief. He lay on his back and cried just a little, distracted by his mind, which was forming new thoughts for the first time in twenty hours. He realized he hadn't had a sense of humor in days. He emailed his mom saying he'd visit for eleven weeks, walked south in the post-storm, anionated air, and enjoyed a productive day in the library.

Biking home on a Citi Bike, he thought about his novel's structure, alternating between Taiwan and New York. It was like a human night, alternating between quiet and dream sleep. Humans spent a fourth of sleep in dreams, and he'd been spending a fourth of life in Taiwan.

Back in 4K that afternoon, Li watched a documentary that argued against the theory that everything emerged in an explosion 13.8 billion years ago. The documentary seemed compelling, but Li, valleying on cannabis and caffeine, fell asleep. His last thought was that the true version of history seemed harder than ever to know—the past kept growing and the theories about it kept multiplying—while personal histories, archived on computers and the internet, seemed more accessible than ever.

The next day, Li bought *The Big Bang Never Happened* by Eric Lerner. First proposed by Edgar Allan Poe in 1848, the Big Bang theory became popular after World War I, wrote Lerner. Society, he observed, influenced cosmology, which in turn influenced society. In a century of chronic, global war, the Big Bang, postulating a finite, decaying, meaningless universe, made sense.

The theory's main problem was that structures existed that seemed older than 13.8 billion years. A supercluster complex found in 1986 required a hundred billion years to form, and things up to ten times as big, like the Hercules–Corona Borealis Great Wall, had been found. Another problem was that the theory required ten to a hundred times more gravity than stars, planets, and other known matter produced—gravity that was attributed to "dark matter."

The main alternative to the Big Bang was plasma cosmology, whose most known proponent was Hannes Alfvén, a Swedish Nobel laureate. In plasma cosmology, the age of the universe was unknown (it seemed to be at least a trillion years old, and was possibly infinite in space and time); dark matter and dark energy (an antigravity effect the Big Bang also required) were electromagnetic forces; and plasmoids, not black holes, were at the centers of galaxies, which explained why seemingly all galaxies rotated, at their outskirts, once per billion years, like clocks: they were electric motors.

As belief in the dominator model of social organization had led to quadrillions of dollars of destructionalia, belief in the Big Bang had led to thirty thousand particle accelerators (costing up to five billion dollars each), which collided particles to try to simulate the Big Bang and find dark matter—goals that were possibly hopeless and that seemed, in Lerner's view, unhelpful to society. Put into plasma cosmology, the same attention and money could, he felt, lead to society-and-nature-helping electromagnetic technologies, like clean energy.

Reading a biography of Nikola Tesla, whom plasma cosmologists respected, Li learned of the term "free energy," which seemed to have been coined by a journalist in 1896 to describe Tesla's ideas for obsoleting fossil fuels, including by converting cosmic rays into electricity and transmitting it wirelessly through the ionosphere. Tesla's funding from J. P. Morgan was cut off when, according to one source, Morgan learned

Tesla wanted to give free electricity to everyone. Tesla lived in hotels for the last four decades of his life. When he died in 1943, the FBI confiscated his papers and equipment.

Researching modern-day Teslas, Li found John Hutchison, a Canadian who began to experiment with electromagnetic radiation in 1951, when he was six. In 1979, on disability for agoraphobia, he discovered, while trying to replicate Tesla's work on wireless energy transmission, a set of phenomena that became known as the Hutchison Effect: using thirteen tons of equipment powered by a wall socket, he was able to levitate heavy objects, make metal rods wiggle and go transparent, heatlessly combust and melt metal, transmute elements, and create aurora-like clouds of light.

Hutchison gave around seven hundred demonstrations, including one for the U.S. Army in 1983. Videos of his effects—which seemed to be generated by electromagnetic interferometry, the interfering of beams and fields of photons, and which to Li seemed close to gravity control, time travel, and other potentially history-ending capabilities—were widespread online. In 1990, the Canadian government confiscated most of Hutchison's lab—millions of dollars' worth of electrostatic generators, Tesla coils, and other things he'd amassed from junkyards and military surplus stores.

Hundreds of people, Li read in the Hutchison biography *Mindbending* and other books, had worked on free energy, inventing Moray devices, Hendershot generators, N-machines, and other overunity systems, which, like mitochondria, generated more energy than they consumed, but none of the inventions had reached mass production. It seemed that four trillion dollars a year in gas, coal, oil, and nuclear power; a century of investments in pipelines, electric grids, and other leaky infrastructure; and the addiction of energy corporations to monthly payments had led to the suppression—or at least the significant slowing of the development and use—of free energy.

Li didn't think anymore that he was going down "rabbit holes" when he researched nontrivial topics through individuals, papers, and books. He felt more like he was tunneling up out of the small, underground, man-made hole where he'd been born. Reading around 150 nonfiction books and 250 papers since 2013, he'd continually learned his worldview was too simple and/or vague. His skepticism had turned. He'd begun to distrust what he thought he knew, instead of everything else.

On August 12, Li and Kay walked to Stuyvesant Square Park and sat on a bench. Kay was a little anxious about her press's relaunch event that she was hosting in five weeks.

They crossed the street to the other half of the park, which seemed almost tropically lush, and stood in front of a statue of the composer of the *New World Symphony*.

"I've been reading about something strange," said Li. They'd emailed near-daily for two weeks—sharing classical music links; discussing a book of essays Kay had divided into four parts and edited based on how much time she had; reminiscing about their childhood piano lessons—but Li hadn't mentioned any of his recent research.

"Okay," said Kay. "What is it?"

"The Hutchison Effect," said Li. "Someone named John

Hutchison does it." He explained the effect and its possible uses. It could destroy nuclear weapons midair, protect the planet from natural impacts, transmute radioactive waste to inert material, propel spacecraft, and be used to build free energy machines. Li explained free energy.

"So it's not really free?" said Kay.

"No. It's just cheaper and cleaner and there'd be no power lines or gas pipes or oil spills or blackouts. People could get electricity from small machines in their homes."

Kay asked how he'd encountered Hutchison. Li said he'd clicked a documentary on the Big Bang, then had read about plasma cosmology, Tesla, and free energy.

They walked east, past a twelve-acre gas-and-oil power plant, to the East River.

Kay pointed at the water, and her pointing seemed to spray invisible things into it, making little splashes.

"That's weird," said Li.

"It's the Yoshida Effect," said Kay, whose last name was Yoshida.

Li smiled widely.

Kay did it again, with the splashes happening this time at a delay. Li tried it and nothing happened. Kay tried it again, holding a stick like a wand; nothing happened.

Li said the Hutchison Effect was also unpredictable. Hutchison had worked on it for years before he could generate it consistently.

On the walk home, Kay said another aspect of the Yoshida Effect was when trees' trunks branched to create the letter Y, which seemed funny to Li because of how widespread it was.

They met again two weeks later, when Li had returned to researching himself—organizing his selected notes from the Year of Mercury into scenes and chapters.

They ate cannabis, walked to a movie theater, and saw the movie *Gook*. "I turned in my divorce forms today," said Li on the walk home. "They said they'll mail me confirmation in three to six months, so I'm not moving until after that. How is your divorce going?"

Kay had gotten an initial agreement from her husband. They'd been emailing about taxes and boxes. Her books and CDs were in boxes at her husband's parents' house.

In 3A, Kay sat cross-legged facing Li on her sofa. Li felt himself looking ahead instead of at her, and when they parted they didn't hug goodbye, unlike every other time.

Four days later, Li woke, drank cold coffee, bused to the library, and emailed his mom, answering a question on what he'd been eating: "Bone broth, fermented cabbage, nuts and seeds, raw eggs, raw-milk cheese, vegetables."

"I need to make a new jar of fermented vegetables, probably cabbage, did you make the cabbage yourself?" she replied.

"I bought it. It's more convenient and I have more variety. I also have kohlrabi and other fermentations that I made." Ten minutes later, he sent her an email that he felt sick in his heart and mind while typing: "When I say what I eat, it is to share as friends, not to get negative feedback. Feels like I'm reporting to an authority figure when I say what I eat and you ask questions that make me feel I should change. I ask that you trust I'm eating well and know my diet is always changing since I'm still learning. I know you probably don't worry about this but I wanted to tell you to make sure."

"Li, you misunderstood me, I was just asking questions, of course I know you eat healthy, you need to understand that so you won't think I mean anything bad."

"I knew I probably misunderstood. I often get paranoid and feel you are criticizing me. I know this and have been working on stopping it. Thanks for explaining."

"I would never criticize you. You should never fear me or Dad. Okay?"

"Okay. The reason I said what I did is because whenever I mention fermented vegetables, you ask if I buy or make. I've told you that making is better, so I feel I am disappointing us by answering 'buy.' But buying can be better, it depends."

"Li, please don't feel I am disappointed in what you do. Don't worry about what other people might think, it is your life, need to understand that to feel real freedom."

"Thanks for telling me that, I agree, I rarely care what others think. With you, I care because I don't want you to worry. If you are not worried, then good."

"You have been teaching us how to be healthy, so it is you who always worry about us, so never worry that I will worry about you."

Seated on grass in the park, Li smoked cannabis. "Emailed mom mindlessly while feeling a certain post-caffeine way," he wrote in a notebook.

Gazing at a squirrel, he collapsed epochs, seeing it as a

stretched rat and, as it scratched its head with a back foot, a shrunken, bigheaded dog.

Walking home, he watched food-seeking pigeons leap and fly away on sidewalks and streets to narrowly avoid people, bikes, and cars, and imagined putting himself, an animal with metaphysical aspirations, into equivalently risky situations.

In 4K, he termed his malfunction that morning "mild brief insanity," viewing it as the second resonance of when he felt insane for a full week in June. The first resonance—in July, when he couldn't stop worrying about how long to visit Taiwan—had lasted a day and a half. Li projected a third lasting minutes or seconds.

He imagined deteriorating to a season of it. Becoming too worried, agoraphobic, and/or brain damaged to go outside or communicate online. It seemed like he'd need to deteriorate to a week, then a month of unconsciously generating despair to reach season-level insanity, but he could also, he knew, become electrosensitive, making him nonfunctional in cities, or pass a disabling toxification threshold.

He transcribed his and his mom's 9:22 a.m.–to–2:22 p.m. email thread from his phone to his computer, whose Wi-Fi wasn't working. He felt troubled and vaguely amused that he seemed to have acted more insane than he'd felt.

"Today, I thought that I for sure don't want to be in a relationship now," he typed in his notes, thinking of Kay. "I still have too many problems. I want to focus on my recovery and novel." He wanted to try to compile a draft of its first three parts—

- Year of Mercury: Ten weeks in Taiwan and eleven months in 4K with trips to Barcelona and Florida.

- Year of Pain: Eleven weeks in Taiwan and eleven months drafting his nonfiction book.

- Year of Mountains: Twelve weeks in Taiwan and the seven months he was five months into.

—before going to Taiwan to live the final part, which he'd begun to think of as the Year of Unknown.

Variations

Li went to Kay's room and she didn't initiate a hug, which to Li meant, "I see, and that is fine/good," regarding his not hugging her bye five days earlier.

They sat on her bed and watched a Science Channel show in which John Hutchison used rocks to make a battery that he said could last for a millennium. Due to a lack of funding and equipment, he'd stopped working on the Hutchison Effect. He was disturbed that the military-industrial complex had the technology. "Mankind tends to want to fight each other all the time with wars, whereas Mother Nature rolls on with great energy and power," he said.

Seven days later, on the way to dinner with Rainbow, Rainbow's girlfriend, and five other people, Kay asked Li if

Çatalhöyük, the largest and most advanced Neolithic settle-
ment, where up to eight thousand people had lived from
9,100 to 7,500 years ago, was real. Li had emailed her a passage from his nonfiction book on the partnership-dominator
fall, and she'd replied, with other thoughts, "Dominator culture seems like this term and concept that I've been unknowingly waiting for."

Li said it hadn't seemed real to him at first either. He'd
learned of Çatalhöyük, which archaeologist James Mellaart
noticed in 1952 as a distant mound in south-central Tur-
key, from Terence McKenna in 2014. Excavating 3 percent
of the fifty-eight-foot mound from 1961 to 1963, Mellaart
had found nine hundred years of peace and equality; the earliest known mirrors, metallurgy, pottery, textiles, and wood
vessels; and that, as he wrote in 1967, "a goddess was the
principal deity."

After dinner, in a concrete gazebo by the East River, Li
and Kay encouraged everyone to chant while holding hands
in a seated circle. Li held Kay's right hand and the essay-
ist Kay was publishing's left hand, and everyone said "om"
for five minutes. They varied the activity four ways, chosen
by four people; in the fourth, they stood and walked in an
omming circle that sometimes contracted, laughing.

On the way to a reading the next night, Kay wanted gum,
and Li suspected he had bad breath. In a dream the previous
night, she'd touched his chest and lain on him. In Brooklyn,
they smoked cannabis half a block from the bar venue. Li
said he felt comfortable smelling of cannabis because people
expected him to be stoned and weird. Kay asked how he'd
achieved that. Li said it came naturally.

"Dreamed about Kay again," he typed in the morning.

"Details vague but she was there and I liked it." Two days later, he typed, "Been thinking about Kay constantly. I've been attracted to her hands and eyes. I feel like part of me is turning against my plan to just be friends, but I think I'm still in control with the plan. Seems wise to continue the plan." But he also typed, "I can advance the story with Kay and other parts of my life like I have with my parents."

Three days later, Kay introduced the relaunch event for her press, calling it an alternative to mainstream culture. She wore black. Her wardrobe seemed to feature black, the color of mystery, ink, text, symbols, and other portals—the screen behind closed lids, the background of dreams.

During the intermission, Li went to her and she introduced him to a reader. He found her again and she introduced him to a friend. After the rest of the readings, he found her a third time and she introduced him to three friends. He went to the bathroom, then found her again. She asked if he was leaving. She went to hug him, stopped herself, and they hugged by his initiation.

Walking home, Li emailed himself, "I'm becoming somewhat and unexpectedly obsessed with Kay."

Hanging upside down the next night, Li realized a relationship might help and deepen and complexify, not necessarily disrupt or distract from, his recovery-novel-life.

He picked up his phone from the cardboard box he'd gotten from Kay four months earlier for moving purposes, saw he'd been aloft fourteen minutes, and emailed himself, "Love detour, try relationships again."

Six minutes later, he got off the bar, typed brief notes,

and lay supine in contemplative excitement. Carefully rein-
troducing romance into his life after four years without it
seemed healthy, rewardingly challenging, and like it was
already happening.

"Going to Kay's room," he typed the next night. "I wonder what she thinks about my increasing attraction to her.
Before, I was openly 'friends only' and even distant and slow
to respond to emails. So far, I have no plan. Just going to try
to stay calm and have fun and see what happens."

He went to 3A with radish and raw-milk cheese. Kay
asked if the cheese would help her vitamin D deficiency. Li
said it would help her K2 deficiency and that fish liver oil
would help her D deficiency. They chewed lemongrass, got
stoned, and walked in Bellevue South Park.

Back in 3A, they listened to Chopin's third piano sonata,
which had four movements. Kay's favorite was the slow, third
one.

They went to 4K's fire escape and sat in quiet darkness.
Kay said when she met her husband, he'd kept emailing her,
and she'd eventually started to respond more.

Li asked why.

"It felt safe," said Kay.

After a long pause, Li asked if she could elaborate. She
asked why. He said he was interested in people changing
what they felt about other people.

They ascended to the roof of their six-story building,
which was around the height of the central hump of Çatalhöyük's main mound, which, fractally accreting buildings
over many centuries, had grown into a streetless, alleywayless

city the area of seven Manhattan blocks, enterable only by ladders, through roofs.

Li asked Kay if responding to her husband's emails felt safe, what felt dangerous?

Kay said something about obsession.

The Empire State Building, usually lit white, was red that night. Buildings were in all directions under the starless sky. NYC contained 0.011 percent of the planet's people. Çatalhöyük, which had emerged probably between 1500 and 2500 AR, after the reset, had had around 0.015 percent of its time's people.

Li accidentally grazed Kay's left hand with his right hand, saw her looking at their hands, and held her hand. "How do you feel about this?" he said.

"Good," said Kay.

Çatalhöyük had been founded next to a river, amid grasslands, marshes, and woods with leopards, lions, bears, wolves, pigs, and deer, on a Vermont-sized, volcano-ringed plateau called the Konya Plain, which before 16000 BC had been a shallow lake, and by the sixties, when James Mellaart excavated some of the city-civilization, was a dry plain.

Li said he felt good too. Kay said she liked when they held hands in the gazebo. Li went to hug her and they kissed. He asked what she felt about the kiss.

"I liked it," said Kay.

Mellaart called 40 of the 139 houses he excavated "shrines" due to their abundance of Goddess symbology—paintings of childbirth and excarnation; sculptures of the female form; reliefs and cutouts of zoomorphized breasts and pregnant deities; rows of bucrania set into benches.

Li said he hadn't kissed anyone in four years.

Kay asked who he'd last kissed.

Çatalhöyük had been "the spiritual centre of the Konya Plain," wrote Mellaart, who felt that the city's U.S.-level diversity (59 percent Eurafrican, 24 percent Alpine, 17 percent Mediterranean) had "contributed greatly" to its "extraordinary vitality." A fertility rate of 4.2 children per woman meant "a constant stream of emigration," spreading art, language, religion.

Prefacing it with, "This is really bad, but," Li said a prostitute.

Kay said it wasn't bad.

NYC's population had been rising since the eighties, though its fertility rate averaged around 1.6, and below 2.1 meant population decline. The Big Apple seemed to suck people out of countrysides and suburbs, out of other cities and countries, and toxify their blood and minds, sterilizing and dispiriting them.

Li said he'd been at the end of a weeklong drug binge on a book tour in the UK for his third novel in August 2013.

Kay asked if it had been good.

Çatalhöyükans had decorated their walls with colorful paintings—women carrying fishing nets, flowers with insects, their city and a volcano. Due to the recurrence of patterns and complete repainting of complex scenes, Mellaart suspected they had books of drawings, probably on cloth or felt.

Li said it had been awkward.

"Really?" said Kay.

Li said he hadn't had an erection. He'd been on cocaine, MDMA, Xanax, caffeine, and probably crystal meth. He said he'd maybe send her his account of the night, which he'd typed immediately after on a hotel-lobby computer.

Four days before the book tour, he'd eaten psilocybin mushrooms alone in 4K and deleted much of his internet presence in a trip whose main message seemed to be "leave society." The tour had pulled him back into it, further motivating him to get away.

A week after the tour, Kay, then an editor at *Granta*, had emailed him questions for an online interview. A month later, she'd solicited him for *Granta*'s Japan issue. Over four months and fifty-four emails, they'd produced an essay on his first three times being stoned around his parents, in November 2013, at three restaurants in Brooklyn.

When Li met Kay in April 2014 at the issue's New York release, he'd been earnestly focused on recovery, viewing it as an endless, heuristic practice, for eight months. The next day, they'd talked on the High Line. Li had said he wanted his next novel to end with the *Granta* essay and that maybe his life after that would be "off-limits" to writing. Kay had returned to London, where she and her husband had lived.

That summer, learning what existed outside society by writing a column on psychedelics, history, and nature, Li had decided to go further into autobiographical writing, using it to help him learn and change. In November, he'd flown to Taiwan, declined chest surgery, and read *Cure Tooth Decay*. Nine months later, Kay had moved to Manhattan; twelve months later, into his building.

Thirteen months later, on September 19, 2017, they descended the fire escape; wended through 4K, a hall, a stairway, and another hall; and entered 3A.

———

Their apartments, decorated with a map of Earth (4K), photos of family and friends (3A), and art by friends and strangers, were around the size of the commonest size of home at Çatalhöyük. Bathroomless, windowless, and chairless, Çatalhöyükan homes had had built-in furniture—one to five platforms for sitting and sleeping, with the largest, bench-attached platform, able to fit two adults, being for the woman of the house.

On her sofa, Kay said it had been obvious she liked Li when they met in 2014. "Right?" she said.

"I don't know," said Li. "I feel surprised by what happened. The kiss. This is notable."

Kay laughed. "You've seemed closed off to more than friendship," she said.

Li said he'd liked being alone and also had felt unready for a relationship, and Kay said she had felt that too.

Around 3400 AR, or 8,200 years ago, Çatalhöyükans began to build a new mound across the river, deserting the first mound over two centuries. Five centuries later, the west mound was also abandoned for unknown reasons; maybe people, tired of urban life, had moved farther west to live with the Old Europeans.

Old Europe, by then a millennium old, comprising the Vinča, Varna, Sesklo, and other cultures, continued to expand its non-mound civilization, building five-room houses; multistory temples; and mysterious, hand-sized, inscribed, roofless models of their buildings, while probably beginning to write books on Mother Nature, for another eleven hundred years before groups of horse-riding Indo-Europeans began to invade south and west through Anatolia and Europe—

eventually, after spawning Yahweh and crossing the New World, destroying or assimilating almost every culture.

The dominator invaders were "indifferent to art," wrote Gimbutas. They supplanted nature worship with war addiction, had only male deities, and ranked men above women. Instead of painting the skulls of their dead and keeping the bones in collective burial under their sleeping platforms, as at Çatalhöyük, where homes contained up to sixty-two ancestors, they practiced suttee, burying sacrificed women and children around the corpse of a dominant male.

Li and Kay kissed again. Kay kept her eyes closed, like the first time. She said she usually began preparing for bed when her 10:30 p.m. alarm went off. Li said he wanted to stay but felt they should part to absorb and process what had happened.

The next day, Wednesday, seated at his desk with his forehead on interdigitated hands, Li sobbed from what felt like gracious joy, listening to the Chopin sonata's slow movement, which he hadn't paid much specific attention to before, though he often listened to the fast movements on repeat. He chronically wanted more change and novelty than he got. He was greedy and impatient, troubling qualities balanced by shyness, recurring pain, and alienation from busy society. He seemed to know that change could flow if slowed into a natural resonance, as Kay had reminded him was possible for history, but he somehow felt like there wasn't enough time to slow down.

He'd been trying to decelerate since college—working low-level jobs in libraries and restaurants, reading poetry and plotless novels and ancient philosophy, training himself to be ambitious in Dao, in gratitude and stability and humility, instead of power and influence—and again after the regressive drug phase, becoming a reading-and-drawing hermit, but maybe he needed to go much slower. Get finally out of NYC and be alone in nature or a small town. Wean off caffeine, cannabis, and other drugs. Have no phone. Learn to meditate. He'd never been able to meditate for more than five days in a row. These thoughts sped through him, as they sometimes did, too quick and fragmented to not feel mostly confusing and worrisome.

He could feel his notes and novel pushing him to do things, generate novelty. They were meant to help him, but they often just bewildered and distressed him. He didn't know yet that it would be the notes-assisted editing of the novel in 2019 and 2020 that would finally unambiguously help. Everything prior was preparation, he'd realize in fall 2019, for the lesson-like experience of repeatedly reading and revising a prose model of his life from 2013 to 2018—studying and shaping the story; researching, writing, and weaving in the self-targeted spells of the larger-perspective passages; realizing Kay's preference for slowness was complementary and inspirational and naturalistic.

Life explored with leisurely meticulousness. It advanced over hundreds of millennia by evolving new forms through survivable destruction—impacts, eruptions, tsunamis, earthquakes, cosmic radiation—from its inorganic, ancestral substratum. Wherever it went, it settled. Reaching land, it stayed in water, interconnecting and layering itself, evolving flying fish and aquatic birds. It was prudent and farsighted. When it seemed to have stalled at the stratosphere with high-flying vultures, it had already, long ago, besides probably having sent spores and microbes through the galaxy, evolved warm-bloodedness, starting a 260-million-year, forked path to outer space and an unanticipated domain called the imagination.

Life seemed to want to pass gently through the star-powered portals of planets into immateriality, while dominator culture, which belittled and suppressed the imagination, seemed to want to rush from star to star, destroying and leaving planets as fast as possible—inventing war and corporations and pesticides, exhuming rare metals into weapons and electronics, sending star-blocking satellites into orbit with mercury-raining rockets. On the first day of 2020, Wikipedia's page for phytoncide was 519 words; Old Europe, 1,760 words; imagination, 3,365; turmeric, 3,574; vitamin K2, 4,187; Çatalhöyük, 4,250; forest, 6,849; Xanax, 7,529; Disney World, 8,424; statin, 11,115; nuclear weapon, 11,520; glyphosate, 16,837; CIA, 20,893; Apple Inc., 33,535.

"Can't stop thinking about her," typed Li on Thursday afternoon. "I'm excited," he typed Friday night. "I'm going to Kay's in ten minutes. This will be our first meeting as more than friends. Feels strange because we've been friends so long. Part of me still views her as a friend. Then I remember we kissed."

In 3A, Li told Kay about his realization that he was ready for a relationship. He said it seemed sudden and rash but had been gradual, then sudden. She said she'd oscillated between viewing Li as a friend and viewing him as possibly more.

In Bellevue South Park, Kay said she'd been blushing for

half an hour. Li said he hadn't noticed. He apologized for belligerently promoting fish liver oil, and she confirmed he'd been a bit pushy.

Back in 3A, they kissed and removed their clothing and gave each other oral sex. Kay asked if they were going to "do it." Li said he didn't feel like it anymore. He said it wasn't because of her.

They sat on the floor and lit candles. Li said he liked that Kay didn't wear makeup. She said she liked to keep it simple. They praised the gradualness of their relationship—a season of emails, years of sparse interaction, months of increasing intimacy.

They listened to Beethoven's seventeenth piano sonata, and Li said he didn't like most male pianists because he felt like they were hitting the piano. Kay said Martha Argerich did that.

Li said Argerich played fast, not loud, that he liked Argerich and Glenn Gould because they played fast but not loud. Kay said Gould also played slowly, and Li agreed.

He said he'd recorded when he told her about the Hutchison Effect forty days earlier, on August 12, in Stuyvesant Square Park. He played the recording, felt self-conscious, stopped it, played a recording of his parents, and stopped it.

The next night, Kay invited Li over to smoke one cigarette. She had a headache and a sore throat. Li brought peppermint oil and cannabis balm—a gift from Kathleen—which he rubbed on Kay's temples.

On her fire escape, overlooking 29th Street, they smoked cigarettes rolled from organic tobacco. Li had told her that non-organic tobacco contained glyphosate, radioactive atoms, arsenic, and other toxins.

Inside, Li asked if he should leave. Kay said he could stay for ten more minutes. They decided to see Martha Argerich at Carnegie Hall in four weeks, and Kay bought tickets online.

"It's been ten minutes," said Li. Instead of parting, they read a children's book in which a horse asks a veil of light why he is a horse, and the light says, "Because we needed another horse," then smoked hash and walked two blocks to a movie theater, where they tried virtual reality goggles.

Back in Kay's room, kissing naked on her bed, Li stopped and said, "I don't know what's wrong with me." He stressed it wasn't because of her—he'd only had sex on alcohol and/or pills since 2010 and had been celibate for forty-nine months.

Kay said after the previous night she'd thought they'd never speak again, which she'd focused on accepting. Li said he'd had fun the previous night. He said the last person he'd kissed was actually his ex-girlfriend, four months before the prostitute, whom he'd realized he hadn't kissed.

In a 10:20 p.m. movie, they smiled at each other incredulously during the previews. Walking home, they were energetic and chatty. Li said he normally slept on the floor but would try Kay's bed. He lay awake for around two hours, then returned to 4K. It was 3:24 a.m. They'd spent nine hours together.

The next day, Li typed, "Feel closer to Kay today than any day so far." At night, Kay texted saying she was home from visiting her mom, whom she visited on Sundays. She asked if Li wanted to get his glasses, which were in her room, or if she should bring them.

Li asked if she wanted to hang out.

"I do. Maybe just for a little bit?"

Li went to her room at 7:15 p.m. They decided to part at 8:30, set an alarm for 8:30, and had sex twice. Kay said while biking home from the Upper West Side, where her mom lived, she'd thought that she wouldn't see Li until Friday. She'd also thought she wouldn't plan anything, and that Li had been obsessed with the Hutchison Effect but then had seemed to lose interest. What if that happened with her?

Li said he'd learned of Hutchison the previous month, but had known Kay for four years, and that he was still interested in Hutchison but had gotten more interested in glyphosate recently because it directly affected his body. He'd learned from MIT researcher Stephanie Seneff that glyphosate was embedded in his collagen, receptors, and other proteins—in his eyes, hands, face, brain, and heart—because life mistook the herbicide for glycine when building proteins.

His ongoing, deepening realization that he was very damaged compared to his ancestors from centuries, millennia, and especially tens of millennia ago was a reliable source of encouragement: even with all the damage, there were times of startling clarity and poignant mystery, moments to weeks of serenity, harmony, and happiness.

Kay said it would be okay if Li lost interest in her. They listened to Glenn Gould's extremely fast, 1955 recording of Bach's thirty-variation Goldberg Variations. Kay's mom, who owned a piano, had gotten Kay the sheet music, which Kay felt was surprisingly difficult due to its rhythm. The 8:30 alarm went off.

The next night, they decided to meet from 7:30 to 9 p.m., a variation of the previous night. In 3A, Kay asked Li to teach her a stretch. They did "dry swimming."

They went to Li's fire escape, where they looked at a green-lit Empire State Building and considered what had transpired since it was red, six days earlier.

Kay asked Li where in America seemed to him like a good place to live. Li said Hawaii. Kay agreed and said her friend Diane's brother lived in Kauai, where he earned money by running a rental.

One of the trees by the fire escape had the Yoshida Effect, with a bifurcating trunk. Kay said she'd told her brother about the effect, and he'd said, "Isn't that just a normal feature of trees?" Li said the Yoshida Effect was as important to him as the Hutchison Effect, or more. "I like variation #2 a lot," Kay texted after they parted.

The next night, in variation #3, they ate a cheese-avocado omelet, delayed parting thrice, and spent three hours together. Li learned Kay had all thirty-two of her teeth, and Kay said she felt both calm and excited around him. "It's 11:18 and I keep thinking of Kay," typed Li after they parted.

In 3A two nights later, he found himself unpleasantly daydreaming about the end of their relationship, distracting himself into quiet glumness. Before parting, they talked about Kay feeling overwhelmed at work, and Li suggested she write a book. "Feel weirdly detached," he typed in 4K. "Maybe we could spend less time together. Or see each other when we're not tired."

The next day, he canceled dinner with out-of-town friends. "For some reason, I was critical and gloomy last night," he typed. "I kept suspecting Kay of doing things to get me to like her more. Seems insane. I should be alone when like that." He stared out the window, past autumning foliage, at the brick building. "There's no need to feel bad about losing or changing interest. It could lead to better things."

But in variation #5 they spent ten hours together. On the A train, they bought a drawing of four flowers, three clouds, two trees, and one ground for one dollar from an androgynous child going car-to-car seemingly alone, selling art from a folder labeled "Positive Energy Project." At a Renaissance fair, Li said he liked that Kay had a career, because he also had things to do; his previous girlfriends had had part-time jobs at most. Kay asked if he'd recorded her since August 12 in Stuyvesant Square Park. Li said he hadn't and wouldn't. Kay thanked him and said he could, if he wanted; it wasn't illegal.

In #6, they started a book club and agreed they were addicted to each other. After #7, Li excitedly emailed himself while hanging upside down, "I felt we were doomed five days ago, but now I feel the opposite." In #8, Kay said she hadn't been around her mom, who "wasn't good at night," for more than a day in maybe ten years. Li talked about getting massaged, seeing a chiropractor, and going to a physical rehabilitation center in Taiwan a year and a half earlier.

In #9, a sleepover at Kay's, they read some of the Nicholson Baker novel *Vox*, their first book club choice. In bed, Li learned Kay had a pet snail in kindergarten named Emily who ate lettuce and watermelon. Snails seemed Daoist to Li— mellow, unrushed, at home anywhere. To Kay, they seemed brave, decisive, strong-willed, and resilient. As a last resort, snails could self-reproduce; selfing produced fewer eggs and fewer surviving hatchlings than mating.

In #10, they drank coffee together for the first time, generating a somewhat tense discussion regarding Amazon.com. Li wanted to discuss its unobvious positives. He'd found *Cure Tooth Decay*, *Surviving Evil*, and other illuminating books there that most media didn't cover and weren't in most bookstores. They decided to say "Amazon" to refer to the jungle five times per time they referenced the corporation. Kay said it would be good if they had as many variations as there were bird species in the Amazon.

They biked around the Lower East Side, visiting a bookstore, two parks, and two gardens. In Union Square, they made plans to fast, organize a Joy Williams conference, and make raw-milk ice cream. Li had been ordering raw-milk goods, including yogurt and cheese, from a company Rainbow had told him about that delivered from farms in New Jersey. Most people were allergic to pasteurized milk, a relatively recent invention, but not raw or fermented milk, he'd read in *The Untold Story of Milk*.

In 4K, they got Kay's period blood on Li's sofa during sex, and Li praised the natural substance, saying it was a welcome presence in his nature-deficient, virtual-reality-like room. Holding each other, they reviewed their day aloud, taking turns chronologically describing what happened.

At Angelika Film Center, they watched a documentary on a British gastroenterologist who'd noticed in the midnineties that autistic children had inflamed guts. It was why they curled around furniture, applying pressure to their stomachs. Li remembered hugging pillows to his round belly as a child.

Around 2008, journalists and other people, noticing Li and his characters' stiff timidity, had begun to call him autistic. Autism, he'd learned, was a set of loneliness-making debilities—eye contact and social problems; restricted, repetitive thoughts and behaviors; tendencies to withdraw, minimize facial movements, process and use language literally, and speak in a monotone or not speak.

At first, he'd suspected autism was invented by corporations to sell drugs; autists were given antidepressants, amphetamines, and antipsychotics. Over years of self-observation and research—reading writing by Natasha Campbell-McBride, a former neurosurgeon with an autistic son; Stephanie Seneff, whose autism research had led her to coauthor six papers on glyphosate toxicity; and others—he'd realized autism described real symptoms that were new to the species.

By 2017, he viewed autism as the result, mostly, of chronic brain inflammation from contamination and damage by thousands of old, new, and as-yet-unidentified toxins (in 2020, Wikipedia, aggregating mainstream medicine, implicated pesticides, lead, air pollution, alcohol, cocaine, and valproic acid, an anticonvulsant) crossing leaky gut and blood-brain barriers, meaning it fluctuated in severity—day to day, month to month, year to year—and was varyingly healable.

After the documentary, they walked quietly. Somewhat as a non sequitur, a bleak-feeling Li said he felt like he had to unlearn college. Kay said college had taught her critical thinking. Li said people needed more layers of critical thinking than what college taught. Kay seemed open to his perspective and said she'd also learned in college of the reality of cultural hegemony, but Li felt shy and stopped talking.

Nothing he'd learned in college—where a journalism pro-fessor had reverently brought in a Gawker writer to speak to the class; where the earliest culture he'd heard of was ancient Greece, 2,500 years ago, in a required class on the *Odyssey* and the *Iliad*, thick books on glorified war; where society had been viewed as benevolent and great instead of insidious, malignant, poisonous, and lie-riddled—would be in his two books, except for what he'd found independently, researching natural health in computer labs, though he had had helpful, encouraging creative writing professors.

They sat in Washington Square Park. Li began to feel bet-ter while telling Kay that he'd added tobacco, which he'd begun smoking with cannabis in an 80-20 cannabis-tobacco mix, and snails to his book—in a sentence on how snails and other animals had kept living in an eternal-seeming, cyclical trance when humans entered history, and a sentence on how aboriginal people had enjoyed pesticide-and-additive-free tobacco (smoking it, snuffing it, and drinking it as a tea or in ayahuasca) for millennia.

In the morning, they decided to visit Hawaii together soon, then ate eggs and parted. Walking home from the library five hours later, ruminating on the previous night, Li felt himself turning against their relationship—he was trying to leave New York, while Kay, who liked slowness but seemed deep into fast society, working sixty-plus hours a week for a demanding boss, seemed to be settling in, with a new job and apartment and her mom in the city—but the uncontrollable-seeming thoughts dispersed when he got home, read a text from Kay, and got stoned.

In 3A the next day, they made and ate lemongrass-arugula

omelets. Li said he used to be bloated and have pain and discomfort most of the time. He'd assumed he was weaker than other people. Kay said she'd always blamed herself for being slow. Li said he didn't think she was slow, but that she just had a lot to do, and she went to work.

In the park, editing a printed draft of his novel's "Florida" chapter, in which he family-vacationed for five days in Orlando, Li thought about the mystery. It seemed to be almost everything—every life-form, dream, thought, and emotion. It was everywhere except where it was obscured by culture or technology—sitcoms, advertisements, skyscrapers, smartphones. "The mystery is Kay and I in bed naked imagining us as complex squirrels looking at each other's faces," wrote Li on his paper.

He considered the secret. It increasingly seemed to be "Nothing at all is what it appears to be," as Kathleen had said in a 2015 talk. "And I have learned that in my many years not only from taking psychedelics but of working with native peoples who seem to understand that much better than our materially oriented cultures do—that 'everything is an illusion and everything may change from what it appears to be now to something else at any moment' is kind of a rule to live by."

Kay texted, "I think I'm accidentally stoned." Li realized they'd used the coffee grinder he used for cannabis on the lemongrass that morning for their omelets and that being unwittingly more stoned than normal had led to thoughts on mystery and secrets. He apologized and asked Kay what she was going to do. She said she was in her apartment, reading; she'd told her boss she had a migraine.

Three days later, Li's divorce confirmation arrived early, freeing him to leave epicentral society. Teaching and pain had kept him there in 2014 and 2015, the nonfiction book and divorce in 2016 and that year. "One of my first thoughts was that I don't want to leave anymore because of Kay," he typed in his notes.

At city hall, he turned in a card to confirm receipt of the confirmation. In a nearby plaza, lying on a strip of grass, breathing deeply while reading *Vox*, he had a YG. Returning to concrete reality, he realized with excitement and poignant wonder that he was still far from assimilating Kay into his life. He'd been alone for so long.

The next day, on the urban farm where Rainbow's girlfriend worked, Li and Kay put their hands into hot compost, played hide-and-seek, and ate koji-fermented steak. On the way home, they entered a pinball arcade and discussed every machine. Before bed, they watched YouTube videos of *Kid Icarus* and other Nintendo games.

In the morning, they watched a talk on severe autism, which affected more than a million Americans. The talk included video of an autistic child's inflamed intestines, photos of boys who'd beaten themselves unconscious while trying to attack their swollen brains, and a home movie of an adult self-protectively wearing a football helmet, which reminded Li of psychic driving, an MKULTRA technique in which people were forced to hear the same statements half a million times from electronic helmets.

Society seemed to mainly pay attention to functional

autists, whose mild symptoms, giving them new perspec-
tives, could be viewed as desirable. Around half of U.S. children with autism couldn't speak, though, according to the
California Department of Education. A third had epilepsy—
chronic brain seizures. A fourth harmed themselves. Many
would never have a job or partner. Li hadn't ever been that
autistic. For most of his life, he'd been borderline-to-mildly
autistic. He was becoming gradually less autistic over years
through nutrition, detoxification, practice, and cannabis.

Li felt himself and Kay watching the talk with their full
attention, as seemed to be their style. Days later, they'd learn
they'd both cried.

Li asked if she wanted to watch more. She said no; she
wanted to work. She worked at home on Mondays. Li lay
stomachdown on a stomachdown Kay and joked it was a
strategy to keep her in his room. She said he didn't need to
lie on her for that.

He accompanied her to 3A, returned to 4K, and typed
notes. Since their kiss a month earlier, time had felt faster. His
relationship with his mom had been saner and friendlier. His
inflammation had regularly reached new lows, which made
sense because he'd severely lacked social contact, in-person
friendship, hugs, kisses, sex, and other anti-inflammatory,
immune-enhancing human trademarks for four years.

In 4K two nights later, they ate six types of eggplant. Kay's
eyes seemed darker and more charged than Li had ever seen
them as she talked about psychotherapy, which she'd had at
6:30 a.m. "Deranged?" she said. "No," said Li. "I liked it."
Kay had started therapy, in which she mostly discussed her

mom and work, two months earlier on a recommendation from her brother and was considering stopping. She said talking about therapy had begun to "feel like a schtick."

She said the previous night, unable to sleep, she'd read an article titled "Fertility Awareness, Food, and Night-Lighting" and realized her menstrual pains and irregular cycle were healable. The article was by Katie Singer, the author of *An Electronic Silent Spring*. They decided to read *The Garden of Fertility*, Singer's book on fertility awareness, a method of charting temperature, cervical fluid, and cervix changes to prevent pregnancy naturally, next in their book club.

The next night, they ate cannabis, walked to Carnegie Hall, sat on the fifth floor, and watched an orchestra play Verdi's *sinfonia* from *Aida*. Martha Argerich appeared and sat at a piano. Prokofiev's third piano concerto began.

After the first, quiet movement, Li began to feel increasingly worried, struggling to stifle hysterical laughter. Kay seemed to be laughing too.

Li walked past five people to the aisle and left the hall, laughing. Kay appeared twenty seconds later. They listened to the softened, clarified concerto from the lobby.

Walking home, they discussed their first times having sex (both in college in their first relationships), her birth-control history (the pill from 2001 to 2011, causing hair loss, dry hands, weight gain, and a darkened face), porn (he used to be addicted to it; she'd only seen it in passing—the idea to find and watch porn had never occurred to her, she said, which made Li laugh), and that it seemed good and rare that they hadn't had alcohol together.

In bed in 4K, falling asleep with Kay spooning him from behind, Li bristled with startlingly unambiguous love.

———

Three days later, on Li's sofa, they read *Koko's Kitten*, a non-fiction picture book on a captive gorilla's relationship with a cat, then browsed James Mellaart's book on Çatalhöyük. Cattle pens had surrounded the city's perimeter. Around 90 percent of Çatalhöyükan meat consumption had been beef. They'd gathered grapes, pears, apples, figs, walnuts, pistachios, acorns, almonds, eggs; grown wheat, emmer, barley, einkorn, lentils, peas; hunted pigs, hares, birds, deer; and fished. Tooth decay had been rare.

The next day, Li typed a text that began, "My brain was annoyingly telling me that I feel frustrated and alone," and said, among other things, "I feel we should hang out less so you can rest and have time for yourself instead of me or work. You seem so busy." He moved it, unsent, to his notes. An hour later, he typed, "Let myself consider not having a long future with Kay and felt calmingly unworried. I feel calm framing low-hope, blame-focused thoughts within expectable times of despair that I shouldn't trust and am trying to reduce." He reread his text and was glad he hadn't sent it.

In bed, imagining what his novel would be like if the relationship ended, he felt like he was asking a friend for advice. His novel seemed to think the relationship should continue. He dreamed they'd broken up. Kay had gone to Maui, Florida, and, for some reason, Ohio.

He woke feeling less pessimistic about their relationship, but when he got home from printing his 189,983 words of notes from the Year of Pain in the library, he typed and texted her a variation of the unsent text: "I feel I'm getting a tired you, an increasingly tired you, but I don't know, I always have a good time with you and you seem very energetic."

Kay replied an hour later, and they texted seventy-six times. Li apologized for bothering her at work. He resented himself with a tense, morose expression the next few hours—buying groceries, tidying his room, reading about a form of overunity called cold fusion—until his fifth cannabis hit of the day, when he realized he wasn't being patient.

"Patience," he thought repeatedly, drawing dots on a mandala. "Finally regained control of brain," he typed in his notes. "Feel good now. Kay texted she saw a mouse in her room. I texted I made eye contact with one in mine."

In 4K that night, Kay seemed shy and inhibited, but after a minute things seemed normal again. She said she'd only seen her husband on weekends at first due to her desire for alone time. Li asked how long that had lasted. She couldn't remember; maybe a year. She said she'd been trying in her texts that morning to say she was scared of how much she liked Li, but he'd kept talking about nutrition. Li apologized and said he felt insane sometimes. Kay gave him a heart-shaped amazonite, a green variety of microcline feldspar.

In bed, they laughed at a noise that sounded like the refrigerator was trying to join their conversation in an awkwardly belligerent way.

"Sometimes I feel like . . . ," said Kay.

"What?" said Li.

Kay was quiet.

Li asked again.

"Never mind," she said.

"What is it?" said Li, ready to reciprocate if she mentioned love. He couldn't remember the last time he'd told someone in person that he loved them. Maybe it was his mom, when he was small.

"Uh-uh," said Kay.

Entering the library the next morning, Li quietly sang, "Feel closer to Kay again." That night, they walked southeast, past the gas-and-oil power plant, to the East River, smoking spliffs. Li said when he taught MFA students he had to be careful to sufficiently caffeinate and cannabinoid himself to avoid falling into extended stupors. Kay said when she taught "critical reading and writing" to freshman design students, tall male students had treated her like a child.

The next afternoon, they met Rainbow at her workplace, a stationery store, and gifted her a glass jar of kefir with cacao powder and honey. Rainbow said she'd thought MKULTRA was a brand of beer. Kay had encountered it in the movie *Pineapple Express*. Li said he'd first heard of it from a poem by Matthew Rohrer and that he felt like it probably still existed under different names, with improved secrecy and funding.

Walking to the Strand, Rainbow said the closest she'd been to dying was when she got waterboarded for sexual reasons, didn't struggle, and went unconscious.

In the Strand, Li read in *Why We Sleep* that people were sleeping two hours fewer than a century ago, cutting off the last fourth of nightly healing.

In bed, Kay told Li, "Your face is a really certain way." Falling asleep, she murmured words in English and Japanese. "Nonfiction," she enunciated softly. "I woke myself by talking," she mumbled.

In the morning, she said she was buying her Hawaii ticket that day. Li was going to meet her on the island of Oahu for a week after he visited Taiwan, where he was going in six days.

Since July, when his mom suggested he visit for twelve weeks and he decided eleven weeks, he'd reduced the visit to ten and then nine and a half weeks in a remarkably smooth, guilt-free process.

"Excited re many days with Kay," typed Li the next day, a day apart. They had plans to meet each day until he left.

The next night, Kay texted she'd be late. In 4K, she said she'd been typing an angry email. She'd been blamed for lateness caused by others' lateness. She was overwhelmed by her mom, who'd nonsensically said Kay could only be a secretary, and had called her stupid, which she rarely did, though she often called Kay's brother stupid.

"I'm afraid something is going to happen to us between now and Hawaii," said Kay. Hugging her, Li assured her—and felt confident—that nothing would happen.

He woke in the morning filled with complaints, which he began to share while thinking that he should be asleep, working on the negative feelings privately. He felt that Kay was too busy for a relationship. He lamented their book club; they'd read one book in one month. Kay said work could be an addiction for her.

In 3A that night, Li said he tried to be positive and helpful, but Kay seemed to want to wallow. "I feel like I'm getting a tired you," he said, realizing with a sickly pang that he'd already said this in his text messages days earlier.

They were side by side on her sofa. Li's arms were folded helplessly across his chest. Diane, Kay's closest friend, was visiting in an hour. Li said he didn't feel like meeting Diane that night anymore. He felt tenser than ever before around Kay. It seemed disturbing how quickly things could change.

Li felt himself ignoring Kay, who was holding her stuffed snowman Frosty, pushing his bonnet back against his round head. She'd had Frosty since she was five.

Changing to a random-feeling topic, Li said he wanted to talk more, because when he talked more it seemed normal, since other people talked more than he did. He realized Kay might think he was talking about them, since he almost only talked to her. He wondered aloud if excessive tobacco was making him insane.

They tensely ate a salad. Li stared self-consciously at his turmeric-stained thumb. A compound in turmeric called turmerone stimulated neuron growth in rats, he knew.

Kay asked if she should return after seeing Diane in her room.

"If you want to," said Li, and lay on the floor.

Kay said she didn't know when she'd be back. Li said he wanted eight and a half hours of sleep. Kay left.

Li smoked his cannabis-tobacco mix, sat cross-legged, breathed, and was relieved to begin to generate humble, gracious thoughts. He texted Kay, apologizing for being pushy with time. He worked on his novel, fell asleep, woke to Kay's return, and murmured that he viewed his brittle mood that night as the second skip of the stone he'd thrown into their relationship eight days earlier with his texts.

He woke to Kay doing things somewhat loudly with her bag while seemingly talking to herself. "Something's in the refrigerator," she said. "I think there's a mouse in the refrigerator."

"I don't think so," said Li, dimly endeared.

"I'm going to my room," said Kay.

"You could lie down and try to sleep," said Li.

Kay left. Li woke two hours later and went to 3A, where they worked separately, then met on the sofa and talked, facing a wall with various framed art, including an Agnes Martin print and Li's mandala gift.

Kay said she'd felt upset since the previous morning, when Li lamented their book club and her workload. Li said complaining was contagious—he'd wanted to complain after she complained about work and her mom. She said she hadn't been complaining. He said his excitement about nutrition and recovery had been dampened by her response: she'd seemed defensive against his fish oil suggestion for her vitamin D deficiency, which she'd brought up. Kay laughed. Li stared grimly ahead at nothing.

Two hours later, he met Rainbow at Union Square farmers market. She said someone had overturned a table of root vegetables at Norwich Meadows Farm's stand, where Li often bought watermelon and tomatoes and greens.

Three officers were there, talking to the farm's owners, who were religious Muslims named Zaid and Haifa, Li knew from an article in *Gastronomica*. After 9/11, customers had formed a "rotating watch group" to protect their Brooklyn farm stand.

That night, Li and Kay put ingredients into an ice-cream

machine. Kay had visited her childhood piano teacher, whom she sometimes viewed as her stable, supportive mom, that day. They'd watched a Japanese documentary on the kidney.

Kay said she felt bad but wasn't sure why. Li said maybe she was still affected by when he'd complained upon waking the previous day. Kay said that seemed right. "Sorry," said Li.

Kay wanted to leave to be alone in her room, but then the ice cream was ready. Trying it, they began smiling and laughing again. Kay said she got half-hour sugar highs.

The next day, Li baked cannabis with black pepper, turmeric, and ghee to bring to Taiwan. He put the loamy substance in a tinted-glass bottle for a chocolate-flavored blend of fermented cod liver oil and butter oil.

Reading his notes, scrolling back months, he realized the past six weeks had felt like a day. "If I keep being busy, my time in Taiwan could feel like a day," he typed.

At night, Li and Kay shared a long spliff amid the coastal din of building-funneled sirens and unseen helicopters, looking across the East River at buildings in Brooklyn.

If the universe was at least a trillion years old, as plasma cosmologists argued, humans were extreme latecomers. Even if the Big Bang theory was accurate, humans had appeared late on the scene: the Milky Way was already around nine billion years old when Earth formed—old enough for unnucleated microbes to have invented the internet thrice over.

In the morning, Li mailed confirmation to his ex-wife that they were divorced. Kay, who was still working on her divorce, notarized a form confirming Li had mailed the confirmation.

Outside, Kay asked what variation it would be when they met in Hawaii, and Li said, "Tomorrow—I mean the next time we meet—will be thirty-two."

He told her about his time realization, and she agreed it would feel like a day had passed when they next met.

Year of Unknown

Dudu

Two days after Li arrived in Taiwan, his parents left on a ten-day trip to visit Mike's family and attend an eye conference. Dudu seemed to remain calm and content, cuddling with still-surreal friendliness against Li's thigh as he slept.

Biking at five a.m., Li saw groups of elders doing languid tai chi. In his room, he worked on organizing his selected notes from the Year of Pain into a loose narrative. After work, he started a greens fermentation, ordered chlorella for Mike's family, formed a three-week plan to use less caffeine, and took a walk with Dudu. In bed, he missed Kay's murmured sleep-talking. He dreamed he was with middle school classmates in a swimming pool in Florida, wailing, "I can't believe we're all sixty-five!"

Insects, fish, amphibians, and reptiles didn't dream, he read the next morning in *Why We Sleep*. Dreaming had evolved twice, in birds and mammals. Of the primates, humans spent the highest proportion of sleep dreaming. Maybe history would end with people spending increasingly more time in dreams, exploring and acclimating, until slipping permanently out of the universe.

Around noon, Li watched a talk by pediatrician Helen Caldicott, editor of one of the nuclear radiation books he'd read in the Year of Mercury. She said women were more susceptible to the effects of radioactivity (cancer, genetic mutation, reduced immunity/fertility) than men, children more than adults, and fetuses more than children. She felt a major threat to civilization was a teenage hacker triggering a nuclear war.

Dudu led Li on a busy night walk, inspiring him with her casual fearlessness and focused autonomy, ignoring crowds of farmers market customers while sniffing and peeing at select locations. Over 230 million years, as the sun orbited the center of the galaxy once, lizardlike mammals had evolved into primates and invented computers. In another quarter-turn of the starclock, toy poodles could have their own archaeological digs, meta-autofiction, and forgotten past: miniaturized wolves who'd experienced their doting masters' two or more falls into history as surreal shrinking periods, in which bites and growls became eerily ineffective.

To help his body detox, Li began ingesting a gram of powdered zeolite—a volcanic mineral able to adsorb and absorb toxins—each morning with mineral water. He woke in the middle of the night with crusty eyes and an intranostril zit, and remembered often having multiple face-and-mouth sores in different stages of healing as a child.

Lying on his back in the park, he read a printed draft of Rainbow's poetry book, which she'd retitled *But Did U Die?* He underlined "Would u rather be crucified or waterboarded." He underlined "When I die I will become everything," put down the paper, and saw microfireflies in Taiwan for the first time. They seemed denser, quicker, and more transient than in New York.

Maybe the abrupt relocation of metal from the crust to the sky as cities, electronics, militaries, and satellites was visiblizing cosmic rays. Maybe one day the new electromagnetic configuration would chain-reactively destroy everything from the ground to the ionosphere—an instantaneous reset to microbes, plants, insects, subterranean animals, and fish.

Through psychedelics, dreams, YGs, theories, and metaphors, Li felt somewhat prepared to leave his life whenever. He increasingly viewed death—which in Daoism was "a return home," according to Ellen Marie Chen—as a zooming out, like putting down a book. Maybe after reading *Li*, he could read *Earth*, a life-form in another galaxy, one of his parents, or *Dudu*.

In the park, Dudu climbed stairs in vigorous, uniform, pouncing hops. Halfway up, she retracted her right front leg to complete the climb three-legged. Watching this for around the hundredth time, Li finally realized Dudu had leg pain. For years, his mom had said Dudu's right legs hurt; thinking his mom was being negative, Li had viewed Dudu's postures and gaits as endearingly eccentric. Now he saw that when she walked fast, jogged, or ran she slanted left and sort of galloped to center her good front leg, and that she sat with her right leg out at a loose angle, crutching herself with a stiff left leg, due to pain, not personality.

Li woke laughing from a dream in which he snorted cocaine with strangers, then watched someone try to liquefy a watermelon with a weed whacker. He had a wrist rash, a runny nose, itchy eyes, and a fever. He sloughed around with withered posture, bent forward and inward, sneezing onto the floor. He had a pulsing ache behind his eyes, which kept unfocusing as he tried to work on his novel. He woke around fifteen times that night, scratching his throat with tongue undulations that made clucking and froglike noises.

He halved his daily zeolite. He rode a train three stops to Taipei Main Station with Dudu afore his chest in a shoulder bag, which his parents had gotten to replace her wheeled container. Dudu observed her reality silently, with her head out of the bag, as Li meandered in and around the station. Around 4 percent of people were wearing face masks, probably to filter air pollution. On the train home, Li remembered prickling with love in 4K with Kay.

On day eight of detox, he couldn't sate his breath, gulping air through his mouth, obstructed nose dripping like a stalactite. He'd expected detox symptoms but not to this degree. He felt tensely sleepy. He could barely move his neck. His back hurt. He couldn't seem to stop doubting his relationship. Maybe he wasn't ready for one. Maybe Kay wasn't. Maybe no one was—no one in society.

In the morning, he emailed Kay, "I felt lonely and confused last night. The first words I thought today were 'despair munchkins' as a non sequitur." Online, he read that the States had half a million nuclear-and-other waste sites, around 1,300 of which—Superfund sites—were in line to be cleaned. At night, he texted Kay a photo from 1985. She said his face in it—squished, serious, almost glaring—was like one he still made sometimes. She'd never seen it on a toddler.

Li woke at three a.m. with a swollen throat and what felt like multiple unfinished dreams, including a seeming flashback to getting antibiotic eyedrops at birth, streaming through his interrupted mind, which had been breaking down his mental Superfunds to absorb as backstory into beneficial narrative threads, or, more likely, due to low-quality sleep, rummaging through them at random, without protection.

He sat in the bathtub and turned on hot water, scratching pre-rash nodes on his thighs.

"I couldn't sleep and now I'm taking a bath," he texted Kay, who was at work because it was three p.m. in New York. "I have the face in my toddler photo. I feel like I don't like my thoughts but can't think anything else."

"What are you thinking?" said Kay.

"That I've been feeling alone and don't know what to do about it. Maybe it's just because I've been alone, with Dudu."

"I think it would be hard and destabilizing to be alone and not in your own place."

"I feel whiny and doomed," said Li. "I can't just tell you to give me more attention."

"You can tell me that," said Kay.

Li lamented their book club, said it "sucked."

"I understand it is quite defunct. Am I supposed to feel guilty, because I do."

"I feel guilty for making you feel guilty," said Li.

"It was easier to keep up with you when you didn't like me," said Kay about the years before their kiss. "It seems hard if I feel like I need space and you feel alone."

After sleeping six hours, Li listened to an interview with Patrick McKeown, who'd healed his asthma by changing his breathing style. McKeown said most people overbreathed (the opposite of what Li had somehow believed), causing oxygen to bind to hemoglobin, leaving less for the organs.

Aborigines, yogis, and samurai breathed slowly, through the nose, filtering, warming, and sterilizing their air, while modern people—rhinitic, allergic, air-conditioned, degenerate—increasingly mouth-breathed, inhaling too much air too quickly, Li read in *Breathe to Heal*.

He felt surprised, realizing he'd unwittingly sabotaged himself for decades, striving to breathe more after the lung collapses, after deciding against chest surgery, and after other times he'd felt motivated to be healthier.

The next day, Dudu greeted Li's parents by spinning in place, emitting dolphin noises. She followed Li's dad around, jumping and bleating. He put away his luggage and used the bathroom, then picked her up and said, "Ayo-ayo-ayo!" as she licked his face.

It was Dudu's tenth birthday. She settled over an hour into a warm cheerfulness, seeming happier than when alone with Li, when she'd also seemed happy.

Brain

On a walk four days later, Li's dad asked Li how often he and Kay made food. Li said most days. Li's dad advised against washing dishes; it could become a habit.

Li said he liked cleaning things. He photographed a majestic-looking, Yoshida Effected tree to send to Kay.

Li's dad said he'd dreamed they'd lost Dudu. He'd put up flyers that said two kilograms, white, poodle, and 0.1 concentration, a detail from his equations.

Momo's owner was in the distance, strollerless. "Momo died," said Li's mom, sounding scared, sympathetic, and, to Li, slightly amused in a nervous, nervine way.

"The vet said Momo died from a bug bite," said Momo's

owner. Momo hadn't been allowed on grass even with shoes, but he'd gone once. Momo's owner walked away.

"Momo died from too many shots and drugs," said Li's dad.

"I think so too," said Li. "Momo had been bù xíng le for a long time already. Remember when he peed red last year?"

The next day, Li and his parents had lunch with Thin Uncle and Auntie. Thin Uncle's hand tremor had stopped again the previous year after he began taking the liver capsules Li had given him, but had returned again in the past few months. He and Li discussed tobacco being good for Parkinson's. Li recommended organic tobacco tea.

On the train home, the quivering right side of Li's dad's right eye, combined with his other involuntary movements, distributed across his upper body, seemed for the first time more troubling than Thin Uncle's tremor, whose unsettling-ness had faded with time, and which, compared to the eye twitch, seemed farther from the brain.

Li looked past his dad's shuddering right profile to his stable, youthful left eye. He didn't know if his dad's twitches and tics—which he'd noticed more due to cannabis, LSD, and notes—had worsened or not in the past few years.

He reminded himself that his dad was steady and still while writing for hours most mornings in notebooks. Con-tinuous extraneous motion seemed to only emerge in movie theaters, on public transportation, when sleep-deprived, and after trips to China.

In a dream that night, Li felt alienated at a high school

reunion for what felt like hours, seated alone at a picnic bench, until remembering Kay and waking grateful.

The next day was Thanksgiving. Scratching his arm and thighs, Li read an email from Kay, who was with her mom at her brother and brother's wife's house in Connecticut, that said she'd tried to send herself through the amazonite. She'd imagined lying next to Li and touching his chest.

Li emailed her, "Thin Uncle said he sensed our relationship was good. He said it was important to look at someone's parents, seeming to assume yours were together, maybe because my mom had said you'd gone to Yale and Columbia. Later, I said you were divorcing, and I'd divorced, so it was balanced, and he didn't say anything."

"It's funny that going to Yale and Columbia might lead to the assumption that my parents were together. I've always thought I ended up doing that because I was looking for stability that my family didn't offer and I didn't know what else to do."

Kay's parents, like Li's, had paid for their kids' undergrad tuitions, but Kay was still paying grad school loans and seemed to have no more financial or emotional support from her parents. She didn't talk to her dad, and her mom often ranted at her on the phone for hours, criticizing her while wanting more of her attention.

Li asked Kay about work, and she said it was "extremely busy still and a little embattled-feeling, like a video game where creatures are glomming onto me and making my bars go down as time runs out."

————

Five days later, Li and his parents watched *Good Time*, a movie about a man who robs a bank with his autistic brother, then tries to sell enough LSD to bail his captured brother out of jail. The movie ended with the autistic brother following commands—"Cross the room if you like candy," "Cross the room if you've ever been in love"— in a windowless room with other disabled adults.

"That movie was terrible," said Li's dad outside.

"You slept through most of it," said Li, annoyed.

Surprised after weeks of friendliness, Li's dad recoiled.

Li and his mom agreed the movie was good—funny, heart-felt, meaningful, not boring. In one scene, the bank robber had poured liquid LSD, which Li's mom had thought was alcohol, down the throat of an unconscious security guard, who'd woken hours later to officers arresting him.

Laughing, Li tried to say the guard had probably been oozing directionlessly in an unrecognizable hyperspace when he woke to upset police voices and began to emit language-less screams. Li's mom laughed.

Li and his mom were interacting more intimately than at any time yet that visit. Li had felt especially autistic around her that year, probably because zeolite had loosed toxins out of his body's unconscious, into circulation. "Feel weird around Mom sometimes," he'd noted. "Bothered by her looking at me, or trying to talk to me."

On the train home, Li's mom looked around rapidly, unable to find Li's dad, who was seated down the car, phub-bing; public-service ads that said "Don't be a phubber"— a new term for members of the facedown troupe—had appeared that year at street intersections.

"You were like Du now," said Li. "You couldn't see Dad and panicked."

"Heh—I was a little like Du," said Li's mom.

Li sat and unfolded his in-progress draft of the Year of Pain. He opened it to what would become the "Ankylosing" chapter and took a pen from his pants pocket.

When they got off the train, he said, "I'm editing when we went to the chiropractor before we found out I had AS. Do you remember that?"

"Of course," said Li's mom. "Good thing the rehab center's doctor knew about AS. The chiropractor was kind of a scammer."

"He cost a lot, but at least he didn't try to put me on drugs," said Li. "The two doctors we saw wanted me to take drugs."

On the walk home, Li's dad asked Li's mom if she could please not wake him during movies. He said she'd done it three times. She said two. He said three.

"I think letting him sleep is good," said Li. "It feels good to sleep in movies." His mom seemed fine with the suggestion, and Li felt friendliness resume with his dad.

At home, Li's mom said she was going to Cotton Field to buy groceries, then to the bank to pay Li's dad's employee. She asked Li to walk Dudu.

Carrying Dudu to the park, Li quietly told her he'd read that pet dogs at Çatalhöyük had probably been adept with ladders, climbing in and out of homes.

"It's my 25th day in Taiwan," he texted Kay before bed. "Time is going fast for me. What about you?"

"Time is going so fast that I feel like I'm in a race."

_____

A week later, at the bottom of Battleship Rock Mountain, Li's mom repeatedly offered water to a turning-away, annoyed-seeming Dudu.

"This is not understanding animals," said Li earnestly. He'd been troublingly grumpy for two or three days. He hadn't been sleeping well.

"You know animals best," said Li's mom, a bit sarcastic.

"I know," said Li, faintly aware he'd grin if he were in a better mood. He'd gotten less congested and dyspneic since changing his breathing style but was still getting itchier. His wrist rash had expanded crescently down his arm. Other rashes were emerging. Ten days alone wasn't enough to detox—he needed months, seasons.

On the mountain, he began talking and moving his eyes more.

"So we just need to get out here," said Li's mom, noticing the change.

Li's dad kneeled to photograph Dudu as she stretched her back.

"Here there are phytoncides and anions," said Li.

"Nature," said Li's mom in English.

Li photographed a tree whose trunk split into five trunks. He sipped tobacco-honey-turmeric water from a canteen. His mom called the drink a "potion," which made him smile.

"Bad mood dissolves in nature," he thought, swinging his vision across and into fractal montane verdure, feeling like he was scrubbing his eyeballs and parts of his mind clean.

Before history, life had flowed. Fish, turtles, and birds

hadn't wanted hands to pull plastic off themselves. Animals hadn't felt misshapen, incapable, meaningless, or bereft. Nothing had been missing: birdsong, starlight, teeth, soil microbes, survival skills, natural scents, clean air.

"Depression emerges in city," thought Li on a down escalator on the way home, scratching his thighs while inhaling unknown amounts and types of dementogens—forms of matter that caused cognitive decline.

In his room, he read an email from Kay that said she was in "a phase of disorganization and deadlines" and had "fallen asleep without meaning to" half of the past six nights. In therapy, she'd imagined standing and saying, "You're fired." Her only dream recently was one in which she thought, "Oh, incest," after hearing her mom and brother discuss "examining each other's buttholes."

Li responded almost immediately, saying, among other things, "Your dream sounds good. People used to do enemas a lot, it seems, but now they do it less, maybe due to fear of butts/poop. Are you busier than when I was there?"

Kay, who'd seemed somewhat distant since they parted, said she was working two more hours per day. One of her coworkers had abruptly quit after doing work that was wrong and needed to be fixed.

"Sympathize with Kay," typed Li in his notes. "She's in a disorganization phase. Don't overwhelm her, so she can feel desire to contact me on her own, maybe."

It unnerved him to qualify resolutions with "maybe" or "I think" in his notes, made him feel like he needed to start another file of notes, zoom out more.

The next morning, Li got upset when his mom seemed automatically against his dad's desire to fish that weekend.

"Fishing is good," said Li. "It isn't looking at a screen." Fishing seemed to be the only time when his dad wasn't distracted by business and his phone.

Li turned to his dad, who was typing on his computer, and said, "It's not good for me to be here this much. I don't have anyone I can talk to."

"You can go back whenever you want," said Li's mom.

"When I said how long I wanted to visit this year, you said I should visit for three months," said Li.

"That was just a suggestion," said Li's mom.

"I'm spending today alone," said Li, entering his room. If he returned to New York, Kay would be too busy for him, he thought while scratching himself with both hands.

He read an email from his mom saying she felt hurt when he said he couldn't talk to her. He replied he'd meant he couldn't talk in Mandarin at a deeper level. He felt somewhat facetious because they discussed complex ideas in English by email; he rarely talked to non-Kay people in New York; and he viewed writing, not speech, as his means to communicate at "a deeper level."

He emailed her again, saying she should be grateful because he didn't know anyone his age who lived with their parents as much as he did. "I'm grateful for you and Dad too," he said in another email. "If I couldn't talk to you two, I wouldn't spend so much time here. It's my choice. I just can feel unsatisfied being where I don't speak the language or have friends."

But he'd liked being in Taiwan more, on average, since 2014, than New York, he knew he'd thought many times. New York was the epitome of what he wanted to leave, except now for Kay. Li tweeted "fuck" in capital letters with seventy U's.

On a walk, he felt like telling his parents he needed help. The urge dissipated as he wondered what he'd say. Holding his phone low, he emailed himself, "I can't expect to overcome thirty years in four years, even with two catalytic books," thinking that he needed to stop phubbing.

After dinner, he deleted the uncharacteristic tweet, which he imagined his mom had already read. He emailed his friend Dan, who'd been in a relationship for two and a half years, "Do you ever find yourself uncontrollably thinking of leaving your relationship?"

Upset

In the morning, he read Dan's reply. Dan had fantasized about leaving his girlfriend "a lot," but, after concluding he had "dark, fucked thoughts" about everything, among other deductions and inferences, "almost not at all anymore."

"I've thought similar things, that I'll automatically have bleak, negative thoughts, which I should ignore," said Li. "Your email helped. Thank you. I want to feel the influence of weeks and months instead of being buffeted by hours and days."

But he felt neglected again later that morning. Kay hadn't texted in three days, or replied to his email from two days earlier. His mom had emailed: "You are more upset and sometimes look worried this time you come to Taiwan. Besides what we have been talking about, is there anything else that bothers you?"

"No," replied Li. "I don't think I'm more upset. I've argued with you and Dad less this year. I can concentrate better now because I'm healthier. You might be mistaking my concentrating face as upset or worried. It is not."

On a walk an hour later, his mood hovered in a groundless, windy place. "I feel like you keep looking at me," he heard himself say. "It feels not good. Too much pressure."

"No one is looking at you," said Li's mom.

"Nothing the matter, don't look," said Li's dad. "Ayo. Du—our Du—doesn't care if you look. The more you look, the beautifuler she becomes."

Li slowed his pace, walking at a distance from his parents. Minutes later, he began a voice memo, put his phone in his pocket, and walked to his mom.

"I'm not more upset this year," he said. "My face just looks different."

"I said I *felt* something was wrong, not that your face is any way," said Li's mom about her email.

"Felt," said Li's dad, seeming to consider the word's meaning.

"You—I—I'm not happy for one day, and you said that," said Li, half-consciously picking up Dudu. "You don't remember the other days."

"I didn't say you must be happy," said Li's mom at the same time Li's dad said, "He met a girlfriend this year. He's happier!"

"I'm in a not-good mood for one day and you say I'm more

upset this year," said Li. "I'm not." If his mom was right, his main goal for four years—recovery, which included getting less depressed—was failing, he thought pessimistically.

"If you aren't, then good," said Li's mom.

"You need to remember every day. And if I am upset, just let me be."

"Okay then," said Li's mom.

"Don't be so sensitive," said Li.

"However you are is how you are," said Li's mom. "I won't influence or force you like saying, 'Oh, you must be this way, must be that way.'"

"I'm not saying force, I'm just saying you're letting me know you've noticed. Give me more time instead of one day before I need to know you're thinking this."

"Let her down to walk," said Li's mom.

Li set down Dudu, and they reached a duck pond.

"Eh, no, don't go up there," said Li's dad to Dudu.

Dudu jumped down from a short concrete wall.

"She even climbed up to look," said Li's dad.

"What?" said Li's mom.

"Du climbed up there to look," said Li's dad.

Li said, "If you don't say it, then I don't need to think—"

"Right," said Li's dad, turning to look at Li's face.

"—of a reason to tell you, or to address this—"

"Don't need to think about it," said Li's mom.

"—as a problem," finished Li.

"It's not a problem," said Li's mom.

"I'll always be . . . unhappy a few days and happy a few days." Patched-together or hard-won coverings of positivity flew away with ridiculous suddenness, like hats, or else gradually and unceremoniously, over days, like paint. Cheerful talkativeness became mute dissociation. Thoughts went from rational and shareable to infantile and melodramatic. Feelings toggled from magical friends to tormentive enemies. History, the strangest, most mystical, and possibly the last chapter of biology, became unaffecting and dull.

"Right," said Li's mom. "That's always been like that."

"You don't need to talk about that," said Li.

"People have always been like that."

"So don't say it. Let me recover on my own. If you say it, I need to think about it, and then . . ."

"You don't need to think about it."

"I can't just ignore your email," said Li.

"It counts as I didn't say it," said Li's mom.

"When I came back, I ate that powder for eight days," said Li.

"What powder?" said Li's mom.

"The detox one. After eating it, my body released things, and I was nauseated, and I'm still in detox." A sprawling rash had emerged across his tailbone. He pulled up his sleeve, showing his arm rash.

"Are there ones in other places?"

"My throat is very itchy. And . . ." He'd been scratching his crotch in dysphoric fugue states, sometimes in public. He had inflamed hair follicles on his scrotum. "You don't remember what happened every day. I do. I have notes. I'm not more upset this year. In past years, every few days I was upset for an entire day. Not this time."

Realizing his words seemed true, he began to feel calmer.

"Li, my meaning is not that you can't be upset—"

"I know," interrupted Li, upset again.

"Right, then," said Li's mom.

"My meaning is also not . . . ," said Li, confused.

"I know," said Li's mom.

"I'm just saying you aren't giving me time to figure it out."

"Okay then," said Li's mom. "I won't control your situation. All day, control this, control that. Sorry. I know now. Okay?"

"What you said was . . . negative," said Li about her email. "You didn't think that in the past I didn't even eat dinner with you two. Now I do every night, and I always say whatever food tastes good." Stoned, food had regularly been intensely satisfying.

"You're right," said Li's mom. "Also, there's no need to compare. It is what it is."

"So when you say that, I feel that you haven't thought of a longer time," said Li.

"Okay," said Li's mom. "I know now."

"Why are there so many people?" said Li's dad. "People mountain people sea," he said, a Chinese term for crowds.

Loud music played in the bustling plaza. People were singing through microphones and speakers for donations. People were selling sausages from carts.

"In the past, I got up in the middle of the night very upset," said Li, recalling waking in the Year of Mercury at times like three or four a.m., seeking and discarding household toxins in grumpily zombielike fits.

"This year really is better," said Li's mom. "You often sleep until morning. Much calmer."

"Last year, every few days I bickered, yelling at you two in public. This year I haven't at all."

"Right," said Li's parents together.

"You don't now, but in the past, ayo!" said Li's dad. "Last year you were very mean. Heh. This year, with a girlfriend, much better."

"In the past, my face had no expression," said Li. "Now I'm healthier, so I look different. When I work, I also feel my face concentrate. And this year my weed is more spread out."

Six months earlier, he'd finally revealed that he'd been bringing cannabis and LSD to Taiwan. Instead of sharing the secret calmly, as he'd imagined doing for years, he'd typed it quickly, while upset, during the week of insanity, in the middle of an email to his mom about how he needed space from her emails.

"Hm," said Li's mom.

"Last year, I ate a lot at once, so for a few hours I would keep laughing or whatever," said Li.

"Hehn," said Li's mom. "So you're calmer this way."

"This year, I've spread it out to twice per day, and I'm using less." Actually, he'd been eating around the same amount (half a gram per day), but he hadn't brought any LSD, though he had added tobacco.

"Much better this year," said Li's dad. "Eh, last year you ran away."

He'd escalated away from and back to his parents in a guided convulsion.

"Last year, in the subway, you scolded us," said Li's mom, laughing a little.

"I scolded Dad," said Li. "He said the Cotton Field cashier scammed us, and I yelled at him a lot."

"They did scam us," said Li's dad. "Did it on purpose."

A military-looking plane passed overhead.

"Much better this year," said Li's dad. "You're an adult

now, going to have a baby," he said, though Li hadn't mentioned wanting a baby. "So what's there to bicker about? Your brother doesn't bicker because of the baby, taking care of the baby . . ."

"*Taking care of the baby* what," said Li's mom.

"Li, they bicker at night," said Li's dad about Mike and Julie. He imitated Mike: "*Child keeps crying and you don't do anything! I do everything!*"

"Yeah," said Li. "Everyone . . . will bicker."

"Li, Julie was like, *I do everything! Why do I always do the dishes!*" said Li's dad.

"No," said Li's mom. "She was like, *Why can't I rest?* And Mike said, *I have to wash the dishes! And I have to wash . . .* something else."

"Bickering in the middle of the night," said Li's dad cheerfully.

"Mike eats so unhealthy," said Li. "He must feel uncomfortable."

"With children, there's bickering all day," said Li's dad. "In the past, when you kept crying, Mom and I would bicker." He imitated Li's mom: "*Child is crying, and you don't do anything!*"

"You and Mike were different," said Li's mom. "Mike always helped. You never helped."

"Just pick up and rock a little to stop crying," said Li's dad.

"I was crying because my stomach was uncomfortable," said Li.

"Dad never helped," said Li's mom. "You were crying and I already didn't know what to do, and Dad would be there writing equations, scolding me."

"Just pick him up and rock him a little," said Li's dad.

"*Why don't you go ask someone what to do?*" Li's mom imitated Li's dad. "And whatever: *Why do you keep letting the child cry?* As if I was letting him cry. *Never* helped," she said, stretching "never," which in Mandarin was also two syllables, to last three seconds.

"Child cries, means he's uncomfortable," said Li's dad.

"Mike helped beginning to end," said Li's mom.

They passed the Yoshida Effected tree Li had photographed two weeks earlier. Trees resembled neurons, he'd noticed. Nature reused ideas across size and time. Many things were spinning—ice circles, hurricanes, planets, galaxies. Almost everything was dying; only photons, electrons, protons, and neutrinos seemingly never decayed into pieces.

"You really are getting better and better," said Li's mom. "And you're taking care of so many people."

"Other years, I had more to say," said Li, continuing to explain why he seemed more upset that year. "I thought of things to ask you two. This year I'm writing, so I don't want to gather too many more . . . things. So I'm talking less."

Li's mom said, "You have too many notes already," paraphrasing Li, who'd taken more than half a million words of notes in the past four years, deepening his lifelong lesson on the distortions, techniques, creativity, and limits of memory.

"Last year you slammed my computer," said Li's dad. "Can't slam computers. Okay?"

"That was two years ago," said Li. He'd done it in the Year of Pain after discovering his dad was back on statins and that his mom was taking Nexium.

"Last year you were already much better," said Li's mom.

"You slammed it but fortunately it didn't break," said Li's dad.

"It was Mom's computer," said Li. "It was the computer we got for you that you didn't want. I pushed your machines off the table that year."

"In the past, in Banqiao, I threw Dad's computer," said Li's mom.

"Ayo! You influenced him," said Li's dad.

"How could she have influenced me? I didn't know about that," said Li, though he wasn't sure if he did. "I don't know if I knew about that."

It was December 6. Dudu galloped toward their building like a tiny white horse, body slanted left. She liked to go on walks, and she liked to go home.

"My novel is a lot about trying to be stable," said Li. He'd been working on it around five hours a day. He was almost done arranging his selected notes from the Year of Pain into something that he could gradually shape into a story.

"Impossible!" said Li's mom, scoffing. "Only robot people could do that."

"It's about trying to be less unstable."

"Don't be too hard on yourself," said Li's mom.

"When I feel not good, I blame others," said Li. Sometimes he could feel the auto-urge to blame—an unpleasant, precognitive ping. "That's not good."

"It can lead to hating others," said Li's mom.

Li was relatively stable for most of the rest of December. He made a salve from bentonite clay and apple cider vinegar and rubbed it on himself, significantly reducing his itchiness. He tried in a general, unorganized way to practice partnership qualities—compassion, cooperation, listening, patience, gratitude, humility, mending—with his parents so he'd be better at those skills with Kay, and vice versa.

He kept doubting his relationship, but less cripplingly. The feeling that nothing mattered unless the relationship ended or he committed to it 100 percent had fizzled. He and Kay were meeting on January 17. He didn't need to worry.

In bed, mentally exploring the growing world of his novel, he felt consoled and reassured, realizing pain and conflict had peaked two visits earlier and that his four-year climax of parent intimacy might have been the previous visit. He didn't want to get closer to his parents—or do anything—in a restless, straight rise. It was unrealistic and unnatural.

On a bus to Tiger Mountain, looking up from an 856-page ebook on MKULTRA, he saw his mom look at him three times. When he got off the bus, he said once or twice was fine but three times was excessive, but he seemed to be joking—they were smiling. Li's mom said she'd felt like everyone was staring at her until her twenties, and Li said he'd also felt that way until his twenties.

With his dad, he watched the Hutchison documentary he'd seen with Kay three months earlier. Li's dad chuckled at a video of a bowling ball levitating but relented that physics wasn't complete and so the effect could be real. In the eighties, people had said his flying-spot LASIK technique was impossible. The CEO of a competing company had called him a "fruitcake" to the media.

"They're here, no need to cast it far, they're here," said Li's dad to himself, fishing at the bottom of Carp Mountain. Dudu sat thirty feet away, seeming neglected and bored. Li and his mom smiled, discussing Dudu's aversion to fishing. They walked to her. "Dad will be done soon; don't worry,"

said Li's mom, and picked her up. "Dogs are good listeners.
Every time we talk to Du, she looks at us right in the eyes."

At the waterfall, flapping languidly while slow-breathing,
Li remembered their first time there, a year earlier, learning
of phytoncides and anions from the bilingual sign. When he
stopped refreshing disempowering irrationalia, he seemed to
automatically recall positive, affecting memories based on his
present sensory input.

On the first day of 2018, Li considered how he'd felt better
after the "upset" conversation three and a half weeks earlier,
but had somehow habituated himself back into tormented
glumness, unable to stop bitterly arguing with imaginary
people in his mind.

He began titling each day in his notes "feeling bad is
a habit." After three days of consciously attributing hazy
despair, static negativity, and loss of mind control to modern urban society instead of other people, personal failings,
or existence itself, he felt stably in a good mood again.

Repeatedly delving to sleep in a Japanese movie with
Chinese subtitles, he sensed that one conceptually kaleido-
scopic emotion-movie, a single unbroken dream that sometimes almost surfaced to waking life, happened in him from
birth to death. He saw Dudu with corgi legs. Waking from
a dream yelp, he saw rapid ninjas fighting in the leaf-filtered
light, the komorebi, of a forest understory and wished Kay
were in the movie.

In his room, he texted her that if she'd appeared on-screen
he might've thought that the density of human connection
had triggered a property in which cities began to seep into

the imagination. Kay said she felt ready for a new property and asked how to help. Li said publishing books—extremely long, unique sequences of words—would probably help. Words pointed at things in the universe or the imagination, creating new connections in readers' minds.

Maybe overminds were made of books, not minds. Hundreds of millions of books had been published since the Younger Dryas. Maybe the overmind would become self-conscious in the imagination when billions of books existed. Maybe an incipient overmind was downloading books into minds to speed the process; most emergent properties involved feedback, with the new property interacting with its generating conditions to catalyze or sustain itself.

Carrying Dudu in the park, Li told her he'd had only one YG since modeling his breathing on his ancestors. He told her about the Hutchison and Yoshida Effects. Gently petting her head, he told her about a Hutchison quote that he wanted to include in his novel: "Every time you run your hand across a piece of metal, you're taking off several million atoms."

He told her a little about *The Garden of Fertility*, which he and Kay had been discussing by email. The birth control pill shut down women's reproductive systems, making them "available for sex all the time," wrote Katie Singer, who argued that fertility awareness, in which men yielded to female fertility rhythm, had a "bad reputation" because "many people trust drugs and devices more than a woman's observations of her own body's signals."

On a walk one day, Li's mom grasped Li's hand with both her hands, which felt surreally warm. "Your hands are cold," she said. "Mine are warm. Mine used to be cold."

"I know," said Li.

"Are yours always cold?"

"I don't know," said Li, holding his right hand with his left hand. He touched his mom's hand. "Yours really are warm. That's good. It's because you have natural thyroid and cholesterol and other things now."

"We thought it was weird at first, when you started telling us cholesterol is good," said Li's mom. "Didn't quite believe you."

They visited Flowerface, a county in east Taiwan where face-tattooed aborigines had once lived. In a government-run store, organic oranges were next to genetically modified oranges. Seeing the G-gǎi, literally "G-change," label, Li's mom made a fearful noise.

Li said only the United States and Canada didn't label GMOs. Li's mom said she'd always thought food was safest in the States. Li said the States allowed up to thirty parts per million of glyphosate in food, while Taiwan allowed only up to 0.1 parts per million.

Later, in a rural area, Li's mom said when she was on a field trip when she was twelve, she'd been the only student who dared not cross a jittery suspension bridge. She'd closed her eyes. The teacher, holding her hand, had led her across.

Nüwa

Back in Taipei the next morning, Li's dad began watching a serial show on YouTube of *Romance of the Three Kingdoms*, a fourteenth-century novel in which men warred from AD 169 to 280. The novel was based on the third-century nonfiction book *Records of the Three Kingdoms* and was as known in East Asia as the Bible in the West.

In his room, Li printed his 189,983 words of notes from the Year of Mountains. Getting a guava from the refrigerator, he heard his dad, who'd been watching *Three Kingdoms* for four hours, say to himself, about a character portrayed as a villain, "Cao Cao really is very cruel."

On a pre-dinner walk, Li's dad said he wanted to live to ninety. He said he'd been "class head" in high school—when

the class misbehaved, the teacher had hit his mandatorily
shaved head with a metal lock. He said kids needed physical
punishment. Li said Kay's mom had pierced her son's hand
with a pencil once, stabbing down. "Aiyah," said Li's dad.

That night, Li's dad showed Li the website of one of the
two eye journals he edited. Li laughed at his dad's unintentionally vertically stretched photo, which made him look
physically degenerate. Li's dad said he'd recently finished a
paper that corrected a decades-old error.

In bed, Li gazed thoughtlessly into organistically shifting
darkness. The murky outline of a strolling hamster appeared.
Li tried to make it jump ahead, as if over an obstacle, and felt
vaguely surprised as it backflipped in low-gravity slowness,
disappearing instead of landing. After a minute of nothing,
he saw depth and color for around five seconds—farmhouses
and fields, scrolling right afore a red sunset.

Before falling asleep, he remembered his parents renting bags of tapes of *Three Kingdoms* in Florida to watch on
weekends.

The next day, Li's dad woke at 8:30 a.m., his earliest in Li's
sixty-eight days in Taiwan, murmuring that he'd have three
papers published that year. He sat on the toilet, using his
phone. At 8:58, he began watching *Three Kingdoms* on his
computer.

In his room, Li looked at his dad's unclaimed Google
Scholar page—his dad's papers had been cited 1,106 times,
peaking in 2016 with 87 citations—then browsed his draft
of the Year of Pain. He remembered his mom chain-watching
a family-based show that year until two a.m. some nights,

probably to distract herself from his then-mysterious pain. Li's dad by contrast seemed happy in his binge, with no undercurrent of despair.

At two p.m., Li sat by his dad and asked how much he'd watched. His dad said twenty-five of forty-six episodes, which were forty-five minutes each. He'd skipped many parts, he said somewhat defensively. Li asked if the show had women or children. It didn't. Li asked if it showed people eating food. It didn't. Li said as a child he'd played a Nintendo game based on *Three Kingdoms* called *Destiny of an Emperor*.

Before bed, Li read a paper on Nüwa, the oldest known Chinese deity. The Chinese had three basic creation myths, said the paper. According to the oldest, Nüwa, whose name the paper translated as "Snail-maid," created both the universe and, with clay and river water, people. Liking her creations' laughter, she formed the sexes and taught them to love and reproduce.

In a later myth that seemed to encode the Younger Dryas reset, the partnership-dominator fall, and the ongoing, species-level recovery, it was said that when two male deities fought at some point in prehistory, causing earthquakes, floods, and fires, Nüwa emerged from her home underground to repair the world.

In the morning, Li read two more papers on Nüwa, who seemed like a partnership Yahweh. One paper said it was unknown when people started to worship her, but that the 5,500-year-old jade-eyed head from the Hongshan Goddess Temple may have depicted her. The other paper argued that Dao was Nüwa unanthropomorphized.

Face masks arrived that afternoon. Li had ordered them after reading that the cabin air of non–B-787 commercial planes contained engine oil because half the air was warmed through the engines, causing aerotoxic syndrome, which people misattributed to jet lag. Li's mom recognized the mask model—N-95—from when she'd ordered masks in Florida, fearing terrorism after 9/11.

After dinner, Li's dad scooted to his right, said, "Watching this is too good," and started *Three Kingdoms* on his computer.

Two days later, it was January 12, 2018, Li's mom's sixty-fifth birthday. Li gifted her an especially colorful mandala and helped prepare dinner by making a seaweed-cayenne pancake-omelet.

At dinner, Li's mom said when she got to the States at age twenty-four, she'd transcribed sentences from soap operas and practiced saying them aloud to improve her English.

Li's dad, whose four-day *Three Kingdoms* binge had ended the previous day, said, "Reagan," starting his most-told story that year. Seeing Li's smile, he laughed a little.

"Seventy years," said Li, summarizing the story. When Ronald Reagan was seventy-two, he'd said he was two, citing Confucius's adage that life begins at seventy.

"My life hasn't begun," said Li's dad. "I'm negative one. You're negative thirty-three," he said to Li, miscalculating or not knowing Li's age. Li was thirty-four, making him negative thirty-six.

News finished showing public surveillance video of an intersection car crash and began to report on fried-food wrappers, saying they leached toxins into food.

After dinner, Li's dad lay on the sofa where he'd been

seated and said, "Going to rest before taking out the trash."
He'd agreed to take out the trash for Li's mom's birthday.

"Do what you say you'll do," said Li's mom.

Washing dishes, Li was somewhat surprised to see his dad
walking to each trash can, saying, "Paper," and, on the second
one, "They're all paper."

Li's dad asked Dudu if she wanted to go to the basement.
Dudu looked at him from the sofa. Li's dad asked four more
times, picked her up, and left the apartment.

Li entered his room, lay on his back, breathed slowly with
his eyes closed, heard his dad return, stood, and entered his
mom's office. She removed her earphones.

"Happy birthday," said Li, hugging her. "Dad took out
the trash."

"I know," said Li's mom, beaming. She went into the TV
room and said, "Hòh"—a spoken, movable, modulatable
exclamation mark. "Today you're the most obedient!"

"Right," said Li's dad, looking at his computer.

In his room, Li read an email from his mom—"Can't
believe 65 years already passed, feels so fast, just like a blink."

"Mom's birthday was a success," he typed in his notes.

On a walk with Dudu the next morning, Li realized three
years and two months, not "four or five years," as he'd thought
for an unknown amount of time, had passed since the beginning of his novel, when he arrived in Taiwan to see doctors
about his chest deformity. The realization—that time was
going slower than it felt, and so he had more of it than he'd
thought—calmed him.

That night, Li's mom felt cold and weak, as she used to often feel. Li made her a drink with camu camu—a vitamin C–rich fruit from the Amazon—and said her body might be thinking, "I have all this ghee; I'm strong enough to get rid of some toxins now."

"The body is so complex," she said with "complex" in English, and Li said he'd heard from Stephanie Seneff, in a documentary on GMOs, that diseases and infections were sophisticated trade-offs, without which most people in society would be dead.

The flu virus delivered sulfate from muscle cells into circulation, "rescuing the blood from a meltdown," said Seneff. Heart attacks released taurine. Rheumatoid arthritis produced sulfate. Breast cancer produced estrone sulfate. The body was saying, "Maybe temporary weakness or chronic pain or a tumor is better than a fatal thrombosis or hemorrhage."

At a lunch buffet two days later, Thin Uncle said he felt suspicious of Levoxyl, which he'd taken since getting his thyroid gland removed a year before Li's mom got hers removed in 2006, because his friend who also took Levoxyl had also begun to tremor.

Li said he felt it was a factor—everything was connected—and recommended Thyro-Gold. Li's mom, who felt warm and strong again, said she'd give Thin Uncle some to try.

Li's dad said Li was meeting Kay in Hawaii in two days.

"Hawaiians say, 'Aloha,'" said Thin Uncle.

Auntie asked Li if he'd wear a lei.

"I don't know," said Li. "Maybe."

Auntie and Li's mom laughed.

Browsing food at the buffet, Li realized his parents' laughter had seemed more stoned to him in recent years not just because it was, due to increasing health, but also because, as he got more stoned over years, he sensed more social subtleties. He returned to the table with lychee-and-jujube soup.

Putting down his phone, Li's dad said, "Calm water flows deep," quoting someone from *Three Kingdoms*. Loud, talkative people were shallow, like river rapids, he explained. Deep people were quiet and still.

"I've never met anyone who talks as much as you," said Li's mom.

"The saying doesn't apply to me," said Li's dad.

Thin Uncle said a Chinese proverb—empty wheat stalks, those who "don't know," stand tall, while those heavy with knowledge bend in humility.

As a non sequitur, Auntie asked Li if he was happy in Taiwan.

"Yes," said Li, smiling.

"You look handsome smiling," said Auntie. "We're all very happy to see you. We wish you'd visit more. Your parents are happier when you're here."

"Thin Uncle doesn't know," said Li's dad, walking to the train after lunch. "He got two plates of desserts and was still eating when everyone else had finished."

"He ate a lot," said Li.

"He doesn't know: to prevent tremors, one needs to do this," said Li's dad, closing, opening, and closing his palm-up hand.

"No," said Li, surprised.

"No?" said Li's dad. "Then what do you need to do?"

Li talked about detox, nutrition, exercise.

"Right," said Li's dad, remembering.

"If your hands start to tremor, or your mind breaks, you can fix it," said Li. "So there's nothing to fear."

Li's dad said his hand had tremored once.

"When?" said Li, putting a mix of emotions on hold.

"I was pulling in chips after winning big in poker at a casino. Heh—there were so many chips. My hands tremored."

That night, seated on the toilet, Li heard his dad in the TV room say, "When Li gets married, he won't want to come to Taiwan."

"What?" said Li's mom.

"If Li has a baby, he won't come to Taiwan."

"Will," said Li's mom.

Online the next morning, Li found a park they hadn't visited before. They decided to go at 2:30 p.m. At 2:24 p.m., Li's dad was ready, walking around, saying it was time to go.

"He's even rushing us," said Li.

"It's a first," said Li's mom.

On the train to the airport the next day, Li's dad moved continuously in his seat—grunting while torquing his neck up and to the left, as if something was in his throat; swinging a hand above his head and patting his hair; nudging Dudu with his face while petting and sniffing her and saying "hair child," "pig-dog," and "very beautiful."

At the airport, Li's dad kneeled to remove Dudu from her shoulder bag. From above, in the glaring light of the chrome terminal, he seemed to barely have eyebrows anymore. Li tried to hold Dudu but she yelped and squirmed away, toward Li's dad, who put her back in the bag.

"I'll miss you all," said Li, looking deliberately at each parent's face, and they group-hugged. He'd last told his mom he'd miss her when he was maybe ten. He couldn't remember ever telling his dad.

Curse

On a beach in Honolulu at night with Kay, Li felt withdrawn and sluggish, with a dull headache. He told Kay about his new, slower breathing style and aerotoxic syndrome. He'd worn the face mask for only ten minutes on the plane because it had made breathing uncomfortable.

They returned to their high-rise Airbnb, where they unconsciously re-created their New York setup—seated on the floor at a low table, smoking, eating, and talking.

Later, as they kissed naked on the carpeted floor, Li couldn't stop thinking that Kay could sense he'd doubted their relationship for a lot of their time apart.

"I feel shy for some reason," said Kay.

Li stopped moving and looked down.

"I feel stupid now," said Kay.

"Don't feel stupid. I feel bad for making you feel stupid."

"Now we're doing the thing," said Kay.

"What thing?" said Li after a pause.

"Making each other feel bad."

As Kay seemed to sleep, Li missed his parents. Howling winds buffeted the building. Li found himself thinking, "The Curse," which he'd never thought capitalized before. He was Cursed to be unhappy in relationships. He was going to be alone again. Reclusive, celibate, fixing himself, caring for his parents. He remembered feeling cursed before the relationship too—sending his mom incoherently accusatory emails in the library, cathecting confused despair in 4K.

He felt better the next day. They climbed an umbrella-shaped monkeypod tree and swam in the ocean. They laughed, analyzing a literary figure they adored's intros to writers on his radio show—"One of my favorite guests, actually"; "I'm extraordinarily overwhelmed"; "All sorts of people tell me they have special ways of knowing whether or not I like the book I'm talking about; you don't have to wonder today."

Walking to a health food store, they noticed half the population was Asian and said maybe they should move to Hawaii. "Dudu would like these wide sidewalks," said Li, missing Dudu. They bought papaya and kratom and rode a cab to Chinatown, where they sipped kratom water while browsing a grocery store. Outside, people lay on dark sidewalks next to their belongings.

Busing back to the apartment, Li showed Kay photos on his phone, which he'd somehow felt blocked from doing in their relationship until then. They looked at photos from Taiwan and LA, where Kay had been the past week, attending one of her authors' events and visiting a friend.

In the morning, Kay answered emails and talked to her boss through her computer. Li read his Year of Mountains notes, choosing ideas, details, emotions, scenes, and days that he especially wanted to remember, which was only sometimes obvious.

Around noon, on their way to Diamond Head, a volcanic tuff cone, Kay walked uphill on disconnected lengths of concrete. Li held her hands from behind, matching her speed, slightly leaping to each new piece of concrete. They switched positions, continuing until a small girl, arms out for balance, approached in the opposite direction, looking down.

They sat on grass and smoked cannabis and did Bridge Pose, then climbed the tuff cone and picked the last house along the coast as where they wanted to live. On the way down, Kay said on the plane a couple near her had talked the whole time. It had made her happy.

"How old were they?" said Li.

"In their thirties," said Kay.

Li still felt quiet and somewhat closed off, like on the first day. The Curse and his weeks of doubt were rippling through him, bothersome and mocking, his own creations.

Later that day, they cabbed out of the city to a rural area near the island's north shore. They put their stuff down at their new Airbnb—a bed-containing tent next to an outdoor kitchen in someone's backyard.

Walking toward a mango farm, they saw flower-dotted green in all directions. A giant monkeypod tree cast a shadow across the two-lane road. Kay answered a phone call. A car containing three elders stopped.

"Get in," said the front passenger, a woman. "We'll give you a ride."

"Okay," said Li. "She's on a business call."

They got in the backseat with a man.

"This is a dangerous road," said the driver, another woman. "There are no lights on this street. It's going to be dark soon."

"Thank you for picking us up," said Li.

"We didn't want to read that two tourists had been killed on this road," said the driver.

"We were going to buy mangoes," said Li.

"Mangoes don't start until March," said the driver.

Kay finished her call.

"We live in New York City," said Li.

"We thought you were Japanese tourists," said the front passenger.

"Have you tried papayas?" said the driver.

"We have," said Kay.

"With lime," said Li.

The driver invited them to a Chinese restaurant for dinner. Li said they had plans to cook.

They alighted at a yellow gate and walked on a dirt road toward their tent. Twilit butterflies looked like wayward leaves. A wall-like mountain spanned their whole view, its tallest parts reaching the clouds. A sign said, "No Trespassing. No Exceptions." Kay said she hadn't decided if she was stopping therapy or not. She said she'd thought of her therapist as a leech before.

They took turns using an outdoor shower, then Kay rubbed bentonite clay on Li's butt rash, which by then rarely itched but was still uncomfortable to sit on. "I think that was my favorite activity we've done in Hawaii so far," she said after finishing, and Li said, "I think it was for me too."

In bed, they listened to wavily droning insects, intermittent barks from distant dogs, and the white noise of plants. Different species, played by the changing wind, made subtly different sounds. Together, the grasses, herbs, bushes, and trees sounded a little like an enormous, faraway waterfall.

Li woke from a dream in which he was in precalculus in high school and needed to pee and hadn't studied for a crucial test that kept being about to start. He unzipped the tent, walked away, peed into darkness, and returned to bed.

"I love you," murmured Kay.

"Huh?" said Li.

"I said I love you."

"Are you awake?"

"Yes," said Kay.

Li realized he should say, "I love you too," which, alloyed with steely dreams, he didn't seem to feel ready, especially after the delays, to say.

"I love you also," he said.

Dustwinkling

In the morning, Kay read a submission of a novel set at a poetry MFA program. Li read his transcript of the day in the Year of Mountains when Dudu became catatonic and he and his parents discussed the story in *Zhuangzi* in which Zhuangzi, a student of Laozi, said, "How do you know that I don't know the fish are happy?"

After work, Li told Kay about the fish story, and they invented the verb "Zhuangzi"—to present a larger perspective on a situation—then ate starfruit, saw a wild pig, and planted four avocado seeds. Kay said she'd been afraid they'd hate each other in Hawaii. Li said even if they hated each other for a few days, they could remember their nine weeks of near-continuous fun and focus on their high success rate.

They walked to downtown Waialua, which had around ten stores, including a surf shop and a soap factory. As they paid for a lighter and a hat, Li talked about facial degeneration. Kay said narrow faces were conventionally viewed as more beautiful.

"Yeah," said Li. "But now I feel that wide, aboriginal faces are more beautiful."

"That's convenient," said Kay, who had a less degenerate head than most people.

"Or actually that both can be beautiful," said Li. "I've realized more the malleability of beauty."

In Waialua Public Library, they read the first sentences of romance novels, praising the clarity and flow. They bought a used hardcover book called *The Forest* for a dollar.

Outside, they wandered into an area with farm vehicles.

"Are you guys looking for the beach?" said a man.

"We are," said Li.

They got in the man's truck, which had another man in front.

"This is as far as we can take you," said the driver after ten seconds.

They got out and saw another "No Trespassing" sign. It began to lightly rain. Crossing a field, they passed a hot-pink thing sticking out of the grass and theorized it was a new species of life that wouldn't be noticed due to seeming plastic.

They climbed a fence and walked on a bike path parallel to the road. Li held his wet glasses. It gradually stopped raining.

They entered an area of houses and saw a bucket labeled "Helpful Bucket." Kay sang a song she'd improvised as a child about a bucket she'd kept by her bed. She laughed.

"I just thought of last night," she said.

"What happened last night?"

"When I said . . ."

"What?" said Li.

"I feel embarrassed."

"What did you say?"

"I said I love you. And you asked me if I was asleep."

"You seemed asleep," said Li.

When they finally found a path to the beach, they walked along the coast, passing a man holding a fishing net, then cautioned and encouraged each other onto a slimy concrete tube going fifty feet into the ocean. Li went sideways like a crab. Kay snailed ahead in a careful crouch. Foamy waves soaked parts of them.

They sat on a barnacled, algaed square at the end of the tube, amid convolving water. Glimmering solar veils fell through the sky, which was partly dark with storm clouds. Li said he'd care for Kay if she fell and were paralyzed.

He remembered hospital life. His mom's wet face. Watching *Survivor* on morphine. Eating McDonald's. Listening to music through earphones.

Riding in a car back to the tent, they looked at Kay's fertility charts. She had three months of partial data on her temperature, bleeding, copulations, and mucus levels spread across three apps. Her cycles the past three months had been fewer than twenty-five days each, not enough for accurate fertility tracking, but she'd grown warmer.

Walking home from the yellow gate in moonlight, they saw a hazy glow atop the wall-like mountain and imagined John Hutchison being there, working on his effect. Li said he'd friended Hutchison, who was in his seventies, on Facebook.

After they made and ate dinner, Kay talked to her mom on the phone, then Li tried and failed to remember the evidence against the Big Bang theory. They decided to watch the documentary he'd fallen asleep watching five months earlier.

In the documentary, Halton Arp, the compiler of *Atlas of Peculiar Galaxies*, recalled being banned from a telescope after finding evidence contradicting the Big Bang. An animation showed a galaxy self-reproducing, like a snail, by ejecting a quasar that would grow into its own galaxy. An astrophysicist named Margaret Burbidge said Big Bang theorists were "worried about their jobs." Kay said, "I don't know why I'm getting sleepy." She curled until her head was in Li's lap.

As Kay slept in the tent, Li worked flittingly on his novel, editing paragraphs from his growing draft at random. Working on the novel daily over the next two and a half years, he would sometimes feel almost able to see the final draft, which from somewhere in the future was bidirectionally transmitting meaning and emotion, backward toward him and ahead to the end of his life.

He got up four times to eat tuna, which was soaking in garlic and vinegar in the refrigerator. He noticed Kay in bed in the tent, seemingly looking at her phone. Minutes later, he saw her phone on a table, not in the tent. He smoked baked cannabis, as he'd learned while in Taiwan was possible. His recent trip was the first when he hadn't run out of cannabis. He'd deliberately saved some for Hawaii.

The mystery was revealed through connections, he thought, looking out into moonlit darkness. Mountains, microbes, leaves, and faces had all emerged by joining electrons, protons, and neutrons into around a hundred different types of atoms and then uniting those in various ways. Connections were spells, creating new things with properties that were unexplainable from their parts.

In the tent, Li said cilantro jostled toxins out of storage, so maybe that plus the mercury in the tuna had made Kay sleepy. "Did the guy who was banned from the telescope write *The Big Bang Never Happened*?" murmured Kay. Li said no, that was someone else. Rain pattered the tent in a unique pattern, creating new neural pathways in their brains. They imagined being the only two people alive in the morning.

The next morning, they lay in bed listening to birds—some sounded like weapons in shooter video games; some were like squeaky toys being squeezed; some seemed to be meekly asking questions—then Kay rubbed clay on Li's rash again.

She asked him why he thought it was a detox rash. He said because he'd ingested zeolite and that it matched his other rashes, which had healed over time.

They worked, ate eggs, and decided to go collect leaves. Traversing a house's side yard, they noticed a medium-sized brown dog, approaching with a low, scanning head. The dog silently bared his teeth, then led them off his property.

They accompanied the dog as he sniffed and peed along a dirt road. Li said the dog was refreshing and commenting on websites on the dog internet.

———

Back at the tent, foliating a square of land with thirty-four leaves, Li began to feel confused and top-heavy. Both his and Kay's voices sounded strangely mechanical. He went to get something to stand on to photograph the leaves. He found a wooden bookcase by the tent.

Standing on the bookcase, he photographed the leaves, then said he felt like resting. He held Kay's hand, leading her into the kitchen, dimly aware his behavior seemed capricious and strange.

They sat at a table holding hands, looking at each other. Li felt dumbfounded and restless. Kay seemed bored. Li led them to a sofa, where they lay and began kissing, then stopped.

"I feel weird," said Li, smiling tightly.

"How?" said Kay.

"I don't know," said Li, and stood. "I just feel like I'm very stoned, in a mushroomlike manner." Kay's face seemed masklike and unamused. Things seemed faintly nightmarish.

Li sat on the sofa, laughing a little. Maybe he'd ingested aprotinin, a drug injected in surgery to control bleeding. Since 1992, the government had allowed corporations in Hawaii to plant, in undisclosed fields, crops engineered to synthesize new drugs, he knew. Microbes spread genes, and wind carried microbes, so the chance of unknown drugs being in anything had emerged.

"What do you want to do?" said Li.

"What do you want to do?" said Kay.

"I don't know," said Li. "How do you feel?"

"I feel like there's something you're not telling me."

"I think I'm thinking too much," said Li.

After a few minutes, he began to realize, in an internal thread that had advanced slowly beneath the confused dialogue, that he was indeed very stoned. He remembered putting baked cannabis in the honey-tobacco water he'd made that morning and had almost finished drinking.

Walking north toward Haleiwa, he felt himself sloughing off multiple curses he hadn't known were on him—ones for being reserved and repressive, minimizing novelty, viewing everything defensively.

They talked garrulously on new topics. They skipped and galloped. They saw a monkeypod tree with the Yoshida Effect. Kay described a short story in which a husband brings home a talking female head and tells his wife it'll help their financial situation. The head was always subtly on the husband's side.

Li wasn't sure if Kay had written the story, partly because she was talking more confidently about her writing than ever before, as if it were someone else's writing. After inferring she'd written it, he began to feel entranced by her voice and to remember other times he'd gotten lost in her words.

The story, which she'd written while getting an MFA in fiction, ended with the wife's sister taking the head away.

An hour later, they unexpectedly arrived at a near-empty beach. They lay on cushiony sand, each grain of which contained up to a hundred thousand microbes, and Li said he could feel his feet "resting, in the middle bottom."

"The arches?" said Kay.

"Yeah. It feels good."

"My feet are pulsing," said Kay.

"Mine are too. In the arches."

Clouds formed the mask from *Scream*, a dragon's head, a person's head with the eyeballs bulging out and floating away, Dudu's head, and the letter Y. The shape-shifting, cloud-colored moon seemed rocklike to Kay. Li felt a demurring awe, sensing Earth flying slowly and exactly around the sun, as if in a bright room, which was actually a small, motioned light in a huge darkness, which zoomed out was actually a part of the brilliant disc of the galaxy.

Li saw microfireflies, which he hadn't thought of yet in Hawaii, and which he hadn't told anyone about. He described them to Kay, calling them "like tiny tadpoles." She saw black threads, gray spots, and squiggly shapes that seemed to be in her eyes. Li said he saw those too—question-mark worms and other things—but the dots, which he'd first seen in Washington Square Park in the second half of the Year of Pain, when wonder had flowed as pain ebbed, didn't seem to be in his eyes.

Kay saw them. Li said maybe no one could see them unless someone else described them. Kay said Li had seen them. They discussed starting a religion around them. Li would write instructions on how to see them. He'd write what had happened minutes earlier. Gazing at the ocean horizon, he saw the lucent dots for the first time as a static, screen-covering "twinkling," as Kay was describing them.

Li said the dots might be the first noticeable evidence of a new emergent property. Maybe the whole solar system, starting with subatomic particles, was immaterializing and would soon vanish in a halved twinkle, then reappear elsewhere and casually perish, like most gametes, or survive to reach millions of dimensions.

Leaving the beach, Li asked Kay what she'd name the dots. She said "dustwinkling" or "microstars." Li said he'd called them microfireflies in his notes but liked her names more. "Microstars" reminded him that stars could seem and be minuscule from higher dimensions. "Dustwinkling" sounded calm and friendly.

In Haleiwa, wild chickens walked idly around, like Manhattan pigeons. Roosters crowed intermittently, stretching their necks while emitting the comically specific noise. Palm trees—one of the rare types of tree that seemingly never showed the Yoshida Effect—rose vertically out of the ground like tasseled wands. A helicopter passed by loudly in the near distance like a giant, grumbling, zombielike bird.

They sat in front of a restaurant to wait for a car to take them home. Dustwinkling, they realized, could be dust winkling or dus twinkling. "Winkle" meant "to extract with difficulty," they read on Kay's phone. "Dus" wasn't a word in English; according to Urban Dictionary, it was an acronym for "driving under the shrimpfluence."

In bed, they tried to imagine a fifteen-million-year history. A history modeled more on nature than Yahweh, who'd rushed by a factor of a billion, spending days instead of eons to make everything. After Earth was protected from impacts and powered by clean, inexhaustible energy—was detoxified, denuclearized, undominatored, and sustainable—then what?

History could be like a yearslong stay in a forest-garden,

observing and enjoying and learning, instead of a crazed visit, running through in an hour, out of breath and confused, yelling and killing. Maybe slowly was the only way to reach the other side of matter—not crashing through with time machines or electromagnetic interferometry, but crafting a planet-sized art object, a context lasting and magical enough for greater magic to appear.

The final, history-ending spell could be a book or a relationship.

Fruitresting

In the morning, Kay had a bladder infection. Li had mild hip pain. They worked for two hours, then baked kratom-almond cookies and moved to a different Airbnb on a nearby property with five one-room houses, an outdoor kitchen, an avocado grove, a citrus orchard, and a yoga deck.

"I can see dustwinkling with my eyes closed," said Li, supine on the deck, looking at his ochre-red, sun-backed screen. "Can you? Probably not with your face covered."

"I don't want to move my shirt off my face," said Kay, and they discussed other things for around a minute, then she said, "So that means they can go through your eyelids," reminding Li they often continued dropped threads.

They discussed opening an Airbnb in Hawaii with a

library and a garden. Kay said she should stay at her job until 2019 because equity would be shared then. At first, Li had viewed her as bluffing or wishfully thinking about moving, but she'd seemed increasingly serious. They decided to visit the dog they'd met the previous day.

On the dog's property, they heard a woman behind a picket fence with three or four children say, "What is wrong with you all today?"

"Hi," she said through the fence.

"Hi," said Li and Kay.

"Hi," said the woman, head appearing over the fence.

"Hi," said Li and Kay.

"Can I help you?"

"We're just walking through," said Kay.

"You can't walk through here. It's private property."

"Sorry," said Kay.

"Sorry," said Li, noticing the dog bringing him a new, price-tagged toy, which he threw. The dog ignored it and a thrown stick. He looked at Kay and Li's hands, which held many flowers, and at their eyes, then led them off his property to the dirt road.

They approached a row of person-height trees, spaced ten feet apart. The dog ran around one. Li copied him. The dog did it again. Li focused exaggeratedly hard on exactly following the dog's path. Kay laughed and joined the game.

They chased the dog in three increasingly complex patterns before giving up. The dog arced far afield, drawing three more ways, then jogged away.

———————

Back on the property, spooning meat from a coconut, Kay said being in a place like where they were, in an outdoor kitchen in Hawaii, could make her feel existential. Li asked what she meant. She said it made her feel like, "What is the point of life?"

Li said he felt that way sometimes during physical activity; as he focused fully on movement, part of him would still be able to think, "Is this it?" He said winkling coconut meat was making him feel existential, and Kay laughed. Li said maybe they'd feel less existential as they spent more time in nature.

They sat at the counter, ate kratom cookies with coconut meat, and decided to read five two-page spreads of *The Forest*. Li felt detached from the first, fall-themed spread. They constructively criticized the second—a confusing drawing of varied animals in one landscape showing all four seasons.

On the third spread, which had a photo of a live bird stuck in ice up to its neck, Li began to feel surprised by how much fun he was having reading a forest book with Kay. He felt like an unself-conscious child who was also an adult who was nervous and giddy with requited love. He imagined he felt like Kay had the night she blushed for half an hour.

The fourth spread was on monarch butterflies, which crossed the country annually by working together over four generations. The first three lived around seven weeks, flying southwest from Canada. The fourth, living seven months, reached Mexico, overwintered, and returned to Canada.

The fifth spread was titled "How a Tree Trunk Grows." Only a microscopically thin, cylindrical layer called the cambium grew; new cells became wood (on the inside) or bark (outside). The cambium was like the present, feeding the accruing wood of the past while maintaining the shedding bark of the future.

After reading, they arranged and photographed fruits and flowers on a picnic bench, then sat.

Kay laid the side of her head on a grapefruit, facing Li, who put his left profile on an avocado.

"I don't think there's a fruit I don't like," said Kay.

"Me either," said Li. "This feels good."

They rested on pomelo, tomato, lime, and four types of oranges. They smelled each fruit, suckled their juice through fingernailed slits, and went to get more limes.

In the orchard, they looked at the moon and the stars. The nearest non-sun star was Proxima Centauri, a red dwarf that couldn't be seen without a telescope.

Back at the bench, they spoke a narrative of their day, taking turns adding to it, sometimes with digressions. They remembered collecting flowers, chasing the dog, reading *The Forest*, and fruitresting.

In bed, Kay told Li about when she feigned surprise at a surprise party for her that she'd accidentally foreknown. Li fell asleep to her falling-asleep sounds—language fragments, isolated teeth-clomps.

In the morning, they ate eggs, discussed their plan to start an Airbnb as a controllable and satisfying source of income, washed dishes, fed trail mix to chickens, began kissing, and returned to their one-room house, which fit a bed and a dresser. After sex, Kay, then Li, showered. When he got back to the house, Kay was putting on clothes.

"I *still* don't feel right," she said.

"Bladder infection?"

"Yeah," said Kay.

Li laughed a little.

"What?" said Kay.

"I just imagined if you were saying that about your life."

"What if I was?"

"I would think you were joking."

Rubbing clay on Li's rash for the third time, Kay asked why it was on his butt. He said he'd rarely moved his sacrum from 2005 to 2016, so maybe toxins had accumulated there.

They made a smoothie and walked around eating it with spoons. They fed some to chickens, flinging it on the ground. Kay accidentally covered a chicken's head in smoothie. Li laughed at the chicken's confused surprise.

In a cab to Sunset Beach an hour later, as Kay talked to the driver, Li looked out his window at rain and verdure, dwelling on how happy he felt compared to how hopeless he'd been in Taiwan and when he first got to Hawaii.

He thought generally of all the times in the past four years that he'd recovered from wanting, for seconds to weeks, to hide and whimper, to abandon complexity and novelty and drift into another drug phase and/or bleak novel. Realizing he'd probably be able to recover from himself, his nearest source of despair, in the future too, he felt a calming, poignant joy, which dilated, touching all parts of him.

At Sunset Beach, they hid under a bridge. Raindrops entering water seemed dustwinklinglike. They bought a purple umbrella from a gas station and sat under it in sun showers on the beach. Around twenty surfers in black wetsuits idled in waveless waters, seated on their surfboards, looking away from land, like a cult waiting for a sign.

When it stopped raining, Li and Kay walked west on the sand, stopping to listen to addictively portentous-sounding waves and to ask a hoodied man to photograph them with a rainbow behind them.

Walking on a bike path, they discussed their plan. Kay said it was an effective motivational strategy for her to tell people she was doing something; she'd told one friend that she wanted to move to Hawaii. They kneeled to examine a large snail crossing the path.

Continuing to walk, Li said he'd write five thousand words on their trip, which he was counting as one variation (#32), to protect himself from convincing himself to stay in New York and to not forget how good it'd been.

They rode a bus to the yellow gate—where the next day, before temporarily parting, Kay would say, "I love you," and Li would blush and realize he'd reddened from love, not awkwardness, and say, "I love you too"—and walked home.

On the property that night, Li FaceTimed his parents and Dudu. They'd gone to the waterfall at Carp Mountain that day. Li's dad had caught four fish. Li's mom said Thin Uncle had decided against Thyro-Gold, somehow fearing he'd get cancer without Levoxyl. Kay said hi to Li's parents through the phone's screen. "Bye-bye," said Li, waving.

They made a fluffy, bitter, kratom-tobacco-egg-almond pancake, which they changed into a pizza by adding tomato and cheese, then read *The Forest* and watched some YouTube videos, including one in which a man squirmed through an apartment like a worm after smoking *Salvia divinorum*.

Kay said she wanted to smoke DMT. Li said when he smoked it two and a half years ago, he'd felt like a microbe on a grain of sand inflating into a person on a beach. "My mom read my account of it and emailed me asking how DMT was beneficial to humans," he said. "She seemed worried. I haven't responded yet but I want to."

His still-forming answer was that DMT produced awe and wonder, but so did reading nonfiction books that referenced ideas outside the mainstream, and that reading seemed better for stability and recovery and was maybe even more life-changing and suited to him, as a way to explore and learn, than dimension-rending psychedelics.

Li woke at around three a.m. to Kay saying she'd thought of a plan—they could return to Hawaii the next winter to find a place to live, then move another year later, in 2020.

"That seems too slow," said Li.

In the morning, they made a garlic-heavy salad for Kay's bladder infection. They sat eating on the yoga deck. Dust-winkling made clouds seem extradimensionally sparkly. A gecko startled Li, standing on his hand. He said maybe Kay's plan wasn't too slow.

"Will this be leaving society?" said Kay.

Li said he'd been viewing leaving as a relative thing. They lived in midtown Manhattan, so almost any change would qualify.

They discussed leaving in parts, leaving mentally and chemically, carefully and gradually. Going beyond, as Kathleen said in a talk, instead of away.

Kay's ride to the airport was in seventy minutes. Li was staying in Hawaii for another week, which he'd spend writing about the first week.

They decided to visit the dog before walking to the yellow gate for Kay's ride. Li asked Kay what they should call him. "Lemoncake," she said after around forty seconds.

Lemoncake led them off his driveway to a clearing with bunches of plants, which he hopped over in an exaggeratedly bunnylike manner, pogoing in various directions. He barked for the first time. A single bark, like a greeting.

Li pet Lemoncake cautiously, remembering when he'd bared his teeth when they met three days earlier. Lemoncake lay and rolled onto his back. Kay rubbed his stomach and he seemed delighted. He stood and walked to the dirt road.

"I feel like running," said Kay, and Lemoncake followed her as she ran. Li walked and jogged to them.

Lemoncake lingered with his head down, seeming to subtly, without eye contact, direct their attention to a small plant that looked different from the others.

Li took a leaf.

Acknowledgments

Thank you to my parents, parents' dog, brother, nephew, aunt, uncles, friends, partner, editor (Tim O'Connell), agent (Bill Clegg), publicist (Angie Venezia), and publisher.